"I'm here to apolog[___] we've had," said Cruz.

"On the trail, and in general in the conversations that have gone sideways, I don't claim to be the cheeriest of people, but I don't aim to be rude, or harsh."

"Thank you for saying that. I'm sorry, too."

He sat back in his chair, surprised, "Really?"

"Yes." Eva bit her lip, and the innocence of it sent heat to his core. "In the last couple of days, I've just been thinking about how I handle things, and that maybe I could do things a little better." Her eyebrows bunched together. "It doesn't mean that I'm not upset that the trail feels like open season on my property—"

"And the repercussions of all of that, I know I had something to do with it. That thing with Brian was just horrible for you, and I wish it hadn't happened."

Her body seemed to relax, and a smile graced her face. "I accept your apology."

"Oh, you're that easy?"

"Ha." Eva leaned in with mischief on her face. "I am anything but easy."

That feeling in his core flared so heat filled his entire midsection, but he swallowed it down with a sip of his drink. "If there's anyone that knows that fact, it's me."

Dear Reader,

Welcome back to Spirit of the Shenandoah and Peak, Virginia! *Love Letters from the Trail* tells the story of Eva Espiritu and Cruz Forrester, who, despite being settled in all matters of career, are searching for answers to their existential questions. They find solace on Spirit Trail and, specifically, in a trail notebook, where they, unknowingly, find friendship in one another.

I have done a tiny share of hiking and found that time, in commune with nature and the sound of my footsteps, soothing and healing. Today, I follow hikers who document their trail hikes on their social media platforms, and I yearn to get back out there. Until then, there is *Love Letters from the Trail*. In this book, I wanted to explore the connection between hikers and one of the lessons learned on the trail: that while everyone is on their own journey, companionship and camaraderie are vital. With Eva and Cruz, who, in their fifties, are sometimes stubbornly independent— with reason—it is a lesson relearned and that promises to lead to a deep and meaningful romance.

Special thanks to Travis T., avid hiker and trail steward, for his expertise in all manners of trail maintenance, which you will read about within this book's pages. All mistakes made are mine!

Happy reading, friends!

XO

Tif

LOVE LETTERS FROM THE TRAIL

TIF MARCELO

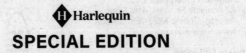

SPECIAL EDITION

Harlequin®
SPECIAL EDITION™

Recycling programs
for this product may
not exist in your area.

ISBN-13: 978-1-335-40223-3

Love Letters from the Trail

Copyright © 2025 by Tiffany Johnson

 Harlequin Enterprises ULC
22 Adelaide St. West, 41st Floor
Toronto, Ontario M5H 4E3, Canada
www.Harlequin.com

Printed in Lithuania

MIX
Paper | Supporting
responsible forestry
FSC® C021394

Tif Marcelo is a veteran US Army nurse and holds a BS in nursing and a master's in public administration. She believes and writes about the strength of families, the endurance of friendship and heartfelt romances, and is inspired daily by her own military hero husband and four children. She hosts the *Stories to Love* podcast and is the *USA TODAY* bestselling author of adult and young adult novels. Learn more about her at www.tifmarcelo.com.

Books by Tif Marcelo

Harlequin Special Edition

Spirit of the Shenandoah

It Started with a Secret
Love Letters from the Trail

Visit the Author Profile page
at Harlequin.com for more titles.

To those searching for their answers
in their daily steps through life

Prologue

Hey there, Rolling Stone,

I don't know where else to go but here. To this notebook. To you.

Do you remember that drama I wrote you about months back, about an important person from my past betraying me, and then finding out about it decades later?

I thought I could handle it.

It happened so long ago, after all.

But there were repercussions that I have to live with, every day.

Admittedly, they haven't been all bad. My family and work have been improved by it.

I should be grateful for this fact alone.

Instead, as the months have passed, I'm just becoming more hurt and angry.

I have tried to find peace, but I can't get there. I've been doing all the things I need to desensitize myself, to look at the bright side. I've given it time. But nothing is working.

I don't understand why I'm still a mess while everyone around me has moved on.

I know this isn't our usual note to one another. You were probably expecting a neutral update of Peak happenings since your last hiking trip.

I'm sorry. I promise the next note will be better. It will be another fun fact about flora, or fauna, or movies, or music. I'm even debating tearing out this page.

Then again, it wouldn't seem right. It would seem like I was cheating this notebook, which is a silly thing to write, but I know you get what I mean. We've written so much the last year. Surely we had to finally come to something more personal, right?

Safe hiking, Rolling Stone. Write whenever.
Blue Moon

Chapter One

Evangeline Espiritu fanned the pages of the trail notebook, filled with her and Rolling Stone's handwriting. They took up at least three-quarters of the pages of the basic college-ruled spiral notebook, the entries spanning up to a year before.

A year of short notes back and forth, but would Rolling Stone answer her last entry? It was the most vulnerable she'd been, and all about the family drama that had consumed her as of late. Before now, their entries to one another had all been about his hikes and her random observations about life in small-town Peak, Virginia. When she'd embedded the notebook in a box in the trail shelter just off an unmaintained trail behind Spirit of the Shenandoah B & B, the establishment Eva built and operated, the last thing she'd expected was for someone to write a full-on journal entry in response to hers.

Trail notebooks weren't rare. They were placed in specific markers throughout major trails like the Pacific Crest Trail, the Continental Divide, and the popular trail a stone's throw from Peak: the Appalachian Trail. Most notebooks, Eva had experienced, simply had signatures of hikers—of their trail names anyway—and maybe a couple of encouraging statements. They were a testament to the humans who had walked past that marker, a reminder that so many others before had their own journey to travel.

But that aforementioned unmaintained trail behind the

B & B? It was a hot mess of a path. Barely wide enough for one person, where long grass and poison ivy took residence and flourished, she had never seen anyone hike it. It was unlike the other trails that were adjacent to the B & B that led to the Appalachian Trail. This small trail—Spirit Trail, as Eva had dubbed it more for herself—had been long forgotten and was no longer included on official National Park Service trail maps, which only accounted for maintained trails, and Eva liked it that way. Not only did she abhor hiker traffic within the line of sight of her cottage, but the foliage added extra privacy for the B & B, shielding the view of the outskirts of downtown.

Truthfully, Eva had hidden that notebook just for herself. A diary of sorts that she'd always addressed "Hey there, Random Hiker."

While writing in that notebook, she wasn't a single mom, a widow in midlife, and an exhausted business owner.

She was Blue Moon, someone who was special and cherished. Her trail name was given to her by her late husband, Louis, because hikers generally didn't use their real names. She'd always joked that had it been up to her, she would have named herself Bug Spray, because she bathed in it before hikes.

To her surprise, another hiker—Rolling Stone—had not only found the trail and the trail shelter, but also the notebook, and answered one of her entries, along with citing their hiking résumé of completing the Appalachian Trail twice. Twice!

Eva and Rolling Stone had become like old-school pen pals; theirs was an easy, breezy friendship of sorts that was an escape from reality. And she hoped that they continued to be after this TMI note.

"I hope you write back." She said the words aloud to herself, then winced while shutting the notebook, and tucked it back into the metal box. Rolling Stone was the only one who she could speak, er, communicate with, though vaguely, in a way in which she felt like she wasn't being judged. The anonymity of it all—since she didn't know who they were, what they looked like, their gender, or even how old they were—was a bonus.

Sometimes, she just wanted to vent, to be heard, without trying to be fixed.

Mariah Carey's "All I Want for Christmas Is You" trilled through the trees like lightning bugs in the dark. Per Philippine tradition, brought over by Eva's grandmother when they immigrated from the Philippines, September meant the start of the Christmas season. Eva had grown up with red, green, gold and tinsel and the Christmas tree up in its full decorated splendor, with Christmas songs on auto play in the CD player in all the *ber* months: September, October, November, December.

It was a tradition her daughters had glommed onto, and currently, the music was coming from her eldest daughter's cottage. She was having a tree-decorating party the family and the B & B staff had been invited to...

Along with Jared, the son Louis had with another woman he'd had a fling with when he and Eva had been on a trial separation.

Jared, who was older than Eva's daughters. Who had arrived six months ago under the guise of applying for the B & B chef's position.

And was now, by default, her son too.

Repercussions indeed.

The dustup had been heartbreaking and beautiful all at once. Her daughters and the whole family had received Jared with open arms. They'd created space for him and treated him as if he had been in their lives from the very start.

Eva, on the other hand, was still rocked by it.

More than that—bowled over. Destroyed.

Eva stuffed the notebook in a plastic zippered bag and

slammed down the cover of the metal box to drown out the sound of the music and to squelch the rise of acid in her throat. It wasn't Jared who she had issue with. It was Louis.

A person who she could never get closure with.

"You've got to get over this," she said aloud. Yet, after exiting the trail shelter, with the intent to head back to her daughter's cabin as previously planned, her legs objected. They went rogue altogether, turning to face her away from her intended destination. Her heart and mind battled between what was the right thing to do, and what she was capable of doing.

She instead hiked down Spirit Trail, toward the junction that would eventually lead to the Appalachian Trail. The opposite direction, and against all common sense.

Because she was in running shoes, not in hiking boots, for one thing. For two, she only had her phone flashlight and not her trusty headlamp. Finally, she was only wearing a windbreaker and did not have her well-loved hydration pack.

Not exactly safe, and against everything she learned about hiking.

But she didn't care. She couldn't face her family right now. How could she, when all she had thought to be true wasn't. It was a crack in the mirror of her life, where she couldn't trust the image that it now reflected.

In the dark, her tears began to flow. Her vision swam, and the bright stream of her phone flashlight did nothing but to help her stay the course as she stumbled every few feet.

A few minutes later, Eva arrived at the junction that, if she went left, would lead to the blue blaze markers of the Appalachian Trail, and if she turned right, would lead to the side lot of the B & B, and then to the main road that would lead through town.

She wasn't yet ready to return home. So, she plopped on what had been dubbed by hikers as Let There Be Rock, a waist-high, arm's-length rock at the intersection. For the mere reason that the rock was a sign that civilization was near.

At the moment, Let There Be Rock served its purpose. It gave her a moment to breathe, because her heart was hammering a steady beat, from the hike and from her tears.

Only one thing could make her feel a little better.

Two things, to be honest, but since her husband was gone and couldn't explain himself, this would have to do.

She fished out a thin, silver, rectangular case from her pocket, engraved with the letter *E*. She popped the latch, revealing a line of seven Marlboro lights. Bringing it up to her nose, Eva inhaled.

Usually the smell of what had been her vice eased her thoughts. She'd been a pack-a-week, only-while-drinking kind of smoker, though if she'd had more money in her pockets she might have stoked the habit more. But she'd quit after Louis died, understanding she was the only parent left.

Right now, though, scent was not enough.

No, she wasn't going to smoke. She didn't even have a lighter on her. She also lived in the woods; fire safety was paramount. But she had to satiate this gaping emptiness in her chest.

She plucked a cigarette out and rolled it between her thumb and index finger, feeling the smooth paper. Along with the comforting scent of tobacco as it wafted into the air, she took a shuddering breath.

The cigarette between her lips was like a warm hug, and she was instantly brought back to sitting with Louis over three decades ago in the back of their pickup truck, young and carefree, looking up at the blue moon. Their families lived in a rural town in Oregon, where there were acres of nothing but grass and small farmhouses. They'd been holding hands. She'd turned to spy his profile as he blew smoke rings into the air.

She'd never been able to do that trick, though she would continue to try time and again as the years passed.

You're my blue moon, he'd said. *That's why I'll never let you go.*

"Why, why, why," she lamented now while the cigarette bobbed between her lips. Her chest welled up with regret. Why had he slept with another woman? Why hadn't he told her?

Why couldn't she get over it?

A light flashed in Eva's eye and she leapt from the rock, one hand going straight to her carabiner of keys, where her Mace resided. Hikers were common throughout the year, day and night, and most were considered safe. Peak was a known stop. Hikers brought business, and hundreds passed through each year for a shower in the public facilities built for them, to eat in one of the walk-up diners, or to use the mailroom for packages sent to thru-hikers, or hikers intent on doing the entire twenty-one hundred miles of the Appalachian Trail, needing supplies.

One usually heard them steps away; one could also smell them.

Still, one could never be too safe.

She raised another hand to block the light. "Hello?"

"Are you smoking on the trail?" a deep voice asked.

Eva couldn't make the person out except for the outline of his tall and slim form. "What?"

"You. Smoking. On the trail."

She recoiled at the tone. It was more accusatory than fear-inducing, but she didn't like it just the same. "Take that light off my face before I point my Mace at you."

The bright beam swept away from her eyes to the ground between them, though it took Eva a beat to adjust to the dark.

"That damn thing could start a fire." The man remained in his spot. "It's completely irresponsible."

"And I don't like being accused. In case you can't tell by the lack of smoke in the air, the cigarette isn't lit. And where I'm standing isn't part of the trail system. This is private property."

He snorted.

The audacity, Eva thought, but she was used to this. Of being completely underestimated. Of people talking over her, of assuming what she was saying instead of asking for clarification.

But this person wasn't going to get away with it. Tonight was not the night.

"What's that about?" She raised her voice.

"What?"

"The snort."

"I didn't snort."

"Whatever." She rolled her eyes. Now, getting back home was forefront in her mind. Even if home, at the moment, had become a black hole of swirling drama. "I'm leaving. Best stay where you are and quit skulking. I'm not afraid to protect myself."

"Shows how you know me, lady, because I'm not that kind of person. Nor do I have any inclination to *skulk* after a person who would even consider smoking on the trail. Or smoking in general. You know that causes cancer, right? Among another things."

"You're right. I don't know you and I hope to never." She wanted to say more, that he had no right to judge her or anyone, and that she had the freedom to do what the hell she wanted. But a second more in his presence wasn't appealing an iota. She spun and trudged up the trail to the B & B, looking over her shoulder once to check to see if she had been followed.

The circle of light remained at the junction.

It wasn't until Eva arrived at her doorstep, when she unhooked her carabiner of keys, did she realize that she'd dropped not just the cigarette but her cigarette case along the way.

* * *

Cruz Forrester hung by at the trailhead seconds after the outline of the woman disappeared over the hill.

He shook his head in disbelief. He'd been in his head coming up the trail. Hiking was his life, but hiking at night was a next-level experience, and he'd allowed the hooting owls, the crickets and the sound of his footsteps to take all his thoughts away.

That was, until he'd spotted a figure sitting on Let There Be Rock with a cigarette in their mouth, and his momentary peace drained out of him.

He couldn't tolerate the thought of anyone smoking around him, not that he could realistically control that—and he knew it. But smoking on the trail, of all places? Well, he wasn't about to keep his big mouth shut about the dangers. While it wasn't illegal to smoke while hiking, there were additional ethical reasons at play such as fire or pollution of these beautiful forests. And selfishly, if he could avoid a little second-hand smoke, well, that was a bonus.

Cruz shook himself out of his thoughts, now concerned at the state of the trail. It had been at least two weeks since he was down this route, and this junction, generally subjected to extra littering, was a hot mess, literally. The woman was right. Where she had been sitting was private property, but guests staying at the Spirit of the Shenandoah B & B were like all tourists—they just didn't care. A majority were hobby hikers who left wrappers and their unmentionables on the trail. Not to mention those who smoked.

Cruz dug out a sustainable sack from his backpack. Might as well clean up while he was here. He swept the flashlight's beam left and right, picking up trash along the way.

Light reflecting from an object caught his attention and he walked to the start of the trail. A silver canister rested next to the offending cigarette.

The woman had not lied—it wasn't lit.

Guilt tugged at his insides. Perhaps he shouldn't have come on so strong. But he'd learned that being polite only got a person so far. Better that he was an advocate—he staked his life on it.

He stuck the cigarette in the bag and picked up the silver canister. Made of steel, the letter *E* was engraved on the front. The latch on the side popped the cover open and revealed six cigarettes.

He frowned. "People."

Another reason why he retreated into the trails. There were too many of them doing whatever the hell they wanted.

As if the world was trying to make its point, the phone in his front pocket vibrated.

Cruz already knew who it was before he looked at the screen. She was right on time. "Hi, Millie."

His little sister gasped. "You answered."

"I'm on a…break, and I thought, why not subject myself for my daily nag session." He smiled into the phone.

"Can't blame me for wanting to make sure you haven't gotten lost somewhere. Now, if you'd turn on your location, I wouldn't have to bother your Zen."

"Today's hike is only a couple of hours."

"At night." She sighed. "I'm glad you at least have service where you're at. Are you making good time?"

"Not at all. I got held up by someone…littering." He caught himself before saying more. Only two other people felt heated about smoking more than him, and that was Millie Forrester and their mother. Riling her up wouldn't serve a purpose.

"That's disappointing."

"Yep."

A beat passed. "Listen. I'm glad you answered, since…we need to talk about Mom."

"Millie," he warned, tucking the silver holder in his cargo pants pocket, "I'm on a hike."

"But when are you not?"

"Fine. Make it quick."

"She really wants you to come home."

"I am in the vicinity of home—it's 1655 Windy Way, Peak, Virginia. Approximately one point nine miles away."

"I mean your childhood home, jerk."

He chuckled. "I'll be there soon enough. I have my appointment in February."

"Cruz." His sister's voice switched to her big sister tone despite, at forty-six, she was his junior by four years. Clearly, it was time to get this conversation over with.

"I don't know what you want me to do. I've got to make sure Cross Trails is on solid ground. And, I have another club to start up in Dawsonville. These things don't happen by themselves. I'm needed here."

Cross Trails number 2 in Peak was his second privately owned hiking club that had two missions: to partner with local trail conservancy groups and to introduce people to hiking and nature.

"Well, we need you, too."

Cruz bit the side of his cheek and allowed his steps to fill the silence. He understood what his sister wanted—their mother was in her eighties.

But thoughts of returning to his family home made him recall being stuck in a sterile room. It reminded him of the time when he couldn't hike to his heart's content.

Still, Millie's pressure was palpable through the phone. Had it been another person, Cruz would have told them to pound sand. But Millie was as important to him as the trails, despite the way he had been avoiding speaking to her.

It wasn't her fault.

It was everything else.

The rush of his past life and his responsibilities made him inhale deeply; it propelled him forward toward the entrance of the unmaintained trail to the right, a half-mile trek that opened up to another path leading to downtown Peak.

Spirit Trail.

"It doesn't have to be all or nothing," she continued in his silence. "You coming back isn't about you moving into your mother's basement. Just…visit."

"Right. Have I mentioned I'm running my own business over here?"

"How about I come to you?" Millie asked.

"You? Take a vacation?" She rivaled his work ethic. She was married to a busy attorney, a mom of two and a CFO. She also added more to her plate as a volunteer at her kids' schools and the homeowners association. "Do you even have time?"

"You let me handle that." From her side of the world his niece let out a scream, followed by the laugh of his nephew. "I don't know. It would be kind of nice to be able to take off for a little bit and have Max handle everything around here. Say yes?"

As if Cruz had a choice now.

Then again, it had been months since he'd seen her. And perhaps, having her over would satisfy her overprotective nature and his mother's curiosity.

"Okay, fine," he said.

"What?" She yelped. "Yay! Okay. I'll call you with details. Keep your ringer on."

Cruz imagined his sister doing a little hop for joy. She and her youthful heart.

Him on the other hand?

He trudged forward, pushing a wayward branch out of his way. Thinking these thoughts would only slow him down. He was already behind in this hike. "Bye, Millie."

"Bye, big brother."

After zipping his phone back in his pocket, he took his first steps into Spirit Trail, taking a breath to steel himself. One had to pay attention entering this danger zone, but not only was this the fastest way into town, but in the middle of this trail was his happy place.

He tripped over a rock after a few feet, grunting while he righted himself. In the last year, this trail had increasingly become more precarious to manage, even as an advanced hiker. To the novice hikers he'd met in town, he had been adamant at warning them off this trail. It could be dangerous.

With his flashlight leading the way, Cruz stepped methodically over rocks and pushed away the overgrowth of foliage. The bright light, however, didn't allow for him to see the full scope of the path in front of him, and he focused on keeping one foot in front of the other. To his relief, the shadow of the trail shelter came into his view, and he treaded over leaves and fallen branches to get under its slanted wooden roof.

The trail shelter itself wasn't in great shape; the wood was rotted in areas. It was a shame, really, to witness the trail slowly being swallowed up when it had the potential to bring more nature lovers to the valley.

After his first hike through Spirit Trail, he had submitted a request to the powers that be at the Appalachian Trail Conservancy for it to be maintained. For the betterment of hikers in the area, he hoped it would come through.

Once Cruz sat down in the built-in seating of the trail shelter, he set his flashlight so it faced up; the shelter lit up dimly. Then, he reached for the metal box behind the bench. From it, he fished out the notebook, which was protected in a plastic zippered bag.

It had been a fluke that he'd found the metal box. A year ago, he'd gotten himself turned around during a rainstorm and sought shelter under the wooden structure. He had unloaded his pack and his sleeping bag so he could nap until the rain stopped. After lying down, he had caught sight of something under the seating.

At the time, there were a few entries by only one hiker, named Blue Moon. And instead of a simple sign-in or a quote, these entries were more like letters.

A sentence in one of the entries had snagged at his insides:

Have you ever missed something so bad you could conjure it in your hands?

Blue Moon had been talking about snow, but Cruz had been feeling vulnerable—rare, for him. His mind had gone straight to his childhood home.

His innocence. That's what he had missed.

But he'd responded with a fun fact that because of global warming, snow now smelled different. Then, he went on to say that he could smell when snow was coming and asked:

Can you tell when something's afoot?

He'd signed the note off with his trail name, Rolling Stone, and left the notebook the next day. When he hiked through a month later, he found a note on the next page addressed to him.

Right now, with his hand on the cover, he took a deep breath.

Had Blue Moon written him back? Their correspondence had never been regular or predictable, and opening the notebook was as exciting to him as a new trail to explore. After months of what could've been considered neutral written correspondence, and the occasional mention about something in their personal lives—though nothing about who Blue Moon was—he felt more at peace expressing himself through their letters than facing anyone in real life.

Right then, after being riled up by that smoker and then by his sister's small request, he wanted to read the words of someone who knew a slice about himself that he didn't show just anyone.

He turned the wrinkled pages to the very last. His heart leapt—there was another new entry, which he read.

Then, he began to write.

To Blue Moon,

I think we need to set a ground rule here. You can share what's bothering you. Though I know we've just gotten to know one another, as much as we have with you having to read my chicken-scratch, I kind of think that we we've got something good going on here. If you can't vent to me, someone who doesn't know you from the next oak tree, then who else can you go to?

Being serious now: I don't know how much time has passed since you wrote this note, but I hope you're feeling better. Or, that when I'm writing this, that my words are getting to you somehow.

Was that a little woo-woo?

Also, since we're revealing more about ourselves, I am not woo-woo. I am definitely hiking boots-on-the-ground, breathe-in-the-real-fresh-air kind of person. But for the sake of this note, I hope you're doing okay today.

While I can't speak to betrayal, I know what it feels like to have the whole earth give under your feet. Is that kind of what you mean? Sometimes, I still feel some of the aftershocks. Not to overload the metaphor and all. :)

Sometimes I wonder what we're supposed to do with all that memory. Are we supposed to forget about it? Or are we supposed to do something about it, even if I'm personally scrambling just to do the everyday things in life.

I'm no help, right? HA!

Know this, though. I'm not just a good hiker—a pretty damn good one, in fact—I'm a good listener. So if the note-book's here, I'm your guy.

Rolling Stone

Chapter Two

Eva emerged from her cottage and shut her eyes against the cool, October wind, and for the first time in a couple of weeks, felt optimism wash over her. Autumn was her favorite season, and the flash of red and yellow in the trees were like a gift.

It was also helped by the last note from Rolling Stone, which she'd read this morning. She'd had an hour to squeeze in a hike and swung by Spirit Trail. Though she wasn't sure when the note was written, its contents floored her.

I'm your guy.

She squelched the excitement from rising her chest. Rolling Stone wrote *guy*. Was the term written neutrally? Casually, in a "hey you guys" way? Or was he truly a man?

Should it matter? Should she care if it did? It shouldn't make a difference if Rolling Stone was a man, should it, because he was a pen pal. A trusted one.

She inhaled to reset her thoughts.

She supposed that her excitement was because he'd shared personal information. Then again, she had been vulnerable first.

What was most important was that he was there for her.

He had her. He wished her well.

From her front porch, Eva refocused her view to the B & B's back property, which crawled with people. Guests taking their brunch on outside chairs. A couple headed down the path to the beginning of the trails. Then, of her youngest daughter Gabriella helping unload a trailer full of pumpkins.

Pumpkins?

Eva briskly marched down her walk, waving hello to guests and keeping her composure. In her arrival to the flat meadow on the northeast side of the property, she found it already teeming with pumpkins, many more than what could be considered proper to decorate the property with.

It almost looked like a…

"It's a pumpkin patch!" Gabby all but yelled, struggling with a large pumpkin in her arms. "Do you love it?"

"Oh my gosh. Be careful." Eva rushed to her daughter and helped her set the pumpkin down against the short brownish grass. They'd had a couple of frosty mornings, but October never really did know what it was in the four season spectrum. While at the moment it was sixty degrees, yesterday it was fifteen degrees cooler, and grass had begun to turn. "It's all so festive but…there are so many of them."

"It's for the fall festival." She wiped the sweat off her forehead with the back of her hand, and straightened her clothing: a plaid long-sleeve shirt, a B & B branded khaki ballcap and the most adorable worn overalls.

Nostalgia rushed back with a small gust of wind. Of Eva's younger self at the pump station filling up her Nissan with gas, and a motorcycle rumbling up to the pump next to her. She'd swung around to look at the person climbing off said motorcycle. It was a guy wearing a slim-fit leather jacket and aviator glasses. She'd swallowed at the sight of it—the machine and the man. At Louis.

Eva had worn overalls that day, except back then, only one strap was buckled, and the other hung loose.

"You recognize it?" Gabby pulled her from her thoughts.

Eva's vision righted. "Should I?"

"It's yours, Mom." She turned left and right, and lifted a foot, proud of herself.

"Wow." She reached out and touched the denim, fingering the marred shoulder buckle. "I didn't realize I still had it. You look great in it, honey."

"Thanks. It was in a plastic tub next to Dad's trunks, those industrial-looking ones from the army. Anyway, these washed up nicely."

Eva knew those trunks well. When they'd moved homes whenever he was reassigned, permanent changes of stations, or PCSs, the movers used to groan upon seeing the trunks. They were massive, bulky.

They also held all of his military gear.

They also probably smelled the same: musty, with a little bit of tinge from the desert. With every deployment rotation, Eva had thrown away his socks and brown T-shirts because there had been no way to get the smell out of them. His gear, though. Though Louis was gone seventeen years, Eva had yet to bring herself to donate his gear to the surplus store.

"What were you doing in that part of the attic?"

"I was looking through boxes and tubs to see if we had anything we could use for the fall festival, and let me tell you, I didn't find much. Especially in proportion to the Christmas stuff we put out every year. Though I did find a couple of flannel shirts and old pants that we can use to stuff scarecrows."

This year's inaugural fall festival, aptly named The Peak of Fall, was Gabby's brainchild, after her successful first public event at the B & B a few months ago: the solar eclipse event. It had brought in such a significant profit that quarter that Eva couldn't disagree that opening the property to the public once a quarter might help the business's bottom line.

"Christmas is our most favorite holiday after all." Eva smiled, inhaling to fill her lungs with the present moment. It was going to be a good day, if she could keep her mind on task.

"But I thought this was supposed to be an adults-only event?" It wasn't that she was against small children—she loved her grandson and every cell in his mischievous body—but the point was to provide a twist on the usual pumpkin patches in the area. The draw of The Peak of Fall was that it would cater to adults. Gabby had partnered with a winery and a hard-cider distillery to pair their selections with the festival menu.

"Mom. You don't think adults want pictures with pumpkins, or to purchase pumpkins?" Her brown eyes trailed to over Eva's shoulders. "Even *he* would take a picture with a pumpkin."

"Speak for yourself," a low voice answered back.

Eva turned to Nathan Paul II, trudging up their way, a pumpkin under each arm.

"How can someone who works in an orchard hate pumpkins so much," Gabby replied. "Heck, you sold me these pumpkins."

"I love pumpkins. But using them as decorations and props? It's silly."

"Being silly every once in a while wouldn't hurt you. Do you know laughter extends your lifespan? At this rate, I'm going to outlive you by fifty years."

They continued to banter, and the palpable tension between them told Eva everything she wanted to know. Nathan the second worked for the elder Nathan Paul, proprietor of Cloud Orchards. Nathan and Gabby's are-they-or-aren't-they status was too complicated to follow even for someone who had witnessed their back and forth the last few years. Though, at the moment, Eva would guess that they were off again, which, in her quiet opinion, was a blessing. This younger Nathan was not as upstanding as his very respected father.

This also meant that she couldn't discuss this new pumpkin patch feature with Gabby right this second, because whatever was happening was messy and complicated.

"Well, looks like you both have it covered." Eva smiled and left without pretending to make conversation.

She sighed. Young situationships.

At times though, Eva wished for it. The excitement of the *what if.* The wonder of the unknown, even if it *was* messy. Thinking of that special person at all hours of the day.

As if you have the time for that.

Heaven knew the B & B brought in enough drama.

But Rolling Stone…

The thought flew in, rendering Eva a little unsteady and warm. Where had that come from? Rolling Stone was her friend. And yes, though she'd made no mention of him to her family or friends, his support was real. Had her point of view changed when he'd realized he was a man?

Admittedly, yes.

But how she thought of him was wholly different from what Gabby felt for Nathan. There was no romance in this. Eva would need to meet him, to see his face. This wasn't that reality show where one chose their mate solely by the sound of their voice. Eva had to see the person.

And that was never going to happen. She couldn't even muster up the courage to fire up a dating app.

Her attention was wrenched by the universal sound of the word *Mom*. More specifically *Mommmmmmm!* Eva turned to watch her eldest daughter Francesca stride across the back patio. Her thick brown hair was like a cape behind her—how Eva loved her girl's hair—and there was a mission to her aura.

Frankie was thirty, but this view was Frankie at every age, as a toddler careening toward the pool, an elementary schooler running across the playground, as a young mother chasing after her son.

A force, her daughter was.

Frankie spoke feet away, waving a piece of paper in her hand. "Great news! Finally, *finally,* the eyesore's gonna be gone."

"What's going on?" Eva extended a hand; the paper was slapped onto her palm. The Appalachian Trail Conservancy logo headed the top of the page.

Eva scanned down the note.

This is notice that there will be increased foot traffic behind your place of business due to trail maintenance.

"Trail maintenance?" Eva asked.

"For Spirit Trail." Frankie pointed to the second paragraph on the note. "Or technically Peak Loop 1."

Eva crinkled her nose at the "real" name of the trail. "Why are they maintaining it? Who said it needed to be maintained?"

"Who knows? But the trail's looking worse by the year. It's a hazard."

"I like it just the way it is." Eva continued to read, half listening.

The trail will be maintained by Cross Trails Club 2, located on 55 Main Street, Peak, Virginia.

Maintaining a trail meant clearing the brush, the rocks, and establishing a walking path. And once the trail was cleared, then it would naturally become a path that hikers could take to and from Peak and the Appalachian Trail.

"The last thing I want to see from this patio is hikers," Eva continued.

"We see hikers every day anyway." Frankie shrugged. "If anything, I think it's good business. Those hikers can come back and stay with us."

"Or *they'll* be the eyesore for everyone." Eva thought of the strangers who would soon be visible from her back balcony. At the moment, her view was only of trees. With her life surrounded by people, familiar or guests of the B & B, she cherished her privacy.

"What if hikers set up tents from where we can see?"

"I'm sure that'll be few and far in between. They could very well set up in places that are visible now, but they don't. Anyway, there's nothing we can do about it now. It's public land, Ma."

Eva locked in on the address of Cross Trails Club 2. She didn't get to this point in her life without at least asking questions.

"I have a question."

Cruz looked up from his scribblings on the whiteboard in the Cross Trails Club main office, to Chip Lowry. Chip was white, in his late twenties, and was the most enthusiastic of the small but mighty five-person team Cruz employed at the Club, but also the one with the most questions. About everything.

Then again, this was why Cruz had a soft spot for the guy, and why he was meeting with him. "Yep?"

"So…let me get this straight. You're leaving us for a couple of months?"

The whole office smelled like a dry erase marker, from Cruz mapping out the plans for the rest of the year, from the upcoming trail maintenance and hiking events, and his short trip back to Colorado with a stop at the future Cross Trails site in Dawsonville. It was the scent of progress, of plans being made, of the future being laid out like the yellow brick road.

But by the look in Chip's eyes, it was as if Cruz was throwing down the gauntlet.

"I'm not *leaving* leaving. I'm simply going to be out of town. But we have phone, video chat, text. And of course, you'll have Dean." He gestured to the man standing off to the side, arms crossed in his usual no-nonsense demeanor.

Cruz had recruited Dean Charles from his flagship hiking club in Boiling Springs, Pennsylvania, to cover for him. The club had become a massive success with Dean managing it, and Cruz had no qualms about leaving Cross Trails in his hands.

"But, no offense, Dean—" Chip cleared his throat and nodded at the man "—you won't exactly be in town every day, either. Just once a week or so, right?"

"But that's why *you're* going to manage the office, Chip." Cruz redirected the conversation to what he knew was the crux of it all. "You are capable."

"Okay, but—" Chip's lips wiggled into a hesitant smile "—am I though?"

Cruz threw his head back in a laugh, further accentuating that Chip was right for the job. "You are. Undoubtedly you know what you're doing on the trails—you've been an outdoors person all your life—and you've got a way with people. You're going to do just fine. Our systems are in place. I'm not leaving until just before Christmas and all of our trail maintenance duties should be completed by then. We won't have any hiking events scheduled. You'll need to keep up with the retail side and perhaps some of the correspondence that comes in, but you'll be good."

"Okay." Chip blew out a breath, standing from his chair. "Thanks. For the chance. I didn't expect it at all." He offered his hand.

"Absolutely." Cruz shook it and ushered him to the door of his office. "You're gonna do great. Though, as a reminder, we're not telling the rest of the staff about it yet. Not until we have all the details hashed out."

"No problem, boss."

When Cruz shut the door behind Chip, Dean snorted out a laugh. "You sure he can do it?"

"I hope so," Cruz said. "I like him. He's a good guy. A little unsure on the outset but he runs a couple of short-term rentals and is a part-time bartender at Mountain Rush. He's got layers."

"Well, we'll be tag teaming the situation, so if anything comes up, surely one of us can get here if needed." Dean sauntered to the white board and gestured to it. "My real worry is all of this. It's ambitious. Especially since the upcoming maintenance job is pretty big. Spirit Trail, is it?"

"That's what it's known as, since it's behind the Spirit of the Shenandoah B & B. Peak Loop 1 is the official name. Apparently it hasn't been maintained for a good seven years. No one's asked about it until I came along last year."

"Hmm." He was quiet as he looked over the plans.

Cruz wished he could read Dean's mind. Dean was Black and in his midthirties, formidable from years of outdoor work. He'd been a thru-hiker of both the Appalachian and the Pacific Coast Trails, completing both in his twenties. Though these days, he stuck to day hikes and was a hiking influencer.

"'Hmm'? What do you mean, 'hmm'?"

"Do you have enough volunteers?"

"Not yet, but we're putting a call out to other volunteer clubs. More hands, less work." Cruz hadn't thought the approval would come so soon, but that was neither here nor there. He didn't back down from commitments. "I guess that means we need to recruit."

"That is the truth." He grinned, shaking his head.

"What?"

"Peak is half the size of Boiling Springs, and every person in this town is probably multitasked already." He tucked the pen behind his ear.

"Are you telling me that the legendary Dean Charles can't pull recruits? Aren't you up to, like, fifty thousand followers?"

His lips lifted into a smile. "Sixty K."

"Not that you're bragging."

"I certainly am not. Because half of those sixty are bots."

"Leaving you with thirty—"

"All right I get it. I suppose I can put a call out."

"Good man." He pointed to his friend.

"As if I have a choice. You are intent on clearing Spirit Trail."

"To better the valley with."

"Uh-huh. And this has nothing to do with smoking out your pen pal?" Dean leveled him with a mischievous grin.

"I knew I shouldn't have told you about that." Cruz's admission had been a moment of weakness after a long day of work and a couple of beers. That, in fact, he was curious, almost giddy, at imagining who Blue Moon was. For him, striking a connection didn't just happen. Even with the Forrester family connections, and his extroverted family members, only a few got to who he was.

Or better yet, there were few that he felt for.

I'm your guy.

A line in this last note flitted in his memory. Had that been a good idea to reveal what his gender was? Would that change anything for Blue Moon? And did he really want to know what gender Blue Moon was, and would it matter to him?

His anonymous friendship to Blue Moon had been free of romantic undertones and he'd wanted it to remain, despite his curiosity. But he couldn't deny that he hoped Blue Moon was a woman.

Was he foolish to hope? Admittedly, the vulnerability of Blue Moon's last note changed something for him.

"So it's true." Dean's eyebrows lifted.

"No. No, it's not true. The relationship is purely platonic."

"Who said about anything being romantic? If it were me, though, I would have already asked to meet. People who get you are few and far in between."

Inwardly, Cruz bristled at his friend's advice. He lived a

solitary life, and while for the most part it was he who erected boundaries, sometimes it got lonely.

"I have one vision." Cruz pointed sideways to the statement hanging on the wall, to snap himself out of these thoughts.

To beautify and spread the love of America's trails.

Dean burst into laughter, just as a knock on the door took their attention. Sydney, a college kid and one of their part-time hires, popped her head in. "Um, Cruz, someone's here asking to speak to the owner."

"What do they want?"

She shrugged.

"We're not done with this conversation. And until I return, it would behoove you to memorize that vision, verbatim," Cruz said, standing.

Dean's lips curled into a grin. "Whatever you say, boss."

Cruz left the office and entered the retail space, cozy and just short of a thousand square feet. From the walls hung backpacks and other camping gear. Every few feet stood a rack of clothing, ranging from convertible hiking pants and quarter zips. Then, toward the eastern wall was a chest high countertop, where they served their customers.

And where a customer was standing now, speaking to Chip, with her back to Cruz. Her dark hair was rolled up in a messy bun, and she was wearing a long caftan-like number that reached her ankles.

Not quite outdoors-wear, but he felt himself light up anyway. Everyone was welcome here at Cross Trails, just as everyone was welcome on the national trails. In his opinion, the more people were invested in the outdoors, the better the world would be.

His own life had certainly been bettered by it.

His phone buzzed, and looking at the screen, he saw that it was his sister. He sent the call to voicemail—she was probably following up regarding her visit, but customers came first.

As he approached the counter, he caught the last bit of the current conversation.

"... Spirit Trail," the woman was saying.

Spirit Trail? Was she a volunteer? Satisfaction flooded through him. He knew it would work out. It always did.

Until it didn't, the devil on his shoulder said.

He shoved that devil off, because yes, he'd had some tough times, but his life had recently been on a downhill run, with the world around him zipping by in an exhilarating rush.

"Um." Chip's cheeks were red, a sure sign that he was flustered.

Cruz had better save him.

Cruz raised a hand; Chip met his gaze. "Here's Cruz now."

"Finally," the woman huffed.

Someone was impatient.

Cruz swallowed his snort. "Can I help you?"

The woman turned, and for a beat, Cruz was transfixed. She appeared to be of Asian descent, with brown skin, and a lean build. Her serious expression, etched in the faint lines in between her dark brows, stopped him in his tracks, and the disdain on her mauve-stained pursed lips sent him right back to the junction on the trail the other week.

Recognition sparked in her brown eyes. "You."

The goodwill and the flare of attraction—damn, where was his mind—dissipated between them. "You. What're you doing here?"

"Definitely not smoking."

Apparently, she didn't want to sweep this under the rug. From behind her, Chip raised an eyebrow.

He cleared his throat. "How can I help you?"

"I received this in the mail, at work." A piece of paper materialized in her hand, and she shook it out in front of him to take, stepping forward. A foot away, he now realized how much shorter she was. Probably a foot shorter than his six-foot frame.

Heh—she had seemed taller.

It must have been the shadows cast in the twilight.

He took it, peeking up before diving into the words. He wasn't great at telling ages, but she looked to be around his age of fifty with the gentle lines around her mouth and eyes.

Except nothing about her was gentle. She radiated scorn, and he darted his eyes down to the task at hand.

He read down the letter, picking up every few words, knowing what it said. It was a form letter, a notice for maintenance, and three-quarters of the way down, he spotted the words Spirit of the Shenandoah B & B.

That was why she was at that junction. She worked there.

"How do I stop this?" Her voice jarred his thoughts.

"Stop what?"

She poked at the paper. "Stop the maintenance. It says here that you are who I need to speak to."

"I know what it says." He glanced down at the paper and met her eyes. "Our club is doing the maintenance, but we are not who to speak to. It's the Appalachian Trail Conservancy you need to speak to. They're the nonprofit that works with all the government red tape for these kinds of decisions."

"Fine. I'll call them. But you can't work on Spirit Trail until it's sorted out."

"What?" He was befuddled by this demand, by her assertiveness. He took a breath, handing back the letter. "Look. We have our instructions, and we'll be there next week."

"So…that's it?"

He crossed his arms over his chest. "That's it."

"This is ridiculous." She spun on her heel and took a few steps. The caftan billowed around her and in her departure he felt the same sense of relief.

Goodness, this woman was just something.

Then, he remembered. "Stop."

To his surprise, she halted. She, however, did not turn around. "I have a name."

"I don't know it."

Her sigh was heavy and impatient. "What else did you want from me?"

"I have something of yours." He walked toward the entrance of the shop, to a box labeled lost and found. "When I'm *skulking* through the trails, I tend to run into a few things. You'd be surprised at what people bring, or think they need." He dug around, under a flask and a vibrator, to the cigarette case. The silver was cool against his fingers.

Standing, he lifted up the case, and the woman gasped.

"Oh thank goodness." She rushed at him, and the scent of her laundry detergent hit his nostrils, and for a beat, her face softened into a sincere smile.

It was nice.

More than nice. It was pretty.

Then, she frowned. "Well. Thank you...for finding this. But... I'm still going to call that number."

He raised both palms in peace—and what the hell was he doing checking her out? "Good luck."

She strode out the door, the bell signaling her departure. It was only then that Cruz was able to breathe deeply.

A whistle sounded to his left. Sydney. "She definitely lives up to her reputation."

"She has a reputation?"

"Yep. Heart of ice."

"Ice, huh?" The nickname surely fit.

"And if there's anyone who can stop the maintenance, it's her."

"I don't even know her name."

"Eva Espiritu."

"Espiritu?" *E* on the cigarette case, as in Eva or Espiritu.

With his small knowledge of Spanish, he said, "Spirit. As in Spirit Trail."

"Also as in Spirit of the Shenandoah. Also as in how she roams that place and those trails like a spirit." Sydney lowered her voice, her tone conspiratorial. "She's a widow." Her voice returned to normal. "But anyway, if the maintenance goes as planned, I don't think this will be the last time you'll see her, especially when she finds out that you requested the maintenance."

Cruz watched as Eva Espiritu strode across the street to an older flatbed truck and disappeared inside of it.

Whether or not it would be the last time he saw her, he certainly wouldn't forget her.

Rolling Stone,

Now there's more drama. It's hard to explain, but I feel like everything is being taken away from me. Literally.

My privacy, my space, my peace of mind.

And people are so frustrating. Especially the kind who refuse to help, who relish in their position of power.

Ugh, are you sick of me yet? I'm sick of me right now.

Let's write about something else. What have your adventures been like? The weather has been beautiful. Have I mentioned that fall is my favorite season? But what I love most is that first frost, which is always a surprise. It could be at the end of October, or maybe not until December. The only downside is when the wildflowers hibernate.

That is, except the honeysuckle. That can go ahead and disappear for seasons. #breathes

And, because you opened the door... I'm a woman. Does this matter to you? This doesn't change things, does it? I don't want it to. You might be the only one who knows all my business. That's kind of special.

Before I run, I wanted to mention that Spirit Trail is going to be maintained, despite my outright objections.

Feel free to relocate this notebook. Or, you can keep it, if you'd like, for the time being. If necessary, leave the box with a note in it for me. I'll find you again.

For some reason, despite everything going on in my life, I trust this.

Safe hiking, Rolling Stone.
Blue Moon

Chapter Three

Eva hiked a hand above her eyes to shield the sun. She peered, shut one eye and then the other, and tried to switch perspectives. Still, she grumbled. "It's ruined."

Her entire view from her cottage was demolished and tarnished. Sure, the backyard was dotted with guests who travelled far and wide for the Peak of the Fall Festival, and the foliage had turned a magnificent combination of gold and maroons and oranges. And yes, the festival was running smoothly and was already a success, with local vendors and their booths scattered among the grounds and the buzz of conversation in the air.

Even the adult pumpkin patch had been well received, with social media-loving guests taking advantage of the backdrops, already tagging the B & B with their photographs. Sales this morning saw increased bookings through the fall. But beyond, loud enough for Eva to notice, were the sounds of trail maintenance: of the whirring of chainsaws, of people stomping through the foliage, of whacking at bushes, and the occasional yell of instructions among the Cross Trails workers.

This had been going on for two weeks. And she was over it.

"It's really not that bad," Frankie remarked, coming up Eva's front porch stairs. She was wearing her trademark gardening hat, a massive straw behemoth that shielded even her neck and upper chest. "And honestly, it does look a little less like a jungle out there."

"It's supposed to be a jungle."

"Um…we have a fake pumpkin patch in our backyard. Not exactly a jungle."

Eva turned away from the abomination. With each sunset the last few days, a section of the trail had revealed itself, and with it, she felt a little bit of herself exposed. Would the workers take down the shelter? She would need to check on the notebook soon.

Eva had meant it when she'd written that she wasn't worried about losing the notebook or Rolling Stone. What stressed her out were all these strangers. Strangers working in her backyard. Strangers sure to hike past her cottage in the future.

"And don't say that you no longer have privacy, because look at this place," Frankie continued, the intuitive she was. She was every bit as jagged as she was vulnerable, and never hesitated to call things out.

"So how can I help you, my dearest daughter?" Eva heaved a breath, having had enough. It was only ten in the morning but her usual cravings for a cigarette had kicked in as soon as she spotted the first of the workers from her back patio.

What would help was a good, sweaty hike, and Morave Chimney Trail had her name all over it. Somewhere she could be alone with the trees, and her thoughts.

Though that wasn't on the docket until after today's event.

"I was just with Jared, and he and I had a great idea about expanding the garden."

"That's great, honey." Her answer was automatic, and so was the smile. A quarter turn, and the garden was within her sights. Her B & B manager, Matilda Matthews, stood in front of its gate, facing Jared, her face tilted up slightly to meet his eyes. Her employee for five years, Matilda reminded Eva of herself, serious and focused, wise beyond her years.

They were a sweet couple; their relationship had unfolded at the B & B six months ago. Unbeknownst to Eva, the two had kept his identity as Louis's child from a former one-night stand he'd had years ago, early in their marriage, a secret for a good month before they'd admitted the truth.

Honestly, they were perfect for one another. Much like Eva and Louis had been, Matilda and Jared were inseparable.

That was, except for when Eva and Louis *had* informally separated and he'd slept with Jared's mother...

A swirl of unease began in her belly. And when Jared reached over and put his arm around Matilda's waist, that swirl took on a hurricane-like quality in her chest. She might as well be looking at a photograph of Louis at that age. How she hadn't spotted it the first time he'd arrived at the B & B, she didn't know. Jared had the same profile, with the round nose and prominent chin. And with the way he had his ball-cap tilted to the back, the bill bent in the sides so that they almost touched.

It had been how Louis had worn his army headgear.

For a beat, her nose picked up the scent of his starched uniforms. Remembered the way his strong, broad shoulders had looked when he was in full dress. How those strong arms used to embrace her when they were alone in the dark.

How he'd betrayed her with another woman...

"...how do you feel about it? We can break into some new ground. We have the room," Frankie continued.

Eva turned to her daughter. "Room for what?"

"The garden? Jared's thinking of expanding it so that we're more reliant on our own produce, and I agree. Now that we're stretching our farm to table menus so we've introduced some Filipino-inspired dishes, it would only make sense to tailor our gardens to them. Like string beans. Or Chinese cabbage. Heck, I'm even thinking about bringing in a few chickens so we can have our own fresh eggs."

More changes.

Heat clambered up her neck, despite the logic that told her that all these changes were good. While Gabby had the nose for marketing, for business, Frankie possessed the vision needed to sustain the internal processes of the B & B. "I'll think about it."

Frankie scoffed. "What's there to think about?"

"Frankie." She buried her fingers into her hair. She couldn't do this right then. There was too much going on. The upheaval overwhelming.

"Fine. Okay. Sorry." She raised both hands, properly putting Eva in her place.

"No, *I'm* sorry." She reached out to her daughter's hands, rough from work. At the contact of her warm skin and the callouses on her fingers, Eva's heart rate settled down.

Frankie was one of the hardest-working people she knew. A true hero, if she was telling the truth. A single mom raising a son, and in many ways taking care of her mother.

Because Eva was a mess. And these days, more than ever.

"Mom, what's wrong?"

She looked into her daughter's eyes and opened her mouth to admit this turmoil that had taken permanent residence in her chest.

But this wasn't Frankie's problem. It was solely Eva's. Frankie, Gabby and Jared were now thick as thieves. They'd bonded and spent time; they'd accepted each other as part of the same family tree, well before they all took a DNA test that undeniably connected them as siblings.

Eva, on the other hand, had given every excuse to create distance from Jared even after she'd spoken to Sharla, Jared's mother, regarding her one-night stand with Louis and the sibling DNA test. She still couldn't fathom that her Louis, a steadfast soldier, had been impulsive enough to stray during their marital break.

She couldn't put her burden on her daughter.

"Do you miss him? Dad?"

Eva could only nod and spoke the most honest truth. "I think of him every day."

These days I curse him out, she continued in her head. *Sometimes, I want to fight with him. Sometimes, I wish I could throw him out of my thoughts.*

This was blasphemous, wasn't it? To be angry at someone when they were already gone? To speak ill of the dead, even if in her head, had to be bad luck somehow.

"He's here, though." Frankie smiled, which slowly turned mischievous. "Especially in the garden."

And, they were back to the original conversation, in which her most direct and insistent daughter knew exactly how to get to her. Louis collected and kept succulents in their young married life, and he'd passed on his green thumb to Frankie, who could revive the most pitiful of plants.

Eva heaved a breath. "You're right. Expanding it is a good thing. Draw up some plans, along with cost?"

"I knew you'd see it my way. Jared already has the plans laid out, with cost and everything. He's prepared to present it."

"Have him email or text it to me," Eva said through gritted teeth.

"Oh really? I would have thought you'd want it to be official, for the team and all."

"No, no need." She looked at Frankie's nose, so as not to give her thoughts away.

That just the thought of having Jared around her for an extended period of time made her heart ache.

"Easy enough." Frankie leaned in and kissed Eva on the cheek. "Thanks, Mom."

"Uh-huh." And despite her best efforts, she melted at her daughter's nearness. She shut her eyes and savored the kiss. Frankie was never much of a hugger, not even as a child. Every

effort to try to wrangle her on her lap had been met with resistance. She had been stubborn from day one. So every kiss,
every hug was meaningful.

But when she opened her eyes, her happy thoughts took
a nosedive. Cruz Forrester, the very same from Cross Trails
Club, was walking toward the B & B patio. He was dressed
as he had been when she'd met him, in long pants and a short-
sleeved olive green shirt.

Both the shirt and the pants were…fitted, accentuating the
curves of his pecs and roundness of his butt. He wasn't sin-
ewy muscle, but lean and solid, an evident result of miles on
the trails carrying a large pack rather than time in the gym.
He wore a ballcap that covered his reddish-brown hair, which
he removed from his head. He swiped his forearm against the
sweat on his forehead.

Eva's throat went dry. It was the carbon copy reaction she'd
had when she saw him at Cross Trails the other week. She had
been simultaneously shocked that he had been the same person she'd encountered on the trail, and stunned at how good-
looking he was.

Just because she was fifty didn't mean she no longer *looked*.
And yes, she still *felt* things her body chose to remind her
that yes, Cruz was a man. A man she might very well be attracted to.

She was a living, breathing human being after all.

But she was also a B & B proprietor, and Cruz was on
B & B property.

"Excuse me, anak." Eva brushed past her daughter and
stomped across the patio and then to the field below, to an
open area where they had had benches installed for festival-
goers to eat and rest. Posts marked the space, and string lights
hung in between for nighttime visibility and were wrapped
with ribbons to give it a whimsical feeling.

Eva would have normally relished those small details, but at the moment, a certain hot hiker had to be put in his place.

No, not hot.

Eva shook her head to clear it of that foolishness.

At her approach the couple that Cruz was speaking to raised their faces to her, beaming. It was Helen Singh of Valley Jewels, accompanied by her younger sister Veronica. Helen was one of Matilda's closest friends.

"Hi, everyone." Eva plastered on a smile. "Just checking in. I hope things are going well?" She cast a sideways look at Cruz, attempting to channel her most inhospitable vibes. It was against her general good nature to feel this animosity, but he'd had two chances at amicable encounters and had failed them miserably.

"Everything is fantastic. Food's delicious and it's a perfect day," Veronica said.

"Made even better by meeting *the* Cruz Forrester," Helen said, pink cheeked. Her eyes didn't stray from Cruz's face, in a full fan-girl moment.

Though Eva couldn't imagine why.

Now, she allowed her eyes to follow Helen's gaze and let it linger on the soft features of this man. His fair skin was tanned; he had full lips and thick eyebrows, deep wrinkles around his clear blue eyes, and with the way he was smiling—so unlike what she knew of him—his laugh lines were captivating and charming. He had the beginnings of fuzz on his chin and cheeks, which Eva could tell would grow red with flecks of silver.

He was probably her age, maybe a little older.

But nope…he bore no familiarity to anyone famous.

Helen spoke up as if she'd read Eva's mind. "Though, you were hard to recognize. Usually, you're all spiffed up in a suit wearing a fancy Forrester watch with Manhattan in the background." She posed, as if she was buttoning cuff links, lips pursed as if the camera was on her.

The image materialized in front of Eva. Of the iconic photo that had circulated through all the fashion and bridal magazines, of a dapper man displaying a watch. A Forrester watch, one of the finest luxury watch brands that Eva couldn't even think of buying.

Her youngest daughter Gabby's incessant love for pop culture then came to mind, about the playboy son of the Forrester watch dynasty. Jet-setting to all parts of the globe, breaking hearts in his wake.

And he was standing in front of her.

Cruz reflexively swung both hands behind him as this woman, Helen, spoke, his right hand clutching his left wrist, and gripped the watch he was currently wearing.

Still, he kept smiling. Did he hate it when people recognized him? Each and every time.

But it didn't give him permission to be rude. It wasn't their fault that Cruz hadn't bought enough snacks for the crew, and instead of driving back to the office, he'd decided to venture up the hill to the B & B. With the festival, he'd thought that they'd have snacks for purchase.

He'd also thought that no one at Peak would recognize him. He'd been an on and off resident for a year now, though these days more on rather than off, and not one person had found out his identity.

Also, it wasn't as if he was truly in hiding. He was just... taking a break.

When he'd been stopped by Helen, who had the sharp eyesight of a hawk, he had no choice but to stop and turn *it* on.

The persona. The smile.

Forrester was to watches what Tiffany was to diamonds. In both cases, the idea, the image of grandeur and luxury and ease was built into both brands. Which meant that everyone who worked for these brands were 100 percent genteel and absolutely aboveboard in public. Baked into his genes, with his great-grandfather starting the company, and outfitting the Barclays and the Russells and more at the turn of the nineteenth century, his body had snapped to attention as soon as the two women recognized him.

But by the look of Eva's face, which had gone cold, she didn't care an iota.

It shouldn't have mattered what Eva thought of him. And yet, the fact that she wasn't impressed elevated her in his eyes. That she seemed true to herself. She was consistently nonplussed.

It was time to wrap this conversation up. His crew was getting hangry, though now, he would need to go through Eva.

"Well, folks, I actually came up here to speak to Ms. Espiritu, so if you'll excuse me."

"Before you go, can I have a picture, please?" the younger of the two women—Veronica, he remembered—asked.

He internally groaned. *Noooooooo.*

The last thing he wanted was for his disheveled self to appear on social media. Yet, what came out of his mouth was, "Sure."

Because responsibilities.

"Could you take our picture, Eva?" Helen pressed her phone into Eva's hand, and that cold face turned into stone.

"Of course." A look of boredom flickered across her face, which turned the curiosity knob in his conscience to high.

After Sydney had called her an "ice queen," his interest had been piqued. He hadn't been able to stop thinking about her. It was intriguing, this reputation, and to manage this B & B, which he'd researched—okay, maybe it was more like snooped, on their website and socials—as a growing favorite in the east coast, especially for weddings. Eva was also a single mom to two daughters, and a grandmother, too.

It didn't make sense how those two images fit into one person. How could an ice queen also be all of those things that required love, and dedication, and emotion? She didn't run away; she wasn't like him, always feeling like he needed to be on the go.

He was knighted his trail name, Rolling Stone, by another hiker, named Quicksand, on his first go at the Appalachian Trail. They'd tackled a twenty-five-mile section of the Appalachian Trail together, until Quicksand had decided to detour and take a week's break. Cruz had been new to hiking and in those twenty-five miles had learned so much from the guy. Quicksand had noticed that as soon as things got the least bit personal in their conversations, Cruz had responded by increasing his stride, by stepping out quickly.

His mind wandered to Blue Moon—why was she dubbed that name? Trail names were given to hikers; hikers didn't name themselves.

A hand on his shoulder woke him. Helen had her arm around him. Discomfort traveled through his body, and it took every bit of him not to shrug her off. That, too, wasn't Helen's fault.

It was him. All him. He couldn't handle strangers touching him, not after the years of being prodded while sick, of having his bubble invaded. From head to toe he had been examined. There were no parts of him that belonged to himself.

It was just one more thing cancer did.

Gritting his teeth into a smile, he stuffed his hands in his pockets, until Eva lowered the phone.

After the requisite farewells to the two women, Cruz turned to Eva, ready to explain, but she beat him to the punch.

"Mr. Forrester, I would prefer that if you needed anything from the B & B, that you come up to the front entrance."

"Call me Cruz, please. And noted."

She gestured to him with a hand to continue. Damn, she was good at being straightforward.

"I wanted to buy some snacks to bring to the crew."

She nodded. "We have our staff inside who can help you."

"That's it?" He frowned.

"What else did you need?"

"Well, I asked you to call me Cruz."

"Yes, you did."

"Aren't you going to offer your first name, too?"

"Oh, I didn't realize that there was a requirement for me to do so."

His brain did a stutter step. He didn't understand why this conversation was going to hell in thirty seconds. "Look, Eva."

"Ms. Espiritu."

He heaved a breath. Good golly. "Ms. Espiritu. Can we start over?"

She threw her head back and cackled. "Start over? You want to start over, after you chastise me on the trail—"

"I thought you were smoking."

"And yet, you didn't believe me nor did you apologize after I told you I wasn't. Then, at Cross Trails you didn't show any kind of empathy for my needs. You all but laughed in my face."

"But I couldn't do anything—"

"It wasn't about you being the solution. It was about you being nice to a fellow business owner."

Nice? It was his turn to cackle. Life was too short to be nice. Life was about doing something in the world, making an impact. Nice went only so far. Nice was actually an excuse for inaction.

"Why are you laughing?"

"You're complaining about me being nice. You?"

"Are you saying I'm not nice?"

"That's exactly what I'm saying."

She shook her head, her face contorting. "Mr. Forrester, I suggest you get what you need and head back to where your people are."

Shit. She was mad. He took off his cap and rubbed his forearm against his forehead. What was it about these conversations that always went south? "Eva."

She shot him a look.

"Ms. Espiritu. This is all coming out wrong. I don't mean to make you angry."

"That's the thing with intentions. Sometimes it's not enough. It's about the execution of it all. It's about doing the right thing."

"And I have done the right thing, by helping to clear that trail. You should be glad that we're available to do this for you. I have a group of great folks working so hard out there, to preserve the land."

"I don't have an issue with the people being told what to do. I have an issue with people making decisions for me. The trail was perfectly fine. The trail hasn't been touched for years and it should've stayed that way."

"As evidenced by how unsafe it is. Believe me, I've hiked it more than a handful of times the last year. After I almost broke my ankle on a felled tree, I put in that trail maintenance request myself."

Cruz had been on a roll, and he hadn't realized what he'd said until Eva's eyebrows rose.

He winced and waited one breath, then two…

"*You're* the one who put in that request?" she asked.

"Yes." Resigning to what he knew was coming—fury—he braced himself. "It was the right thing to do."

"You didn't think to discuss it with me first?"

"That trail is public property. What was there to discuss?"

"That maybe it was important to me for the trail to stay the way it is. That maybe, just because you had an inkling to slum it here in Peak and try to, quote, do the right thing doesn't mean that you know what we need."

"Slumming it?" He snorted. That was preposterous. She hadn't a clue. "You don't know me."

"I know that your family's net income exceeds Peak's and probably the neighborhood town's gross income. And yet, you spend your time hiking and sleeping in tents and now digging around in my backyard and for what? Why are you even here?"

"That's none of your business." A flash of his past life came to mind, though it wasn't really long ago. Five years ago, after feeling confined in his bedroom, in clinics at doctor's visits. Shuttled here and there for claustrophobic imaging exams, he'd discovered the trails and the open space.

Since then, he hadn't been able to leave it, and he wanted everyone to feel the peace of the outdoors.

The trail notebook came to mind, which he had tucked deeper into the trail shelter's bench before the trail maintenance began. Hikers were respectful of trail notebooks and he was confident that it wouldn't have been taken if it was found.

"And yet, you're totally in *my* business," Eva said.

He decided to ignore her accusation, her low blow, because now something else arose. "What I don't get is why you wouldn't want Spirit Trail maintained, when a trail is supposed to be hiked?"

Her eyes shut for a beat as he spoke, as if she was steeling herself.

Believe me, lady, you're not exactly fun.

"People come to this B & B for the privacy, and soon, that will be gone. Soon, people will do exactly as you did, coming up to the B & B from the back, intruding on my property. It will mean people stopping and watching us. Thanks to you."

Cruz didn't know what else to say, nor what he wanted at the end of the day with Eva Espiritu, except that she beguiled him.

His curiosity wasn't enough to deal with her attitude though. This was yet another reason why he preferred trails to humans. With the latter, sometimes, you just couldn't win.

From afar, his name was called by one of the volunteers. He raised a hand in response. Perfect timing, because it was probably better to get the hell out of there.

"I guess we'll agree to disagree then," he said.

"Guess so. Have a good day, Mr. Forrester."

"Ms. Espiritu." He nodded and made his way down the hill toward his people.

Belatedly realizing that he didn't get the snacks he had been intending on procuring.

Blue Moon,

Surprise! I'm here. Did it take you long to find the box?

What do you think of the trail opening up? Do you think the maintenance folks are doing a good job? I'm writing this under a beam of sunlight since there isn't a wall of leaves and limbs blocking its way. The shelter doesn't quite look so haunted.

I'm sorry that there's more drama in your part of the world. I can understand the pressures you're under.

Right now, I don't feel like I'm doing anything right.

An example: I made a decision that seemed naturally like a good idea. Or so I thought. Apparently, I didn't take something—well, someone—into consideration. Apparently, I'm selfish and inconsiderate. Maybe even wrong.

Am I just out of practice, dealing with other people's feelings? Or am I really just an awful human being? I think about my life before I started hiking, when I was around people all the time. When I was really a people person. How did I treat people then? Was I just as callous? I'm realizing what an amateur I am.

Of course, you don't need to answer any of this, because in your way, you would probably try to make me feel better, which I don't think I deserve at the moment. I didn't write all that for you to feel sorry for me.

Still, did it work? Did I distract you from your drama? Ha!

Also, I hope I didn't overstep your boundaries by telling you I'm a man. I fully understand if you want to keep all other personal descriptors out of these letters. Though, to be honest, knowing who you are, that you're a woman, only makes you more real in my mind. But no matter who you are, the result would have been the same. Our friendship remains as it is.

Hopefully calling us friends isn't too much out of line, though.

Rolling Stone

Chapter Four

The bride-to-be scrunched her nose, plummeting Eva's mood.

"It's not to your specifications?" Eva asked, scouring Elizabeth Landry's face for clues to her dissatisfaction. They, along with her daughter, Gabby, who was the wedding planner for the B & B and Elizabeth's mother, were standing at the gazebo, which held the best view of the entire property. Surrounded by the beauty of the valley, alight by the four o'clock sun, about an hour before golden hour, it was the final stop in the venue tour that usually clinched the hearts and minds of future brides and grooms.

But Elizabeth's expression was telling.

"It is, but it doesn't feel…" She trailed off once more, this time stuffing her hands in her camel-colored wool pea coat.

Eva was used to future clients speaking up. By the time they scheduled an appointment to tour the B & B, most wedding parties were eager to make their decision as to where they wanted to spend their special day. Most often, their decisions had been made before they even stepped onto the property, because of word-of-mouth recommendation. Eva had set up the B & B on multiple social media platforms over the years, and Gabby's knack at taking the best pictures made it work perfectly for their purposes.

But not in this case, apparently. Elizabeth had been giddy

indoors, but her mood had cooled along with the dip in temperature since stepping out.

Eva looked to Gabby for assistance.

Her daughter jumped in on cue with a megawatt smile. "I know it feels crowded right now, but for the wedding, we'll be clearing the firepits and the outdoor couches. If you like we can sit and draw out the ceremony layout and reception seating chart. Everything is customizable."

Gabby gestured to the patio where round wooden tables flanked by groups of two or four chairs filled the space, with a dozen guests milling about. A couple was chatting with Jared, and the conversation was animated. All three were speaking with their hands. It was hard to imagine that half a year ago, Jared had trouble adjusting to catering to B & B guests. A former sous chef in Louisville, he'd worked solely in the kitchen.

No, Eva, he had a hard time because he was keeping his identity a secret.

Eva turned away to keep herself from staring at him, and to chase away that errant thought. Yes, he'd kept his secret for about three weeks, but it had been Louis who'd kept his affair a secret all of their marriage.

It wasn't an affair. You were on a break.

What was this, an episode of *Friends*? She shook her head to clear her brain and focused on Elizabeth, who was the most important person at this moment.

The Landry family, an English family originally from London, was well connected in Washington, DC, society. Elizabeth's wedding could unlock another set of opportunities.

"My problem with the place is…" Elizabeth said, blue eyes downcast.

"Before you say anything, how about we head inside for some delicious kalamansi juice," Gabby said, with what Eva knew was a manufactured optimistic tone. "Our version of lemonade, but better. We've been on our feet a while now."

"Oh, okay." Elizabeth seemed to brighten and followed after Gabby.

The two left Eva with Elizabeth's mother, walking a few steps behind them. A good opportunity, Eva thought, to point out some other advantages of the B & B. "Have I mentioned that we have the best partnerships with two inns just down the road? We can easily accommodate the wedding party and even guests with a great group rate."

Mrs. Landry sniffed the air. "Ms. Espiritu, my daughter is too kind of a person to say anything, but this isn't quite the venue that we're looking for."

Eva inwardly winced but kept on. "What do you mean?"

Her gaze trailed to the right. "It's not exactly...up to our standards."

"I assure you—"

"We can see people camping from here." She pointed toward Spirit Trail, now a clear and visible path. Where, among the greenery, flashed a bright yellow tent shell. Then, to the right, two figures hiked east, toward Peak.

Of course Eva had seen that tent first thing this morning. It was hard to miss when she'd taken her morning coffee on her balcony. She'd hoped though that Elizabeth and her mother would not have noticed.

Was it wishful thinking?

Hell yes.

"Oh, that?" She peered, as if the tent didn't glow like the sun. "I can barely see it from here."

"Right. Uh-huh." Mrs. Landry harrumphed. "Is it possible that we can put a sign up, a no camping sign?"

"I'm afraid that's public property, so I can't prevent them from camping." She scrambled for a solution. "I could...fence that area."

Though as she said it, she knew it wouldn't be a satisfactory answer for the likes of Mrs. Landry who wanted total privacy.

Fencing the entirety of the property would be cost prohibitive in the near term.

Eva's chest was heavy with dread with the truth that she had been carrying for months now, not just about this, but with everything since Jared came into town. That she couldn't do anything about it. Not right now, anyway.

But, she noted as they walked toward the patio, that while Jared had come from literal left field, from the actual state of Kentucky with no fault in his parentage, Eva knew exactly who to blame in this instance.

Cruz Forrester.

At the internal whisper of his name, frustration threatened to bubble out of her. Since the maintenance crew had packed up a few days ago, she hadn't seen Cruz, though every time a new tent or a random hiker appeared she immediately thought of him.

It was awful. Because in addition to her ill feelings came this sliver of attraction she couldn't seem to kick.

Eva was a hot mess.

I'm realizing what an amateur I am.

Rolling Stone's last written words came to mind, and it settled her whirlwind thoughts. The vulnerability that he'd showed, vulnerability that she could relate to, had given her some solace that she wasn't alone.

At too many points in her life, Eva had wondered if she had done the right thing. Raising girls on her own in Virginia, despite having the support from her friends and family in Oregon, she had often doubted herself. At times, she'd been angry that she hadn't had Louis to turn to and consult. Sometimes, having to make decisions by oneself was so difficult.

She was *still* an amateur. The thing about grief was that it never ended; it simply took different forms that sometimes knocked the wind out of her.

Knowing that at least she wasn't alone in feeling this was a reprieve.

Though, as Gabby and Elizabeth walked up with Jared, her resolve was challenged once more.

"Before you make your decision," Gabby said, looking straight at Mrs. Landry, "we save the best of our staff members to meet for last. May I introduce my brother, Chef Jared."

Eva maintained her composure even if every part of her wanted to bend over in pain. Gabby had brought Jared to them strategically to win Mrs. Landry over, knowing he could very well save this moment. Compared to the type A members of the Espiritu family, Jared was funny, personable, and charming.

What Eva was stuck on was the word *brother*, at how it was said, so easily and with pride, without a single hitch in her daughter's voice. The tone was of pure acceptance.

At the pause, now realizing that Gabby had lobbed her the ball, Eva cleared her throat. "Yes, our esteemed chef, hailing from Louisville. In addition to your chosen caterer on the wedding day, you'll also have him at your disposal."

"That's right," Jared said, teeth gleaming in his winning smile. "And by next fall, you'll get to experience a new season of menus. We've slowly grown our farm to table concept, and we expect a great harvest next year. Ingredients we haven't grown ourselves will be carefully sourced, of course, down to the coffee we brew. Only the best."

His delivery was perfect, and by the look on Elizabeth's and her mother's faces, it made an impression. Much like how Louis could command a room. He could walk into a party, and in his quiet way could draw conversation. He hadn't had to say much to leave people better than he met them.

Apparently for Jared's mother too.

Eva shook her head to clear the intrusive thought.

"You don't agree?" Jared raised an eyebrow.

Goodness, she had checked out of the conversation. Half-laughing, she said, "No, no. I apologize. I was thinking of… what I meant was…our farm to table concept was Jared's plan, and I only regret that he wasn't on staff earlier, because it promises to be a great success. We should show you the garden."

"No, that's okay." Elizabeth looked briefly at her mother, and then back at Eva. "I think I'm ready to go. I'll need to consult my fiancé, and will get back with you if I have any questions."

This wasn't good. Not good at all.

As the Landry women walked through the B & B and out the front door, Eva was a step behind. "I'd love to hear from you soon, so that we can be sure you get the day you want before someone else books it. Why don't we follow up with you in a couple of days? Or if you wanted your fiancé to have a tour, too, we can definitely arrange it." She felt like she was chasing after them, but she couldn't stop. It was like watching water slip through her fingers, and soon the Landrys' car was speeding out of the lot, leaving Eva with her hand in the air waving pitifully.

"I don't think they're going to schedule," a man's voice said behind her.

Jared.

"No, I don't think so either." Eva heaved a breath to steady herself and turned around, facing his solemn expression. It was like Louis's too, with his dark eyebrows scrunched together.

Every day since Eva had found out that Jared was Louis's son, she had tried. She'd donned a friendly face, said affirmations before the day's work. And for a few weeks, it worked.

She loved Jared. She knew that in her bones.

But she wanted to be okay with this. She wanted to be flexible and understanding. She wanted to embrace this whole situation and be the bigger person.

Still, she felt it in every ligament and muscle in her body— the betrayal.

"There'll be others who won't mind the scenery," he said astutely.

"Not with that kind of clout."

"Do we need clout though?"

"We do. Every business needs clout, needs the recommendation. The word of mouth helps to make us." *And to break us*, she thought.

"But maybe there'll be a different set of folks, still folks with clout, that we'll attract," he said.

He was such an optimistic person. Normally, Eva would have appreciated the perspective, but right then, she didn't want to hear it. They'd lost a client.

"Maybe." She walked past him and climbed the two steps into the B & B, eager to put space between them.

"Um, Eva?"

She didn't turn, but stopped at the doorway. She held her breath.

Please let it be a simple question.

Please just let me go.

After a beat of silence, Jared said, "Did you end up getting my proposal for the extended garden?"

She exhaled. "Yep."

"What did you think? I'm totally open to changes—"

"It's great." In truth, she'd skimmed the plans, trusting that Frankie could help keep the project in check. "Have Frankie check in with me every so often. But, approved."

"Oh…good." Except, his voice lacked his usual mirth. But she couldn't be bothered with that. Not yet.

"See you soon," she said, then scurried into the house.

It went to show that at every stage in her life, even now,

when she was supposed to be a mature person—midlife for gosh sakes—that she *still* didn't know if what she was doing was right.

"How's everyone feeling?" Cruz called back to the three hikers behind him. It was his favorite time of day, when the sun was low on the horizon bathing their surroundings in orange, but by the look of their faces, they were oblivious to the sight.

Then again, it was to be expected, since all three were beginner hikers. Their batteries were drained after a full day adjusting to their twenty-five-pound backpacks.

Now that Cross Trail's maintenance requirements were over, the shop resumed its normal guided trail hikes through the valley. Cruz had organized trips of varying difficulties, ranging from advanced, which were three- to five-day trips traversing large sections of the Appalachian Trail, and smaller adventures like they had today, which was a full day's hike and one overnight in a tent on trails a stone's throw from downtown Peak.

It was a good introduction to hiking: they remained close to civilization and the path was generally flat. Cell phone reception was available for those hikers who weren't ready to unplug, and on this specific route, which utilized Spirit Trail, the ground was even for first time tent campers.

The downside: Spirit of the Shenandoah B & B was in his sight line. Which meant that Eva would be able to see them too.

He shouldn't care, but it's as if he could feel the animosity in the wind, as if he was a trespasser on her land.

It was ridiculous.

"I'm exhausted," Brian, a thirty-something corporate strategist, said. He threw off his pack as if it was a rabid animal and grumbled. "Please tell me we can set up camp here."

"Camp is up the road another quarter mile, into the woods."

Cruz meandered to Brian's backpack and picked it up, gesturing for everyone to keep moving. He'd learned fairly quickly that just because a body was tall and strong looking didn't mean that the person necessarily was. Brian had been the weakest link in their group by far.

Brian shuffled, hands on his hips as the other two hikers passed him. "Why not here?"

The only woman in the group, a forty-something nurse named Mara, slipped her fingers under the straps of her pack. "Because he said so. C'mon. The faster you move the sooner we get there."

Go, Mara. Cruz snickered to himself. Mara was easily the shortest and leanest but the toughest of them all.

"There's more privacy off the road," Cruz added. That, and they would be further away from the B & B. While they had every right to be there, Cruz didn't want to think about Eva while settling down for bed. He wanted to enjoy these hiking trips too.

"Honestly, I'm done, too." Lloyd, a bearded accountant from Winston-Salem, said. "I have blisters on my feet. And there are woods right there."

Lloyd gestured to the flat area of land next to the trail.

Brian whooped in triumph and scooped his pack from Cruz with newfound energy. Lloyd followed him, leaving Cruz and Mara on the trail.

Mara looked up at him and shrugged. "If you can't beat 'em." Then, she walked toward the two men, who were now emptying their packs like they were Christmas presents in sacks.

Cruz really needed to firm up these hiker release forms. It wasn't as if he didn't accept suggestions. So long as it wasn't unsafe, he'd consider them. But he wasn't in the mood for an accidental encounter with Eva.

Their last interaction had been awkward at best, contentious at worst. He'd caught glimpses of Eva around town recently, and every single time, he'd skirted out of her line of sight. One only had enough patience throughout the day, and Eva wasn't the person he wanted to practice it on.

Speaking to her riled up all parts of him that he'd thought he'd gotten under control over the years. The racing heart, the bristling, the constant overthinking.

Which was what he was doing right this second. Instead of wrangling these hikers, he was thinking of *her*.

Stop it.

He nodded decisively to snap himself out of the moment. "All right then. How's this for a compromise. We'll camp here, but even deeper into the brush. I prefer not to have other hikers topple over us."

Cruz was met by cheers; he led the group into the tree line and assisted in assembling their tents. He then cooked up a quick dinner by boiling water and pouring it into a prepackaged meal packet—delicious if he said so himself, though the other three weren't impressed.

As sunset led to darkness, and the chirping of the crickets turned up from three to ten, it became more the world that Cruz was accustomed to. A little solitary, a smidge colder, but a lot peaceful, muting the voices in his head, the complaints of the other hikers, and the doubt that had seemed to surround him these days.

In the last year, his life had gotten busier. When he'd first set foot on the trail, his intent was to find freedom, to rediscover himself and the world around him. Then, as he'd gained strength and confidence, he'd needed more.

New challenges. A purpose.

Giving back seemed like the next step. But after his last conversation with Eva, he'd been left with a feeling like he might have truly done her a disservice, and that didn't sit right with him.

What *was* he doing, anyway? With a prominent family, it would be easy enough to contribute money to causes. He could leverage his platform, could use his cancer diagnosis to bring awareness. And yet, he was running away from it.

He was readying his sleeping bag when his tent wobbled. "Cruz?"

It was Mara. "Yes?"

"Sorry to bother you."

"No. It's fine." He unzipped his tent and crawled out. "What's up."

"It's Brian. He's not in his tent."

"Oh?"

"Yeah, um." Her expression turned sheepish. "I'm a little neurotic, you know. I take care of so many patients on my shifts, and I like to keep my ducks in a row. Anyway, Brian left a little earlier to do some of his 'business,' but he's not back yet. He went that way." She pointed toward the direction where Cruz had instructed them to do their personal hygiene. "Thought you should know."

More rules for these hiking trips. I need to make sure there are more rules.

Like traveling in buddy teams, and notifying the tour guide if they were leaving the area.

"Thank you for letting me know. I can take it from here."

"You sure?"

"Yes, I'm sure." He grabbed his flashlight from his pack, sighing to himself. "I'll head out there just in case. You have my number on your phone?"

"Yes."

"Text me as soon as he returns."

"Okay. I'll stay up until you get back." She hiked a thumb over to Lloyd. "He's sound asleep."

Cruz nodded, smiling for good measure, in hopes to ease her worry. As far as trails went, was it possible for Brian to lose his way? Sure. It was dark, and if he hadn't been paying attention to his surroundings, he could get turned around.

But it wouldn't be too hard to find him.

Cruz swept his flashlight over the areas they'd traversed during a day. Then, he went in the opposite direction, which took him to the junction where Spirit Trail began.

He trained his flashlight down the path, which was now clear of debris. One could see where the trail wound through and around trees, and from where he stood, not a single rock blocked the path.

He smiled, chest swelling with pride. His earlier doubts fell away.

He helped make that happen. Now, people could enjoy the trail in relative safety. They could focus on enjoying nature rather than feel threatened by it.

Like Brian.

Cruz took off down the path. "Brian!" He called out into the dark, and did so every few seconds, waiting for a response though no one answered back.

A quarter of a mile in, he knew that his and Blue Moon's trail shelter was coming up to the right. He hadn't been able to check if there was a response to his last entry, and while he couldn't do so now, he panned his flashlight in that direction, in case Brian had found his way to it by mistake.

Still, no dice. And, there was no text or call from Mara.

"Brian!" He yelled louder now, to match the rising worry within him.

From afar, Cruz heard the sound of voices, a mixture of octaves that echoed through the trees. He jogged down the path, finding himself in the whirlpool of a loud conversation.

"C'mon, lady, I just want to wash my hands."

"And I want you to get off my property."

Cruz stepped off the path to the left, to what he knew would lead to a cottage. He'd once noted how quaint it was during the trail maintenance. It was small, built on a hill so a balcony overlooked the trail. From what he'd been able to tell, the balcony wrapped around to a porch.

Which he now realized also looked over the B & B.

Dammit. This was an Espiritu-owned property.

He jogged down the path until he reached Brian, illuminated by a motion detector spotlight. He was holding the end of a hose.

And when he looked up, there was Eva, one hand clutching the front of her robe, the other holding her phone.

"Of course it's you." Eva's facial expression switched to annoyance when she met Cruz's eyes, or to what he could tell through spots in his vision from the spotlight.

"Evening, Ms. Espiritu," he said, to deescalate the situation. And then, "What's going on here, Brian?"

"It's called trespassing," she called down.

He raised a hand to her as if to say "please, give me a sec," and she huffed. Then, he faced Brian; he was covered in mud.

"I got lost." He shrugged.

"Really?"

"Okay, so no. At first I wasn't lost. But I got a call from my girlfriend, who dumped me mind you, and then I got pissed. And *then* I got lost and then fell into a mud pit."

"Don't forget the trespassing part," Eva added.

"I thought people were nice to hikers. Cruz even told us about trail angels, who bring snacks and water," Brian said. "But you're not an angel. You're kind of a bitch."

"He didn't mean that!" Cruz said to Eva, shutting his eyes for a beat in frustration.

"But you said—"

"Brian, trail angels meet *us* on the trail, and not *everyone* is open to having other people come to use their facilities. Usually there's a sign that says help yourself. You can't just come on someone's property and use their hose."

He really needed to firm up his hiker trip guidelines.

"Great trail guide you have there, giving the wrong information. Are you sure you won't get lost with him?" Eva called, her voice echoing in the night. It grated on Cruz's nerves.

"That isn't necessary," Cruz said through gritted teeth.

"Apparently it is, because you're both on my property." She readjusted her hold on her robe. "You have five minutes before I call the sheriff."

"It's fine. We're going!" Cruz tugged Brian's shirt. "C'mon."

They turned and crunched through the foliage to the path back to Spirit Trail, with Brian cursing behind him.

In the background, Eva yelled, "Four minutes and twenty-two seconds."

"Damn. I was better off before you came. She sure doesn't like you," Brian said.

"No, I guess not."

"Sounds like you need to set things right with her."

That's the thing with intentions. Sometimes it's not enough. It's about the execution of it all.

Eva's words returned to him. Maybe she was right. Had he inserted himself too much in her life? Did he have some responsibility in her unhappiness?

And God, he didn't want that, for anyone he knew.

"You know what, Brian, for as much as you've gotten us in some trouble, that's not a bad idea."

But what was Cruz going to do about it?

At that moment, he needed ideas, another voice in his head. A friend. As they meandered down Spirit Trail, he knew exactly where he could get all three things.

At the familiar opening in the trees, he halted, and so did Brian.

"What are we doing?" Brian said, warily.

"Stay right here. Got it?" Cruz said. "I need to get something."

"In the dark?"

"Yep. It's...work related." Sort of. "Tell me you won't move."

"Right already. I won't move. I swear."

Cruz nodded. Good enough. Then, he stalked into the opening, shining the light ahead of him, to the trail shelter. Then, he dug the box from its hiding place and slipped the notebook out. He tucked it into the waistband of his jeans, and headed back to Brian, who blessedly hadn't left.

Tonight had devolved into a chaotic mess, but at least he had the notebook. He had Blue Moon.

Rolling Stone,

You know, the mere fact that you're evaluating your actions tells me that you're far better than most people I meet.

I, too, have questioned my decisions.

There's one moment in my life that I wish I could take a second chance at. A moment in which I pushed someone away. That break led to a whole host of consequences.

Have you ever thought of the time we have in this world?

Is that my age talking?

Don't answer that. You could be a young man in your twenties and I'm scaring you with morose conversation.

I just think we have a responsibility to leave this world a better place, to do our best for others before we shuffle off this mortal coil, don't you think? At the same time, we can only do so much.

So don't be so hard on yourself, Rolling Stone. From what I know of you, you're not half-bad.

It's been a day, so I'll end it here.

Safe hiking,
Blue Moon

Chapter Five

"As I live and breathe. Is that *the* Eva Espiritu?"

Eva startled at the catcall as she walked through Waterfall Soda Shop's dining area toward the two women in the back corner booth. Both had coffee cups in front of them and were scanning their menus.

As if they hadn't ordered from Waterfall dozens of times.

Eva grinned, and she felt her insides relax. Though she knew she would have to bear some accosting from her two best friends, she was glad to see them. Especially because they would be the only ones to give her sage advice after receiving an email from her archnemesis.

Okay, she might have been overreacting. But after finding him and one of his hikers on her property the other night, and blowing up at them, she couldn't trust herself to decipher the email's intent.

"My God. It has been forever," Kayla Jackson, the woman on the right, said. She was Black, wore her hair in box braids and welcomed Eva with a bright smile and a hug. She slid deeper into the booth, allowing Eva to plop down on the fake leather couch. "How long has it been? Nine weeks? Ten?" She was a retired army wife and a labor and delivery nurse, and as a result tended to think of time in weeks rather than months.

"It's been way more than that." The more headstrong of the two, Joy Punsalan, chimed in. Filipino-American, she had become a close friend of Eva's shortly after the Espiritus had moved to Peak so many years ago. Her expression wasn't quite as open as Kayla's, and the displeasure was clear in her dark brown eyes.

Scratch that—it could be her natural resting nonplussed face. Joy didn't exactly represent her given name. She, too, was a widow; she'd lost Shep about a decade ago.

Eva squirmed in her seat but didn't banter back. She had no excuse for her recent lack of communication. "I'm sorry."

"All of us are busy, Eva, but there is such a thing as texting." Joy picked up a teaspoon and stirred her coffee though she hadn't put anything in it, and it was as effective as her pretending to sip. "You kind of went into a hole."

"I know." All Eva could do was lower her chin to her chest.

"Is it because we're not good enough for you? Now that the B & B's bringing VIPs from all over the place? After that Maggie Thurmond wedding, townies just don't cut it anymore?"

"What? No! Of course not." She pressed a palm on the table to emphasize.

Kayla sipped her coffee. "We read about everything that's going on at the B & B on social media. Unlike you, Gabby and Frankie have the ability to put fingers to keyboard. We know that Spirit Trail was maintained. And that you had that amazing fall festival."

"The sad part is that we don't know anything that's going on with your life specifically," Joy said.

"We're supposed to be in the prime of our lives, aren't we, Joy?" Kayla took a sip of her coffee.

"Yep. With our independent kids. Still healthy, even if menopause is a pain in the—"

"Speak for yourself, I'm still in perimenopause, friend," Kayla bantered back. "Though it's a pain just the same. Yet, despite it, we were going to live our best lives. Together. All three of us. That was the plan."

"Except." Joy raised her eyebrows. "Someone simply stopped answering our group texts. I mean, did she just mute the group chat?"

The guilt trip was as thick as the valley summers. Eva raised a finger. "I answered some of those texts."

"Emojis don't count, Eva. We're supposed to be your best friends."

Eva slumped in resignation. To be honest, thought spirals about Jared and Louis had consumed her. To boot, she felt alone in them. Both Kayla and Joy had been super accepting of Jared too, and Eva wasn't about to bust their supportive bubble by telling them of her woes.

"But we still love you," Kayla's eyes brightened after a protracted silence, and a smile replaced what had been her faux frown.

Relief coursed through her. She looked to Joy, who was the true test. "Really?"

"Yeah, I guess." Her lips quirked in mischief, followed by a slow wink. She set down the teaspoon dramatically. "Oh, come on. You know we can't stay mad. Besides, we kept in touch with the girls, and thought that you'd come around when it was time."

Eva heaved a sigh. And she looked at her friends, cheeks burning at her shame. That she hadn't thought of them enough. "You have every right to be mad. I've been a little MIA."

Kayla nudged her with a shoulder. "We all have our ups and downs, Eva. And we wanted to give you time to sort out what you were feeling. We know it's been a lot, with Jared. If space was what you wanted, then you should have it."

"It has been a lot," she admitted, though she couldn't yet allow herself to crack into her thoughts about Jared. Yes, she'd been able to write down her feelings, vaguely, on paper for Rolling Stone, but to speak it aloud?

"Let's move slowly then. So…what's up? What prompted the text?"

The burn in her cheeks flooded her face. "I'm sorry. I don't want it to seem like the only reason I texted was because…"

"Staaaap," Joy said. "No need for that. We're friends through and through. So, get on with it."

"Okay then." Eva turned on her phone and clicked on the email that she received last night, an email that had kept her up all night long. An email that could only be deciphered by her two dearest friends. "This is from Cruz Forrester, the owner of Cross Trails."

"The hiking company in town?" Joy asked. "I've seen the owner around. He's cute."

Eva's cheeks warmed. "He and I…we've butted heads the last few weeks. He must've found my email address on the website."

She slid the phone to the middle of the table. Kayla read the email aloud.

"I think that we got off to a rough start. It would be great to coexist in a small town, and I would like to apologize, in person, and try to repair what could be a civil relationship between two Peak small business owners. I was wondering if we could have dinner. Maybe at River's Edge Restaurant at six tomorrow? If that's not a good time, please let me know when you're free."

Joy's smile widened. "This meetup feels like it has some romantic undertones."

"It says he 'wants to apologize in person.'" Eva pointed at the words.

"And yet, who requests a time to apologize? They would simply do so."

Eva pursed her lips. Joy had a point.

"Why does his name sound familiar?" Kayla asked, now monopolizing the phone and clicking to show the sender's email address.

Eva braced herself. "Because his family is Forrester Watches."

As she predicted, both Joy and Kayla squealed.

"How in the world did you get involved with *him*?" Joy asked.

Eva jumped into the explanation of how she'd met Cruz and her continued interactions with him. She talked about Spirit Trail and the loss of privacy from the trail maintenance, and when he showed up with his runaway hiker.

But what she hadn't mentioned was that when she had received the email, she'd been equally curious and thrilled. There wasn't a bit of animosity in her veins as she'd read it.

It was…an interesting realization, for a lack of a better term.

Her friends nodded and hummed and gasped through the storytelling, and Eva fell into the moment as she would her favorite cotton sheets. She felt understood; these two had seen her through the worst of her grief after she lost Louis—years after the initial crisis point, long after the flowers had wilted and the freezer meals had been consumed.

"What's your feeling, Joy? Agree with me?" Kayla asked.

"I agree. You have to meet up with him, E," Joy said. "He's a Forrester."

"I don't care about that," Eva said.

"Then think about this: this is a man who wants to spend time with you, even if it's just to apologize."

Eva's heart did a little summersault, which was a betrayal of utmost proportions. "We're supposed to hate one another. I haven't even given him permission to call me by my first name."

Her friends broke out into laughter.

"That's why he called you Ms. Espiritu." Kayla cackled. "How is that even a thing?"

"I don't know," Eva said. "It felt good at the time to withhold it."

"Goodness. It's like you're back in grade school or something. Also, it sounds like he felt bad about the other night." Joy's fingers interlaced in front of her. "Are you going to say yes?"

Eva hadn't even gotten to that point in the decision-making. She was still stuck on his intentions. "Should I?"

"Up to you. Though, you'll have to hear him out and consider forgiving him."

"And, you're not really the best at forgiveness," Kayla added. "At least, not like us."

It was just like her friends to tell it the way it was, and then remind her that she couldn't be a hypocrite either.

"My opinion?" Kayla continued, "The mere fact you came out of hiding to talk to us about this email means that something about this guy piqued your interest. Though, I don't see how you could not be attracted to him. If I wasn't married... Hell, I am married and I still think he's hot."

"I don't know. He's got that rugged, pretty boy thing around him, and that's not really my type." Joy cackled.

"I don't even remember the last time I had a type." Eva mused. She'd had dates and small flings, sure, since Louis died, but he was her one and only love. Louis had been her type, she guessed.

Cruz infuriated her. And she didn't know what to do with that.

"Do you know what I think?" Joy asked.

Eva snorted. "I'm sure you're about to tell me."

"I think that you should say yes. And we should be there." Joy grinned. "After all, you can't go on your first date without having backup."

"This isn't a date."

"Date, shmate, whatever this is, Kayla and I have to be there, too."

"*If* I say yes, I think I'm grown enough to not have chaperones."

Kayla waved down the wait staff. "But who's going to make sure you actually show up?"

"And in the proper outfit," Joy said.

When the server arrived, they placed their orders, and the pause allowed Eva to piece together what her two friends were implying.

Eva shook her head after the server left. "No. This is not an ugly duckling situation. No makeover for me."

"Who said anything about a makeover?" Joy asked. "You're gorgeous as you are. But you've been so busy taking care of others. Taking care of that B & B. Layers of stress. We're talking about uncovering."

"That sounds like another way of saying makeover." Though, at the mention of it, Eva twirled a piece of hair at the nape of her neck that didn't quite make it to her ponytail. Hair that hadn't been trimmed in months. "That's also not a very feminist thing to say."

"Taking care of yourself *is* being feminist, Eva. It's putting yourself first, above the needs of others."

Kayla added, "Just because we're in the stage of our lives when everybody expects for us to disappear into the background doesn't mean that we have to fall into that trap. We are accomplished women. And, Eva, you should enjoy it. You should love the things that you're doing right now. You should be celebrating your life."

What was it about being with such close and honest friends that made Eva want to break down and cry? No one spoke to her like this. Not her children, not her family. Then again, she'd created a life in which her children respected her emotions and gave her space. And she hadn't seen her family nearly enough.

Note to self: call your cousins.

Kayla reached out and put a hand over hers, and Joy did the same. It was a reminder that they would not allow her to fall. They would always hold her to the standard that she deserved. And they would be there for her.

"As long as you promise that there won't be blue eyeliner anywhere in the plans," Eva said. "I know fashion is cyclical, but I don't ever want to relive the nineties, except of course for those high-waisted jeans."

Her two friends laughed.

"But fine. You both can come so long as you're incognito."

Whether or not they were right that Cruz was interested in her, Eva was sure she would need the push on the day itself.

Because if she was being honest, she was attracted to her archnemesis.

The next evening, Cruz fiddled with his phone as he sat at a round table outside of River's Edge Restaurant. Though it was only a little past six in the evening, the sun had set, with darkness tinged in orange. Daylight savings wasn't until next week, and he could feel the change in the air, from fall to winter. Next to his table was a tall heating lamp emitting enough warmth that he'd shed his windbreaker and was comfortable in a thin knit sweater and long casual pants.

What wasn't changing, though, was his current status, of being alone.

Eva was late, and he was starting to lose hope. Unable to sit still in the wrought-iron chair behind the table that held two water glasses and a bread bowl, he repositioned himself while randomly scrolling through his phone.

He clicked on their email thread once more to check if she had canceled at the last minute.

Cruz,

That will be fine. Six o'clock sounds great to me and I will
see you there.

Eva

Her last email had lacked animosity and she'd signed it
off with "Eva."

That was a good sign, right?

The server, dressed in all black and wearing a waist apron,
approached his table. His face bordered on sheepish. Cruz had
arrived at the restaurant ten minutes before their designated
meeting time. So he'd technically been waiting for twenty.
And in that time, the waiter had solicited him twice for his
drink order.

Cruz, in his attempt at being the gentleman, had held off
until Eva arrived.

Now, he wished he had an old-fashioned in hand.

He didn't remember the last time someone stood him up.

"Sir, can I get you anything at all? It doesn't look like your
party is here yet," the server said. Then, realizing what he'd
implied, his cheeks bloomed pink.

Poor guy, Cruz thought to himself.

Hell, poor me.

He heaved a sigh. "Let's do this. How about the carbonara
and a bowl of tomato bisque and pack it to go." Then, Cruz
thought twice. "And an old fashioned while I wait for it."

The waiter broke out into a smile. No doubt he was worried about not getting a tip. "Coming right up."

As the server left, his phone dinged with a calendar invite.
"Millie taking over Peak" was the title. Then, below it was
her travel information, right down to the minute.

His baby sister was arriving in a week. Hell or high water, she was going to be in his tightly protected bubble.

A text came in from Millie herself: Are you ready for me?

He answered, pressing his lips into a grin: You're coming? I didn't think you were serious.

Please, just make sure that I have a bed.

I've got a pretty sweet backyard that's even and without a ton of rocks. Makes for a comfortable surface for a sleeping pad.

There was silence for a beat, in which Cruz knew Millie was sweating it.

Seriously? Do I need to send myself a bed?

I don't know. Will you? Cruz snorted. What did his sister think he was, a caveman? Hadn't they been raised in the same home? But he didn't correct her. Just because.

Laughing and whispering came from the inside and Cruz looked up to see a woman walking in between tables, coming his way.

And she was beautiful.

Straight hair in a long bob that reached her shoulders, it was parted to one side, her head tilted to the right just so, as if appraising him.

She was wearing a floral dress that was tapered at the waist, and hung long, down to her calves. It had long sleeves, but the dress was formfitting. Though the dress itself was casual, the overall look was so…soft, and sexy.

Cruz had been resigned that Eva was not showing up, that it took him seconds to realize it was actually her.

Eva. In front of him.

His heart rate spiked, and with a sudden nervousness, he

stood, the chair leg squeaking against the floor. Behind her were other people—women, he thought—but he couldn't be bothered to find out because there was something different about Eva.

There wasn't a stitch of anger on her face.

At least, not outright anger. Her expression was more wary, more professional, and her eyes weren't shooting daggers at him. Yet.

For a moment he hoped that he looked all right. He palmed the back of his head and hoped that he'd tamed the cowlicks that always had their way.

He was out of practice.

"Wow, hi. You look…nice." The moment the words left his mouth, he gasped. "I mean, not that you don't ever look nice but—"

She shut her eyes like a teacher who'd been delivered a ludicrous line from a student. But, instead of a clapback, she said, "I'm sorry I'm late."

"No, it's fine."

The server, thank goodness, picked exactly that time to come with his old fashioned, setting it on the table and then pulling the chair out for Eva.

"I ordered a drink while waiting. Did you want something?" he asked, first waiting for Eva to sit before he did.

"Sure. Riesling, please. Danbury Winery?"

"Sure thing," the server said.

"The local winery," Cruz noted, when the waiter left.

"Yes, I always want to support the local businesses. Makes for good partnerships. Much like communication—it's so important in small towns, don't you think?"

"Ah. We're here already." Within a minute and she was getting to the heart of their situation. "We haven't even ordered yet."

"Well, I've never been one to waste time. We get too little of it as it is."

He remembered what Sydney at the office had told him about Eva. That she was a widow.

It was only then that that fact had settled in. That maybe her actions were in consequence to her loss.

And maybe why she intrigued him so much, since he'd had his own losses that he'd had to contend with.

"First, can I call you Eva?"

"Yes. Please." Her expression softened. "And before you say anything more, I'm sorry I was so formal with you. I can be a little stubborn."

Her apology took him aback, and he relaxed in his seat. "I didn't exactly make a good impression."

"Impressions." She emphasized the *s* in the word, though did so with a smile.

She was joking with him.

Cruz laughed, though was unsure how to proceed. When he'd emailed her after the Brian and the hose situation, his mission had been to quell this tension between them. To shake on being civil. To tread on neutral ground. But now that she was here, and she seemed different, and amiable, his agenda dissolved, and he wanted more.

A connection, maybe.

Which was something he hadn't had in a long time.

He tested the moment. "I started to worry that I wouldn't get a chance to change your opinion about me. That maybe after the other night, I messed it up for good."

"To tell you the truth, I wasn't exactly sure that I was going to come, but I was convinced," she said.

"What finally convinced you?"

"Curiosity, I guess." She looked down at the table briefly and then back up at him.

Meeting her gaze, something crackled in the air. Her words sounded like a challenge.

And he wanted to meet it.

"Here's your wine." The waiter set Eva's wine in front of her, momentary blocking his vision.

Thank goodness, because he'd needed a moment to think, to internally scan his body that reflected back that yes, he was attracted to this woman. As he watched her biting her cheek as she read the menu, his internal temperature rose. And her lips, shiny and dark red, tempted him.

Not good.

Not the lips—the whole situation. Because this was Eva Espiritu. Not a woman he could flirt with and walk away from.

Cruz had had relationships since his cancer diagnosis, but he'd been careful to be with women who'd understood his boundaries. In his case, these were women who'd been unserious and laxed in their relationships.

Eva was neither of those things.

Cruz was so immersed in his thoughts that he'd forgotten that he'd ordered. After Eva handed the server the menu, Cruz jumped in and said, "I'll have the chicken parmigiana."

The server looked from him to Eva and back. "Sir, should I have the chef plate your carbonara?"

Eva raised her eyebrows, confused.

"Right… I ordered because I thought you weren't coming," he explained. *And, also, I am fully not in control of my brain at the moment.* To the server, he said, "The carbonara will be perfect."

When the server left, Cruz settled back in his chair and restarted his efforts to have his wits about him. "Eva, look, to cut to the chase: I apologize for the misunderstandings we've had. On the trail, and in general, for the conversations that went sideways. I don't claim to be the cheeriest of people, but I don't aim to be rude, or harsh."

She took a sip of her wine, and in the pause, Cruz expected a dismissal.

"Thank you for saying that. I'm sorry, too."

He sat back in his chair, surprised. This was not how he thought this meeting was going to go. "I feel like this is a trick."

She laughed, and the shock of seeing it, at witnessing her face light up, shot warmth through his chest. "It's not a trick. I've been thinking about how I handle things, and that maybe I could do things a little better." Her eyebrows bunched together. "It doesn't mean that I'm not upset that the trail feels like open season on my property—"

"And I know I had something to do with that. That thing with Brian was horrible, and I wish it hadn't happened."

"Yeah, I wish it hadn't happened either. It scared me. And I don't think that will be the last time that that happens."

"That's fair. Looking back, I could've spoken to you about it beforehand. I was eager. I've hiked that trail a number of times, and wanted to make it better."

Her body seemed to relax, and a smile graced her face. "I can't continue to be upset that you want to make Peak better. At the risk of sounding weak, I accept your apology."

"Wow."

"What?"

"I can't believe how easy tonight has been."

"Ha." Eva leaned in with mischief on her face. "I am anything but easy."

Heat filled his entire midsection, but he swallowed down with a sip of his drink. "If there's anyone that knows that fact, it's me." The conversation was unfolding better than he'd expected, so he dug into his mental notes, items he'd thought about when he'd decided to contact Eva. "I have a couple of ideas to help make the rear of your cottage a little more private, if you're interested."

She leaned back and crossed her arms. "Interested."

"A fence, and a tasteful sign near that small path behind your house could do the trick. I can do it in a weekend. I'm pretty handy."

"The watch prince does labor?" A smirk lifted her lips.

"Oh no," he said, shaking his head, though, in fact, enamored by her straightforwardness. "This is where we're going to go?"

"I mean, did you learn carpentry at boarding school?" She tapped her chin with a finger. "Or wait. Do you have specialty watches for those in carpentry? I did see that you had a line for equestrians."

"Ha. We do like to offer our niche customers their own set of timepieces." He leaned in closer. "Just like I have a lot to learn about you, Eva, you have a lot to learn about me."

And at that moment, he hoped that she indeed would.

Blue Moon,

I'm definitely not in my twenties.

And what is this talk about shuffling off this mortal coil? That's pretty grim! I don't plan to shuffle off anything for a very, very long time, if I can help it.

The facts: I'm definitely Gen X. So, there is no fear at all in discussing age-appropriate things.

To answer your question, as to whether or not I believe that people should leave the world a better place: I do very much agree.

To be honest, I have thought about this for a long time. I haven't always been in the best of health. I have faced mortality. I know that sounds a little dramatic, but it's true in the realest way.

Only my family knows, but I am in remission from stage 1 colon cancer. It's not something I talk about, ever. I consider it my baggage, and mine alone, so I'm not looking for pity or sympathy.

I say this to give context that there are many ways I think a little bit differently, and why sometimes people don't understand me. So thank you, for reminding me that I can only do so much. I'm sometimes too eager for my own good.

Blue Moon, I bet my rockstar water filter that you have brought so much good to so many people. But something I learned this last month is that it's not on one person to fix everything.

Rolling Stone

Chapter Six

"Mom! Are you listening?"

Eva blinked herself back to the present, to the massive warehouse of Skyline Drive Superstore. It was the largest building in Peak and its surrounding areas, where they sold everything from couches to lawnmowers to plywood.

Speaking of wood, they were standing in front of fencing boards. "Yes, of course I was."

Gabby giggled. "Right. You weren't, but that's fine. What is it you want for your fence? Cedar or redwood, or pine? Or did you want synthetic…"

Her daughter went on about the size and height of planks, but Eva couldn't form a coherent thought.

I am in remission from cancer.

Rolling Stone's words had continued to cycle in her head since she'd read them early this morning. She'd awoken with newfound excitement for today's meeting with Cruz to buy fencing materials, and a hike to the trail shelter had felt like the perfect activity.

And though she would never admit it to Cruz, Spirit Trail was now a much easier and safer path to traverse.

The vulnerability Rolling Stone had showed—the trust he'd placed in Eva—felt special and important. And she'd hoped that what she'd scribbled in response was worthy of it.

His admission was yet another reminder that everyone had

their own struggles to contend with. And the last line in his note, that she needn't have to fix everything, hit her in the chest. That she couldn't fix what happened in the past.

"Oh, this stain is perfect." Gabby had moved on, apparently, to wooden board samples. "This closely matches your cottage."

"I agree." Eva pulled out her phone and took a photo of the swatch, because there was no way that she was going to remember any of this.

"I have to say, I love that you and Cruz are working together, instead of being mortal enemies," Gabby said, taking out her own phone, scrolling. "You two really turned the corner."

It was a full ninety degrees, if she was being honest. The dinner had been that turning point. Cruz, she realized, was a good person. Presumptive, or eager, as he called it, but good nonetheless.

"Oh my…oh my gosh. Mom!" Gabby looked up from her phone and all but shoved it in Eva's face.

"What is it?" Eva reared back and tried to make sense of the words on the page, but before she could string two sentences together, Gabby pulled back the screen. "Goodness, Gabby."

"Sorry, oh my God. This is so great. The Landrys said yes."

"What?" Eva's jaw dropped, stunned. Gabby had tried to reach Elizabeth in the last week with no response. They'd all assumed that she'd moved on to another venue.

"She says that she's so excited, and the September date is on. Yeah!" She raised a hand up, prompting Eva to slap it.

Eva did so with gusto. This was a major win. It was also a relief. She didn't like to be proven wrong, but if it was the case that she'd overestimated how intrusive the tents and hikers were to the B & B's privacy, then she would take it.

Soon, Gabby started to sway to the song playing overhead in celebration. It was elevator music, but at that moment, Eva didn't care about making a scene. She scooped Gabby's hands into hers; they swung their arms, laughing.

Besides Maggie Thurmond's sponsored wedding earlier this year, Elizabeth Landry was their biggest wedding client.

Someone cleared their throat; she and Gabby turned their heads to the right, breathing heavily.

Eva froze. Cruz.

"Oh, hello," Gabby whispered. "Rugged silver fox in the vicinity."

"Shh." Eva shot her a look. Though it didn't quite transmit what she'd intended apparently, because her daughter simply laughed.

Cruz was wearing his usual: hiking pants and this time with a hoodie. He walked with one hand in his pocket, his gait confident. He walked with the intention of taking up space, with the shoulders back, chest lifted.

At their dinner, Cruz had been insistent at building her a fence at his cost, and despite her pride that hadn't wanted his help, she'd agreed.

Their dinner had been civil, and even comfortable. They'd bantered, and while the wine had let her be flirtatious, she didn't regret it. It was nice to dress up, to have eaten a good meal with someone who made her think, and laugh.

At times she'd even been breathless.

As she was right this moment.

He was looking at her in the same way as he'd done at the restaurant, with a smoldering gaze. Even if she was back in her jeans and long-sleeve flannel shirt.

Gabby got out ahead of her, extending her hand. "You must be Cruz Forrester."

He shook her daughter's hand. "I am, and you're Gabby, right?"

"That is correct. I'm the youngest."

"Morning, Cruz."

He nodded. "Eva. Ready to shop?"

"Yep." She still couldn't look at him straight on, focusing on his nose instead. "Gabby and I were taking a look at all the different types of wood, and I'm not quite sure what I really need. Or even how much I need."

"Speaking of me," Gabby said, holding up her phone. "The reception in here's not so great, and I've got to send a couple of emails. Meet you outside, Mom?"

"Sure."

She grinned at Cruz. "Are you installing the fence, too?"

"Yep."

"Great. You'll get to meet Frankie. That's my sister." Her gaze darted between him and Eva.

"Nice."

There was a beat in which Gabby appraised them both, then said, "I'm glad you're taking care of my mom...with this whole fence business."

Eva peered at her daughter—was she trying to play matchmaker?

Cruz nodded. "I'm just lending a hand. Pretty sure your mom could run around most of us twice over."

A flush crept up Eva's neck from the compliment.

"Good answer, Cruz." Gabby grinned, then winked at Eva. Winked.

Eva internally groaned.

When her daughter finally stepped away, Eva said, "Kids. They say the darnedest things, even when they're full-fledged adults."

He let out a breath. "So it wasn't just me?"

"Nope. She was definitely insinuating that you needed to 'take care' of me."

"At least she thinks I'm okay?"

"Yeah, it's probably safe to say that, though it's very easy to win her over. Frankie on the other hand..."

"Ah…so when I come over to build the fence, should I bring something to smooth over the first meeting. Flowers, maybe?"

"Eh, you'd be better off bringing a plant she can mother instead of cut flowers."

He pressed a finger to his temple. "Noted."

A laugh rippled between them until it faded into silence. And surprisingly, awkwardness did not follow. "So, we should probably get this going," Eva said.

"Yep. So, in regards to your lumber and how much you need, I went ahead and measured and took photos of the area, and you have some choices."

"When did you do all that?"

"The other day. I was hiking Spirit Trail and thought to bring my tape measure with me."

He slipped out a folded piece of paper from his back pocket, revealing a basic sketch. Stepping in next to her, he said, "Not sure how far you want to extend the fencing, but in my opinion, having something here—" he pointed to what was supposed to be the path "—is enough of a signal for hikers to stop. I don't think you'll need to block this entire area. Thoughts?"

"I agree. Though I think it should extend this way about a foot." She drew an imaginary line with her finger on the sketch, though now acutely aware of how close he was to her, their arms almost touching, with him hovering above her.

He smelled like the forest, leaves and wood. Or, it could have been the store itself, but she was swept up into it nonetheless and into the image of Cruz hiking past her window. Of her peeking out and watching him in his element.

Still, she kept on task somehow and picked out the wood—pressure-treated pine for its resistance to rot—and the stain Gabby had suggested. Of all the fence designs, she liked the dog-eared picket fence style. Cruz found a sales rep and ordered the materials he would need.

After Cruz paid, they walked toward the double doors of

the store, which opened automatically, bringing in the cool air. And with the sun at its peak, warming her face, Eva felt content and productive, and completely relaxed.

"That wasn't bad," she mused.

"What wasn't bad?"

"You." The word came out before she could stop it. She slapped a hand against her mouth to stifle a laugh.

"What?" Pure disbelief was on his face.

"I mean, I can't believe that we didn't fight once."

"We didn't fight at all at dinner."

"You're right...but we were both on our best behavior then. We spent more than an hour in there."

He stuck his hands in his pocket; there was a gleam in his eyes. "Do you want to fight? I can find something to rag on if you'd like."

She laughed. "No, that's absolutely fine. Thank you. This was...fun."

"I had fun, too."

Gabby walked up to them, tearing Eva's attention away from Cruz. "How did it go?"

"Well," Eva answered. She noticed that Gabby was tense. "Everything okay?"

"I think I'm hangry." She gestured to a food truck at the other end of the parking lot. "Can we grab something to eat before we head back? Frankie recommends it. They serve paninis. Cruz? Want to join us?"

"Oh, Gabby, he's probably busy—" Eva glanced at Cruz. Everything had gone so well, and departing from here felt right and safe.

"But, Mom."

"She's right, actually," Cruz said. "I need to check into work, since I'll be at your place tomorrow."

"How long will it take to put the fence up?" Gabby asked.

"Just the day. It's only about twenty-four feet we're talking about, and the fence is already premade in sections. So, easy peasy." He looked at Eva. "Then, I'll be completely out of your hair."

I don't want you out of my hair flashed through Eva's head, startling her. She quickly masked her reaction with a flip smile. "Well, I hope you have a good rest of your day."

"I'll see both of you tomorrow. I'll be there first thing, around nine?" He walked backward.

"Absolutely!" Gabby said, waving until Cruz ducked into his car. She gripped Eva's forearm. "Oh, Mom, he is cute."

She wound her arm around Gabby's. "I want you to try not to drool over him tomorrow."

"Oh my gosh ewwww. I'm not drooling over him. I'm drooling over him and you. You should have seen the two of you together. You were both laughing at the same time. It was sweet."

"He said something funny. There's nothing sweet about it. And he's actually far from sweet. He's…" She searched for the word: rough, grumpy, detached?

"Like you. But taller. And also a man. So when a person makes you laugh, it's a good thing." She pressed her hand to her belly. "My tummy's rumbling. Have I mentioned that Nathan made a comment that I was a picky eater?"

A ping went off in Eva's head at her mention of Nate. "Where did that come from?"

"I just remembered. And because unlike Cruz who can make you laugh, Nathan continues to be a pain."

Eva hummed though didn't bite. Gabby was the kind of woman who backed off the more one pursued. From when she was a little girl, Gabby could not be convinced to share her own secrets.

As predicted, her daughter continued. "He's always got something to say."

"Like?"

"So I picked up a tree from their orchard last week, and he kept telling me that I needed to remember to water it. As if I haven't taken care of a real Christmas tree in my entire twenty-six years."

Eva raised a finger. "Technically your dad and I watered the trees. And, last year, you called the orchard back to try to return your tree because you *forgot* to water it."

"You know what I mean." She grunted in exasperation. "He's insufferable. Even the little things get to me. Like how he runs his hands through his hair. Ugh."

Eva raised her eyebrows. Bingo. Now they were getting somewhere. If she hadn't known before, she knew now.

Something was brewing between them again.

Eva changed her mind about staying out of their complicated relationship. On the contrary, she might need to keep a closer eye.

The last time the two broke up, Gabby had been devastated.

For the moment, Eva kept her face as neutral as fence lumber. "Maybe you *are* hangry."

They'd gotten to the end of the food truck line, and the smell of cheese and garlic and onions wafted by. Gabby squeezed herself closer to Eva. "One day, I'd like to be the one who's smitten and giggly. Like how you were with Cruz."

Smitten and giggly?

"And don't even try to deny it," Gabby continued. "You blush every time I say his name."

"I'm not blushing."

Gabby rolled her eyes. "Sure, Mom."

That evening, Cruz shut the rear of his Outback and dragged Millie's two large hard-shell suitcases to his front porch. Looking back, he saw that his sister had halted at the driveway. "What's up?"

"It's so small, Cruz. I mean, it's cute, but it's small."

He unlocked the front door, and tried to see his modern log cabin from her point of view. His childhood home outside of Denver was five times its size, maybe even more. And unlike his cabin, made of wood that blended into the foliage around him, theirs had been regal with its white column frontage, long driveway and manicured bushes.

It didn't bother Cruz that his sister had been surprised by his home. It was that she hadn't understood that it was perfect for him.

He stepped inside, and when Millie finally followed behind him, he presented his abode. "Living room, kitchen, dining area."

Her eyes scanned the space, no doubt taking in the tiny eat-in kitchen. "The bedrooms are…"

"Mine is up the stairs there, next to the refrigerator. It's a loft. And the office is the guest room, behind that door." He gestured to the right. "I have two bathrooms—one in the loft, and the other en suite with the office."

She moved around the space as if she was expecting a jump scare and opened the office door. She visibly exhaled. "There's a bed in there."

"You didn't trust me?"

"It's not that…okay, yeah well, sometimes I *don't* trust you. You were always such a prankster." She looked around, contemplative. Then, she nodded. "And this isn't bad. It's rustic, but not bad. Do you have any food in that fridge?"

"Nope. I was going to order delivery for tonight. Pizza? Mexican? Chinese?"

"Surprise me. I could eat my suitcases."

"Then I'd better get them out of the way." He dragged the suitcases into the office, grunting. "Damn these are heavy. What's in here?"

She shrugged. "A little bit of this. A little bit of that. I didn't know what to pack. And you can't forget my skin care. Turning forty-six isn't for the weak."

Cruz laughed, though allowed himself to really look at Millie. They had the same fair skin and blue eyes, but while he'd allowed his gray to grow in, she hadn't, blending in dark strands and highlights with her blond hair.

"You look great to me."

"That's nice of you to say, but it's about how I feel. So I have a new normal. Resistance training, walks, HRT and retinol, baby."

"What's HRT?"

"Hormone replacement therapy."

"Ah." Though, he only knew a little bit about this season in her life. He could only handle what had been thrust on him years ago: from diagnosis to surgery to remove the tumor, to treatment, and everything that went with recovery. Including the emotional challenges.

He shoved his morose thoughts away.

"Anyway, give me a sec to change out of my travel clothes and I'll be ready to eat and catch up with you."

As Millie closed the guest room door, Cruz called to order a couple of appetizer samplers from Mountain Rush, the karaoke bar down the street. He knew Millie had a penchant for anything fried, and requested delivery ASAP.

The pipes groaned in the house; his sister was taking a shower, so he decided to check his texts, grabbing a sparkling water from the fridge.

He was halfway to taking his first drink when among the bolded new texts was one from Eva: I appreciate your help today.

He felt himself soften. Coming upon her and Gabby while they danced in the aisle was eye opening. Just proved how multilayered she was. And though he'd questioned her surprise at how well they'd gotten along, he, too, was pleased.

He didn't know where any of this was going to go. His intention was to make amends with Eva so that he would feel better, but he found himself looking forward to the next time they see one another.

Thumbs hovering over the phone, he debated on what to write back. Professional or banter? He didn't remember the last time he'd questioned what to text. But getting it wrong wasn't an option.

So, for tomorrow, I like a splash of cream in my coffee. No ice with my lemonade.

Three dots appeared instantly. Cruz couldn't help but grin.

Is that right? Berries in your oatmeal, too? Icing on your cinnamon rolls?

Now you're talking.

I'll get right on it. She added an eyeroll emoji.
He snorted. I'll see you at 9.

See you.

He didn't exit out of this message app, reading her words once more. What was she doing at this moment? Was she already in bed? Or was she still working?

"What are you grinning at over there?" Millie snapped Cruz out of this thoughts. Standing at the doorway in pajamas, she was brushing her hair.

Had he been grinning?

He set the phone down on its face, sipped his water. "Oh, nothing. How was your shower?"

"Amazing water pressure."

"Glad you approve." He crossed his arms over his chest. "Though I don't know why you underestimate me."

She plopped on the couch and nestled herself in. "Can you blame me? In between your hiking trips, you were living in that shack in Boiling Springs."

"Respect. Not a shack. A tiny house."

"Cruz, a tiny house means that there should be indoor plumbing."

"It was a short walk to the outhouse."

"I can't with you." She heaved a sigh. "Anyway, this...this is much better. It could use a little bit in terms of decor, but it's a structure. How long have you had it?"

"About a year now. I was doing a ton of traveling between the two offices. With the third opening up next year, I'll buy another small place nearby, and keep this one open for when I need to pop back in, just like the one in Boiling Springs."

"But is this really what you want to keep doing? Opening shops and then buying little houses where those locations are?" The humor was gone in her voice; apparently his sister was ready to lay into him her first night here.

"As of right now, yes."

"That doesn't sound so...stable."

"Nothing is stable, Millie. I'm doing what feels right for now."

It was fully against everything their father had taught them, against the entire Forrester thought process of getting ahead of the times, of attempting to predict the future and making decisions against it.

Cruz could barely wrap his head around what could happen in February at his next follow-up appointment, much less attempt to think beyond that.

A silence settled between them. To break the tension, he grabbed a sparkling water from the fridge and tossed one to Millie.

She caught it expertly, cracking the seal and taking a sip. She peered at him. "Are you worried about your follow-up appointment?"

The breath left his body. "I mean, yeah. The scan, the exam, the blood test. All of it."

"Have you had any symptoms?"

"No. Then again, I didn't have any the first time." Cancer cells were found during his first routine preventative screening not long after he turned forty-five. Cruz had gone into the procedure without a lick of concern, only to wake to find out that his doctor had removed suspicious tissue from his colon.

Things moved quickly after malignancy was established. He'd had surgery to remove the cancer, and he was lucky to walk away from it with clear margins, but the fear had never gone away.

With every follow-up screening, test, blood draw, or physical exam, Cruz felt the anxiety viscerally. Only spending time outdoors calmed him.

Being outside, hiking, the feel of his boots on the trail kept him from drowning in his worrying, spiraling thoughts.

"You know we're here for you, right?"

He nodded, swallowing hard. "I do."

"We were there for you before."

"I know that too."

And he'd hated it. Not because he hadn't wanted his family's help, but because it was unfair for them to carry his burden. He couldn't stand to see them exhausted and worried. He remembered how sad he'd been when his dad had passed. Timothy Forrester had had a cardiac arrest in his seventies, but living through that and then knowing he was causing Millie and their mother more pain had been too much to bear.

"So why not reach out to us? Or even open up? Mom misses you. You could even just tell her how you feel. She would love this place too." She grinned. "After I clean it up a little. We wouldn't want her to panic."

The humor was back, which meant that Cruz was in the clear. "I think this place is about as big as her bedroom."

"Um...her bedroom beats this main area by at least a hundred square feet." She hefted herself to her feet, sipped on her drink and meandered to the refrigerator, where Cruz had tacked up random receipts and notices. She fingered one out of a magnet. "Picket fence?"

Of all the things she could have pick out. Cruz resisted rolling his eyes. He could see the teasing now. Which meant providing her with the least amount of ammo. "Yep."

"For this place?"

"No."

"You're so forthcoming, big brother."

"Just...work." It was the easiest thing to say. "You know how it is."

"I do know." She turned and leaned back against the fridge. "Will you take me to work with you?"

"Sure." His body lightened with the suggestion. This was the first time she'd suggested remotely joining him on the trails. "Do you have proper outdoor clothing?"

"You're asking *me* if I have the proper clothing? I came prepared. I have a couple of outfits in my suitcase. Even hiking boots."

"Great. Then, yes. Though not tomorrow because I'm working on...a special project. But the day after I can take you on a hike. A short one, so you can break in your boots."

"I'm in. I've got a lot to do for work tomorrow anyway." She winced. "You do have Wi-Fi, right?"

"Yes, Millie. I do."

The chime of his doorbell sounded through the house. Millie leapt toward the door. "Oh thank goodness."

Cruz followed behind, to see that Chip, one of his part-timers at Cross Trails, was delivering.

"Here's your order." Chip raised a hand to Cruz. "Evening, boss."

"Hold on a sec. You're delivering too? Aren't you bartending at Mountain Rush?"

"Yep. But they needed an extra hand in the kitchen, and the bar was slow. I saw your name on the ticket and thought, what the hey, might as well stop by and say hello." He glanced sideways at Millie.

"This is my sister, Millie. Millie, this is Chip. He works at Cross Trails."

"Hi, Chip."

"Nice to meet you. And, boss, I also wanted to see if you needed help putting up that fence for Eva tomorrow morning?"

Cruz frowned. "How did you know…"

"Oh, Gabby told me. Smart idea to put up a fence to block her path off from Spirit Trail. Do you need an assistant?"

"Um…sure, but I'm not getting paid so…"

"Oh, no I'm not looking to get paid. I just like to learn something new. And besides, Gabby and I are hanging out after. So…what time?"

"Nine o'clock." Cruz noticed the blush that had risen to Chip's cheeks. "Gabby, huh?"

"Yep. Well, see you tomorrow, boss."

After they said their goodbyes and closed the door, Cruz took a moment to think about what transpired. Chip and Gabby? Interesting.

He idly dropped the order off on the kitchen counter.

As he unpacked the platters, Millie hopped up on the counter seating. "Hmm…so a picket fence receipt you're cagey about, a special project tomorrow that we now know is you building this fence. You're missing work for this special project because your arrival time is at nine in the morning. Work that you're doing for free? It doesn't take a COO to figure out it's all connected. So who's Eva?"

"Millie," he warned.

She tore open the takeout bag. "Uh-huh. Don't you worry, I have my ways."

Rolling Stone,

Thank you.

Thank you for telling me like it is, for reminding me that I can't blame or hold myself accountable for someone else's actions. I have a bad habit of doing so, probably after a lifetime of taking care of others.

Thank you, too, for trusting me with your diagnosis. I'm sorry that you have had to face that. I have had my own health challenges. I've walked with others with theirs. And I've lost people. So I know what it feels like to grieve and to be angry and to keep things inside.

At the risk of centering myself, I'm honored that you felt safe to tell me your history. I feel the same way about you. I meant what I said in a previous note: I haven't told anyone the things I've written in this notebook. I can barely say them aloud to myself.

Which, now that you've told me that you're a Gen Xer, it makes me feel even better opening up to you. Since you and I are generally the same age, you might have a greater understanding of the breadth of my experience. That we lived through Y2K, and 9/11, and saw the rise of The Internets. :)

Safe hiking, Rolling Stone.
Blue Moon

Chapter Seven

It was only a little after nine in the morning and Eva's family group text was blowing up.

Frankie: I'm going shopping this weekend for Thanksgiving. What should I bring?

Gabby: The silverware

Frankie: Brat! Mom, please wrangle your bunso. Just because she's the youngest doesn't mean she can get away with insinuating that I'm not a good cook

Gabby: It's not me who said it

Eva: Gabby pls don't disrespect your sister. Honestly, I have not thought about the full menu yet.

Jared: Is there a sign-up list? Put me down for anything

Gabby: See? No need to bring anything Ate Frankie. Kuya Jared will take care of it

Eva's heart thudded at Gabby referring to Jared as big brother in the same, natural way she addressed Frankie as her big sister in Tagalog. This time though, she realized that it wasn't out of pain or upsettedness.

Frankie: I can make sisig.

Gabby: Great

Frankie: I'm ignoring that. Also, don't forget the decor

Jared: Fall and holiday decor in one room? Whoa

Eva laughed, then gasped.

This was good, right? Maybe she was moving on from her hesitancy around Jared. She ventured another text: Jared, it'll be a holiday you'll never forget!

Jared: Bring it!

She waited to feel the sting and…nothing.

She smiled. This was due to Rolling Stone's perspective, in him reminding her that she couldn't go back in time, and that there was no need to. Also, his note enabled her to remember that she had to be thankful for the people she had around her.

A separate text came in from Frankie: Hey Mom can you check to see if I still have my elementary school yearbooks? I wanted to show them to Liam. No rush.

I can look now. I have a few minutes.

She wanted to see what of last year's fall decor was left up in the attic anyway, so she climbed the steps up to the second floor. From there, she turned the corner to a narrower door that opened to steps leading up one more flight.

Lit dimly by dormer windows, the room was several degrees warmer. Eva tugged on the string hanging from the ceiling, and the space was illuminated by a single LED light bulb.

What reflected back was the usual mess that she'd never been able to clean out. Each new year, she'd resolve to empty out a box a week, but never did follow through to take care of it.

And she didn't have time for it at this very second, so she walked to the right-side corner where Frankie's things were stored.

The yearbooks were an easy find. The fall decor on the other hand? It was a mess, a result from Gabby going through them for the fall festival.

Eva dug through the Sterilite containers, finding fake greenery, faux pumpkins, a cornucopia basket. She scored, finding a sack full of spray-painted acorns, and beaded garlands made by her girls when they were little.

Then, she opened another container tucked into the corner of the room.

Eva found nonfiction books. A JFK biography, a self-help book about people management, a famous soldier's memoir.

She inhaled a sharp breath. It had taken her a beat too long to realize that she had uncovered Louis's stash of books. Books that her family had packed when he'd died, and because the container they'd used wasn't the industrial-grade trunks, Eva had simply tucked it into a corner when they'd moved into the Spirit of the Shenandoah property.

Louis hadn't been much of a reader, and this was why Eva had refused to declutter his books. For him to have kept them, he'd thought them important.

She sifted through the titles, and to her surprise, she came across a sci-fi novel. She thought he'd hated sci-fi.

She shut her eyes and took a breath. She'd hated learning new things about him.

The way she had him on a pedestal when he died…

She rummaged through the stacked books to shove that last thought away. She sat among the stacks and scanned the spines, coming upon a yellow hardbacked journal.

His recipes.

Eva toppled the books above the journal and snatched it out of the stack. She opened it to a random page, to her late husband's messy scribblings.

She ran her hand on the page and felt the pen mark ridges, willing herself to remember Louis cooking with the book propped on a book holder.

But she couldn't quite pin down the details.

It was getting harder and harder.

"Louis, where are you?" she whispered now.

It was a question she'd asked over the years, time and again, when she'd needed him. When she'd wanted answers, or reassurance, or encouragement, she'd called out his name.

Louis had been good at fixing things. Yes, at times, she'd found it annoying—sometimes all she'd wanted was to be listened to—but she'd grown to rely on it.

Right then, Eva was asking these books to show her the way. To bring her to peace with Jared. To get back the life she'd had before finding out about Jared, which was one that had an immovable foundation. To find a way to move on.

She wasn't sure how long she'd been sitting there, staring off into space, until an incessant hammering pulled her from her thoughts. She stood from the stacks and went to the dormer window, opening it.

Along with the cool air came the hammering and chatter. Eva stuck her head out, and looked down to see Cruz and Chip. Chip was chattering away clearing rocks as Cruz hammered the posts.

"Ohhhh." Her somber mood lifted at the sight. Cruz was wearing a formfitting black T-shirt, with his ballcap off. He laughed at something Chip said, and she could imagine that it was a wholesome conversation, with the kind of guy Chip was.

She, on the other hand, was veering away from wholesome with how she couldn't tear her eyes away from Cruz's biceps, the muscles of his shoulders and back. She could only imagine that he was cut everywhere.

If only she could find out.

When he'd arrived at nine o'clock on the dot with Chip, he'd checked in with Eva via text and got to work. It had been a thoughtful way to announce his arrival, but, to be honest, she'd wished that he'd knocked on her door.

What was happening to her?

She took it back—she absolutely knew what was happening to her. The more she saw Cruz, the more she wanted to get to know him.

To touch him.

Heat clambered up her chest.

Knocking sounded from downstairs, snatching her from her lustful thoughts, followed by voices, calling her name. "Eva!"

Eva's heart leapt. She hadn't been expecting anyone today. She grabbed Frankie's yearbooks and the journal, and padded downstairs. After stashing the books in her office, she opened the front door to Kayla and Joy. In unison, they said, "Surprise!"

Then, they walked right in.

"What are you both doing here?"

"I can't believe you didn't tell us." Kayla dropped her purse on the couch and went to Eva's balcony sliding doors.

"Tell you about what?"

"Today's main event." Joy procured a bottle of wine from her large tote.

"Oh my gosh, what else do you have in there?" Eva said.

"What else? Binoculars. Are the glasses still in the same place?"

"Um…yes?"

She still didn't understand what was going on but watched as her friends flitted around the room. Kayla added an extra chair to the two already on the balcony.

Then she realized. "You're here to watch Cruz?"

Joy was pouring Kayla a generous helping. "Yes. And watch you with Cruz. And to meet him, too."

"How did you even kn— Wait, did you both speak to Gabby?"

Kayla touched her nose as in, Eva had gotten it right. "She was at Mountain Rush last night."

Oh, that daughter of hers. Eva sighed. "Well, nothing much is happening. He's just working."

"We'll see about that."

The two left Eva in her kitchen and walked onto the balcony—Joy with her binoculars—and looked over. From where she stood, she heard them giggle, no doubt ogling him.

Then, she heard Joy say, "Hi, there! I'm one of Eva's best friends. Joy."

"I'm Kayla, the other BFF," Kayla added.

Mortified, Eva sprinted to her friends' side, whispering, "What, are we in high school?" Sure enough, Cruz was holding a fence post, looking rugged and sweaty and beautiful.

"Hey, Eva, we're about halfway through," he said.

"Oh, take your time," Kayla answered.

She elbowed her friend gently, then through gritted teeth said, "Thanks for letting me know, Cruz."

"Are you thirsty?" Joy called out.

"I am." Chip raised his hand.

"Chip, I wasn't talking to you," Joy snapped.

"I'm fine, thank you," Cruz answered, then carried the fence post to its desired location.

Speaking of fine, he was indeed.

Still, this was embarrassing.

Eva all but dragged her friends from the balcony and into the house. "I cannot believe you all just did that."

Joy shrugged, sipping her wine, then plopping down on her couch. "It's obvious he likes you, else he wouldn't be here."

"We're not talking about it," Eva said.

"Okay, then we need to talk about something else— Frankie's thirty-first birthday. She never did her dirty-thirty party this year with how busy she is," Kayla said.

Eva shook her head, pressing her fingers against her forehead. She hated the term dirty thirty, and much more, associated with her daughter. And though Kayla was correct, that was still almost a year away. "I think it's a great idea, but I can't think past Thanksgiving."

"We know how busy you are, too, so we're going to do the legwork on this," Joy added. "We're her aunties after all."

Eva pressed her hand against her heart. Her emotions— they were everywhere today. From Jared's texts, seeing Louis's things, and then her body's response to Cruz—seriously, what was going on with her?—and now this.

Joy and Kayla, besides being her best friends, had always come through for her daughters, even as her girls' second and third mothers.

The fact that they'd still thought her girls important even as adults was…lucky.

"You guys. Are you for real? You don't have to do that. Who knows—she might already have her own plans."

"Still. She's been through a lot the last couple of years, with the divorce, and raising Liam, and basically being your partner at the B & B."

They were right, of course. "What were you thinking?"

Joy beamed. "Let's surprise her with a girls' trip."

"No." Eva shook her head as she grabbed snacks from the pantry. Her friends were sure to have the munchies after their wine. "Frankie hates surprises."

"Fine. No surprises. But how about Vegas?"

"She doesn't gamble or drink."

"Right," Kayla drawled.

"A cruise!" Joy said hopefully.

"You do remember that she gets seasick, right?" Eva said.

"Dramamine for the win. And folks tell me that once you're on the boat, you get used to things."

"I suppose."

"Now here's our question," Kayla asked. "If we do this, will you come with us?"

Eva poured pretzels in a bowl and carried it to where they were sitting. "I'll have to make sure we have coverage here at the B & B."

"You do have a son that you can rely on."

The bowl slipped from Eva's fingers, though she caught it just in time, with a few pretzels spilling out.

"Whoa, butterfingers." Kayla made to stand.

She stuck out a hand. "No worries, I've got it." Picking up the pretzels, she was breathless. Regaining her composure, she set the bowl on the coffee table.

Maybe she *wasn't* truly over Louis's betrayal.

She cleared her throat to reset her expression. To move the moment forward, and to stall until she could be alone. "So, where did you all want to cruise to?"

That evening, Cruz loaded his Outback with his gear, Tetrising extra lumber with his portable wood saw, contemplating for the first time that he should buy himself a gas-guzzling flatbed truck.

"Hey, boss. I'm out," Chip said from behind him.

He turned and shook Chip's hand with vigor. "You were a great help. Don't know how I could have done it without you."

"Oh, I know you would have, except it would have taken a couple of days."

"No doubt. Let me know how I can repay you."

"Eh, it's nothing. It was fun." He backed away. "I'm headed up to Gabby's so…check you later."

"See you." He turned back to car and tried to close the trunk, though unsuccessful.

It was very much that kind of day, a mix of little annoyances with small triumphs. Though he'd accomplished what he'd set out to do, he'd overestimated his skills and underestimated his timing.

Like not properly measuring the distance with each post. Forgetting to factor in the time for the quick-set concrete to be ready, and having to double back to his house for the portable saw and other pieces of equipment, which he was now trying to fit into his car.

A project that was supposed to end in the afternoon had now taken him past dinnertime. He was hungry, tired and a little grouchy, if he was honest with himself.

He'd sensed Eva's presence all day. Their brief exchanges here and there had been pleasant and had only fueled the growing attraction he felt for her. The best thing he could do was drive back to town as soon as possible, before he said something that might dissolve the peace between them.

From behind him, someone cleared their throat.

"Did you need something, Chip—" He turned, but instead of Chip, it was Eva standing there. Her hair was halfway up, lips and cheeks pink, and she was smiling at him. He felt his body unwind at the sight of her. "Hey."

"I got your text that you were done. You could have come up and let me know."

"Didn't want to bother you. I saw how busy you were today."

In between digging, hammering and drilling, he'd seen a steady stream of guests at the B & B walking through the grounds. Eva had been on her feet all day, chatting it up with people, both guests and her staff alike.

Watching her in action at work once more peeled another layer back from who Eva Espiritu was. The more he spent time in her world, the more he admired the business she'd built and how strong she was.

"I would have made time," she said, gesturing behind her. "Do you want to give me a tour of the fence?"

"Yeah, sure." The tiredness left his body as he followed her toward the rear of her property, and pride soon replaced the final bits of his exhaustion when he presented her with his completed work.

"Cruz, wow. This is awesome." She came up to the fence and put a hand on one of the posts.

"Those things gave me a bit of trouble," he admitted.

She shook it. "Feels solid to me. This truly was more than I could have asked for."

"I'm glad. And oh, remember my suggestion of having a sign that marks the beginning of that small path off of Spirit Trail as private property? I think that's the only thing you need to finish this off."

"That would be a great project for my grandson."

Cruz remembered, from the last time he peeked at their website, though he kept a neutral expression. "Oh?"

"Liam, that's his name. The son of my eldest daughter, Frankie. Do you...have grandkids, or kids?"

"Me?" He pressed a hand to himself and snorted. "No. I kind of missed that whole path. You could say that I was a little bit of an, um...explorer."

Mirth passed across her face. "Explorer. Is that what they call partiers these days."

"It's a nicer way of saying it. I was a work hard, play hard kind of person. Forrester's kept me busy and on the go. With that I met a lot of people, and was on a high road to life."

"And now you're building fences and own a trail guide shop."

"Two shops, mind you. With a third on the way."

"Impressive."

"I think so. Not sure about what the rest of the family thinks. But yeah, I decided to pivot." Alone with her once more, as he'd been at dinner and at the home garden shop, he felt completely disarmed of all of his usual boundaries.

"If you ask me, you made a good move. Because this is nice." She made her way up the hill. "Are you sure I can't pay for anything at all? You did a full day's work. You took time away from Cross Trails."

He followed behind her, feeling light at her comment that he'd made a "good move." For his convictions to leave Forrester, it didn't mean that he hadn't carried doubt about doing so, now especially with Millie in town. Her presence had been a mirror to his lack of contribution to the family business. "Nope. This was on me. I offered, and I meant it. We can just call this whole thing even. With the maintenance, and all the arguments, hopefully we can be civil. Neutral."

"Neutral. Definitely." They'd made it to his car, and she tucked a strand of hair behind her right ear. She looked as if she was going to say something else.

"What is it?"

She shook her head. "Nothing. Um, before you go. Hold it right here."

"Okay." As he watched her climb the porch onto her cottage, he shoved the tools in his car in hopes to finally make them fit.

Though what occupied his mind were the words she hadn't said. After tonight, there would be no reason for them to get together. He'd hoped when they were talking that she would have given him a sign that she was willing to meet up again.

He would miss it, the run-ins, the banter. It lit him up, if he was being honest. She was the kind of person he wanted to be, and with her, he could be who he was without having to compare himself to the person he'd been before he got sick.

Then again, who she was, was an entrepreneur and a mother, and he was his own businessperson who didn't intend on staying in one place for very long.

Cruz was simply grateful that he could, at least, find a resolution between them, so he could move on with his next mission, which was Cross Trails number 3.

He shut his hatchback once more, and thank goodness, this time the latch clicked.

Then came the sound of Eva's footsteps. Cruz turned to her as she held up a brown bag. "I know you're probably starving. It's from the B & B kitchen, courtesy of Chef Jared."

From the bag, Cruz detected something garlicky and savory. Tummy rumbling, he accepted it. "Thank you, I appreciate it."

"Of course. It's a nice helping of Filipino stir-fry."

His mouth was already watering. "I haven't had Filipino food in forever. Do you serve that to your B & B guests?"

"Starting to, now that we have someone fully qualified to cook it, and especially in scale to feed everyone."

"Pretty cool to have him around, I bet."

"Yeah, it is." Except her smile didn't quite make it to her eyes.

"Well, I'd better go. Thanks. For the food. See you around town?" He offered her a hand, which felt too transactional and impersonal for the time they'd spent together. But what was he going to do, kiss her?

I wish.

The warmth of her skin pulled him out from his thoughts.

"Yep, I'm sure of it. Small towns." She walked backward.

Belatedly, as he opened the car door, he said, "Maybe I'll see you while I'm on the trail."

She smiled. "Safe hiking, Cruz."

He smiled getting into the car, warmed by the meal in his hand, with the satisfaction of the work he'd done, and her sweet smile. But as he started the engine, the familiarity of her greeting landed squarely in his belly.

Safe hiking, Rolling Stone.

He looked through the windshield and watched Eva climb up her front steps. "Heh, that's funny."

But before he could think more about the déjà vu her words had given him, his phone rang. It was Millie.

"I might have overloaded your circuits. We have no electricity."

Oh, great. "What happened?"

"I don't know. It could have been the air fryer? I was hungry, thought I'd make dinner and—"

"I don't have an air fryer."

"Um…you do now…"

Cruz counted to ten to chill himself out, then switched the gear to Drive. "I'll be right there."

Blue Moon,

Ah, The Internets. I literally just snorted a laugh. I actually watched that presidential debate. In all seriousness, though, I don't like to look back. That is, until we started writing, and here I am telling you my deepest secret.

What does that say about us that we can be so open in a notebook more than we can be in real life? I wonder, if we ever met in person, would we be as open about what we're feeling too?

Not that I'm suggesting it. It might be weird, right?

We've written in this notebook over a year, and it didn't dawn on me until today that you could be someone I've already met. We could have passed each other on the trail. We could have picked up breakfast from the same diner.

Then again, I wouldn't want to change what we have, so maybe ignore that last paragraph. There's no pressure from me to meet, I promise.

Is it obvious that I need a challenging hike to loosen some of the random thoughts in my head? I guess that means I should be off.

Rolling Stone

Chapter Eight

Lemons—check
Flour—check
Vanilla extract—check
Olive oil—check

At Jameson's, Peak's largest family-owned grocery store, Eva pushed the shopping cart as she checked off the items on her list, thinking about the recipes she'd slated to cook for to-morrow's Thanksgiving dinner. The market was full of peo-ple doing their last-minute shopping. But she kept focused, with only a few minutes left before she had to get back on the road to the B & B.

It was, after all, also their busy season. Guests were still arriving and departing, visiting family or vacationing through the holidays.

Her phone buzzed with a text; it was another one in a slew that had popped in since arriving at Jameson's.

Jared: Saw the contractor today. He said that I would be able to move in by Christmas.

Eva stuffed the phone back in her purse and breathed through the swirl of emotions creeping up her throat.

When Jared had accepted the position as the B & B's permanent chef, he'd also opted to live on property. It was part of his contract. However, his cottage had needed a renovation, and all this time, he'd been staying with Matilda.

Jared staying on the property was ideal, in part because he maintained the chef's garden that was so integral to the B & B's farm to table concept. Soon to be married to Matilda, her B & B manager—they were engaged a few months ago—in the end, having her there would be beneficial too.

It also made sense because he was a part of the family.

But Eva wasn't sure she was ready for him to be *right there*, even well after hours.

Eva was so engrossed in her thoughts that she didn't pay attention to where she was pushing her cart, not until she was T-boned.

"Oh my gosh! I'm so sorry." A woman with fair skin and blond hair gushed an apology.

Raising her hand in peace—because these days there was an incredible amount of road rage—Eva said, "My fault. I totally wasn't looking."

"No, it's me. *I'm* sorry." She pressed a hand against her chest. "I completely underestimated how busy it would be, and my mind is everywhere and definitely *not* on my list."

Eva gestured to the space in front of them. "I know how that is, too. Please, go ahead."

The woman heaved a breath. "Thank you. I hope you have a better Thanksgiving than we will."

Eva's attention was caught. Living first in a rural town in Oregon, and then in smaller military communities, and now Peak, had fine-tuned her empathy skills. And sometimes, people and opportunities appeared at the most perfect time.

It didn't dawn on me until today that you could be someone I've already met.

Rolling Stone came to mind—a reminder that everyone was connected somehow, even if it wasn't so obvious on the outset.

Perhaps Rolling Stone had even been a guest, with neither one of them the wiser. Or, he could be here at Jameson's at this very moment, also stressing out about his holiday plans.

So, Eva couldn't let the woman go. "I hope you don't mind me asking, but is everything okay? I'm a local, and I'm happy to help if you need anything." Eva had businesses and resources on her speed dial. If someone needed a meal or someone to talk to, then she was surely able to provide it.

"No, I'm sorry. I am totally overreacting." The woman looked around as if to spot prying ears. "I'm here visiting my brother, and I'm trying to find my footing in what I can make for him for Thanksgiving. I'm a mom so I usually go all out, but I also have a fully stocked kitchen. Trying to dial down the cooking in his kitchen has been a little bit of a challenge. I mean, I practically blew out a circuit the other day." She barked out a laugh.

"Wow." Eva wasn't sure where to start in this woman's sudden rush of energy. "You left your family in order to celebrate with your brother?"

"I did. It was a tough choice. But I'm glad I'm here, for him. For me too because I miss him. It's just been a little complicated, living together, even for these short few days. Working remotely in *his* space. Personalities, you know. And honestly, he's so blah about Thanksgiving, and grumpy about holidays in general." She adjusted the scarf around her neck. "Sorry. Blah blah. I'm usually around a lot of people and, gosh, all the houses are so far apart and he lives in this tiny house. The Teams meetings aren't cutting it for my extroverted nature."

Eva continued to nod, interested, though a part of her was keeping time of how long she'd spent in the store. She tried to wrap it up. "Well, I hope that things look up. I bet with you cooking, he'll get into the spirit. He's lucky to have you."

"You know what?" The woman looked at Eva with what seemed like renewed motivation. "You're right. He's going through something and I want to support him but I have to find my fun, too."

Both Kayla and Joy came to mind then, at how they had allowed for her to process even if they hadn't known what was actually wrong with her. They'd given her space and then welcomed her with open arms.

Eva half laughed. "You should. You can give your brother grace, but you have to give yourself grace too. Your brother, at some point, has to decide for himself how he should celebrate."

"You're so wise." She stared into her shopping basket, which had all the usual suspects: butter, potatoes, carrots, flour. "I think I'm going to cook the dishes I want to eat for Thanksgiving, and if he wants to pitch in his thoughts at some point, then that will be on him." The woman's smile spanned from ear to ear, and her eyes lit. "Oh, and speak of the devil himself."

Eva turned with a smile on her face, ready to meet this brother of hers. It had to have been somebody new that moved in.

Only to see Cruz Forrester weaving around people, headed in their direction. His eyes were on hers.

Her heart beat at double time, her lips spreading out into the same grin he was giving her. In his arms were boxes and cans, but he didn't falter even as he juggled them, his eyes never leaving her face.

Since building her the fence, Eva had seen him every day around town. It was as if she had manifested him each time.

To be honest, she hadn't minded it.

"And I guess you know each other already," said the woman next to her.

It woke Eva up from her thoughts. Her eyes darted from the woman to Cruz and finally landed on the woman's wrist. Sure enough, she was wearing a diamond-encrusted stainless steel watch.

A Forrester watch.

"Wait a sec," Eva said to the woman. "Is he—"

The woman next to her laughed. By then, Cruz had approached them and systematically dumped everything in his arms into the basket. "Looks like the two of you have already met. What's so funny?"

"That this town is truly tiny. Actually, big brother, we haven't." To Eva she offered a hand. "My name is Millie."

"Nice to meet you. I'm Eva." She took Millie's hand in hers, and it was warm and soft. And now, knowing they were siblings, the similarities were uncanny. The soulful, ocean-blue eyes. The wave in their hair. The way they stood, their posture sure and confident.

"*You're* Eva." Millie's eyes darted to Cruz.

"I am." A giggle escaped her lips. "Oh God, hopefully he hasn't said too many terrible things about me."

"No, not at all." To her brother, she said, "Eva and I got in a little bit of a fender bender."

"And she was telling me that someone was a little grumpy." Having peace with Cruz didn't mean that she couldn't not give him a hard time. And with the way he was currently rattled—he was speechless—she couldn't help but dig.

"So, how do you know one another?" Millie asked.

"Let's just say that your grumpy brother was grumpy toward me too."

Millie groaned. "Cruz, you didn't."

"It wasn't all my fault." Cruz shook his head. "But this is a very long story and I'm not in the mood. This place is a zoo."

Millie rolled her eyes. "Spoken like a person who isn't worried about putting Thanksgiving dinner on the table."

"I told you that's not necessary." He gave Eva the side-eye. "Besides, I'm not even sure that my oven works."

Millie's jaw dropped, and for a beat, nothing came out of her mouth. "You never said that."

He shrugged. "I tried to tell you."

"No, you didn't."

Eva was having déjà vu. Oh, the fuss. Like her girls. Like she and her own siblings. These days, when they came in from Oregon, they were all on their best behaviors. And, with losing Louis, it put a lot of their squabbles in perspective.

Still, watching these two caused her chest to swell with emotion. The candid banter, so intimate and yet so common.

She wished for more of it sometimes, for someone to banter with her, rather than she simply being a witness. Once, it was that way, when she and Louis couldn't stop talking, discussing. Yes, they'd had quiet times, but boy could they cut it up. Louis had a way about him, so charming.

Charming.

He had been charming to not just Eva, but to Jared's mother too.

Damn intrusive thoughts.

"How about you both come over to my place tomorrow?"

The words were out of Eva's mouth before she could register them, spilling out to combat her thoughts from forming into a spiral.

Cruz raised an eyebrow. "Really?"

"Immediately yes." Millie nodded. She thumbed into her phone and handed it to Eva. "Can I get your number? I can update you on what I can bring depending on this possible broken oven." She returned her brother's side-eye.

Eva punched in her number. "Honestly, please don't worry. I always have a full house during Thanksgiving and the holidays. I was a soldier's wife…" The explanation caught in her throat, and she tried again. Because this part, no matter what had happened between her and Louis, was something she would always be proud of. "I was married to a soldier, and our house was always open. Especially during holidays, to make sure anyone who needed a hot meal could get one."

She looked down and away to catch her breath. She cleared her throat. She pushed a smile on her face and looked at Cruz. To her surprise, he returned an open expression, one that was sincere, nonjudgmental. "And I insist."

Cruz raised both hands as if in surrender. "As if I have a choice with you two in front of me."

A laugh broke out among the three of them, snapping the tension; Eva nodded in appreciation of Cruz's humor.

He continued to surprise her.

Cruz pressed down on the emergency brake of his car. "Okay, Millie. Out with it."

"What?" Her voice was laced with innocence. Fake innocence.

He eyed his sister. On her lap was a plastic travel cake container. His sister, if anything, was resourceful and had somehow made a caramel apple no-bake cheesecake. After shopping at Jameson's yesterday, they'd detoured to the home store for more equipment and tools. This morning, Cruz awoke to a pretty cheesecake in his refrigerator, with chopped apples decorated up top and drizzled with caramel sauce. "Ask it now or forever hold your peace," he said.

"Is there something going on between you and Eva?"

"Except for the fact that she hated me at first?" He thought about it now, at the trajectory of their…relationship. "To tell you the truth, even *I'm* shocked that things have turned around so well. But no, absolutely nothing." And yet, when Cruz said it, he didn't quite mean it all the way.

"I could've sworn, with the way you looked at her. And the way she was looking at you…" Her voice was wistful. "It's like a sister's dream come true, you know? To see your big brother who you thought had no feelings for anything looking at somebody with those bright eyes."

He snorted. "You're full of drama."

"What do you think our business is? Do you think it's built just on watches? Nope. It's about relationships. It's about love."

Cruz rolled his eyes. "You're too much. You've always been too much. I don't know how Max can even deal with you," he said in jest.

"Don't talk to me about Max."

Cruz did a double take and caught what he thought was a grimace on her face. This was strange. And so unlike his sister, who was optimistic to a fault. "Here you are giving me the third degree but am I feeling something here? What's up with you and Max?"

Her gaze darted down to the dish.

That alone spoke volumes.

"Is this why you're here for Thanksgiving? To get away from Max?"

"No comment."

"Hey. What's up?" Cruz turned in his seat, the leather seat squeaking underneath him. Left arm resting on the steering wheel, he squeezed Millie's shoulder with his right hand.

It had always been Cruz and Millie; they were best friends. When their father had died, it took them both to help their mother and to keep the board of directors from crumbling. They'd juggled their mother's loss with theirs, and though Cruz never really did know if he was doing the right thing, he always had Millie to back him up.

Millie was unshakable. Millie was never the kind of person to run out of words.

"Max and I are having trouble," she said now.

"What kind of trouble?"

"The kind that involves other people."

Anger burned through his body. "That mother—"

"*No*, Cruz."

He sat up in his chair. "Do you mean...you?"

"No. I don't mean that either."

Cruz settled back in his seat. "I don't understand."

"This is about the both of us. We are...considering the possibility of other people. We married so young. How did we really know what we wanted at the age of twenty?"

"Because you just knew." Cruz shook his head.

This wasn't happening. Besides their parents, Millie and Max had been the example he'd always looked at for what a marriage should be. This dynamic played out in their lives, that even though he was the older sibling, it was he who was trying to catch up. Especially in love.

Millie and Max on the other hand? They were it. Or so he thought.

"I know this is a shock, and probably super horrible to hear. But this trip was as much of a getaway for me as it was to help you."

"But the kids?"

She lifted an eyebrow. "Their father is capable of taking care of them. And, for all the business trips that he took and holidays and birthdays he missed, I am not gonna feel guilty about spending a holiday with my brother who I haven't seen in months."

He raised a hand. "I hear you. And that came out wrong. I was just thinking about the kids and how they were doing with all of it."

"We haven't made any firm decisions about anything. But Max doesn't want counseling and I'm tired of waiting for him to change his mind. So while we haven't said anything official to the kids, I'm sure they notice. But yeah, I'm worried about them too." A sheepish smile spread across her face. "But they love that I'm here with you."

"I can't believe you're using me to play hooky. Or that you're playing hooky at all."

"I guess people change."

Her words were like an arrow to Cruz's chest. This was

his current life's theme. For him, it had been about that big change in his health status that would keep him on his toes. He couldn't relax, not unless he was hiking on a dirt road.

But he couldn't think about that now—instead, he leaned in and hugged his sister.

When she sat back, her eyes were glassy and red-rimmed, though she had a smile on her face. "Bet you're glad I came to visit, huh?"

He grinned for her sake. "Actually, I am. This might be the first time you're more of a hot mess than me."

"Ha." She inhaled deeply and then let out a slow breath. "We should really go inside."

"We don't have to. We can cancel."

"And keep me from finding out a little more about Eva? You're joking." She placed a hand on his forearm. "But listen."

His lips curled. "So we're not done."

"No. We're not. Look, I wanted to get away from Max for a little bit, but I'm here for *you*. To be in your presence, because that seems to be the only way I can get you to talk. You're that kind of person, you know? You need that eye contact, the one-on-one conversation and not virtually. But don't wait to have these conversations, especially as February nears. If you need to, talk to someone. A friend. Therapy, maybe."

Cruz thought of his letters to Blue Moon. At how it took a year for them to get personal. But therapy hadn't worked on him. "Hiking is my therapy."

"I don't doubt hiking helps. But connection helps too." She gave him a wan smile. "Just…think about it. Okay."

"Yeah, okay," he said, though to move the moment forward.

They both climbed out of the Outback and walked up the concrete circular driveway of the Spirit of the Shenandoah B & B. This was his first time coming through the front entrance, and the facade was impressive. It was modern, with a wooden and wrought-iron exterior, with clean lines to its architecture. If it was a watch, it would have a gunmetal gray face and with mahogany leather straps.

Huh, where had that come from?

Cruz hadn't thought of watches in a while. In fact, aside from the one he wore, which was given to him by his father, he purposely pushed all things Forrester-related from his thoughts.

It must have been because Millie was here.

"This is nice," she said, as if prompted by his thoughts.

He led the way to the foyer, also impressive, with bamboo flooring and minimalistic design. The scent...he couldn't place it, but it was floral and nostalgic.

Up ahead was a guy in a collared shirt with the B & B logo, but a woman with dark hair appeared from a hallway to the left. Her smile grew. "Hi. I remember you from the other day, putting up Eva's fence. Cruz, right? Can I help you?"

"Yes, um. We're here for Thanksgiving dinner, at Eva's."

Her eyes lit. "Oh! I'm Matilda. Perfect timing because I was on my way to Eva's cottage." She offered her hand, shaking his and then his sister's.

Matilda swiftly led them through the building, and gave them an informal tour—she apparently was the B & B manager—passing a hallway that led to more rooms, a wrought-iron staircase and a modern kitchen. They entered the dining area that extended to a four-season room.

The back of the B & B was all windows, and the sight took Cruz's breath away. Everything he loved was in full view.

All that green, of trails, trees and mountains.

"Wow. Gorgeous," Millie said from behind him. "Do you host retreats?"

"Yes, we do. It'll need some long-term planning if you wanted dates on the weekends, since we're scheduled out for weddings. But weekdays are a little more flexible. Frankie can actually help you with that. She handles our reservations."

"I'm definitely following up. Do you have a ton of people here for the holiday?"

"We're only at three-quarters capacity." They'd made it to the flagstone walkway leading away from the patio, which led to a dirt path. "But it's great for us, because it'll give the whole staff a chance to cycle through Eva's cottage for Thanksgiving dinner."

"That's nice she's inviting everyone for dinner."

"Oh, Eva celebrates everything." Matilda smiled. "And sometimes even a combination of holidays."

"My kind of person."

Cruz felt Millie nudge her with an elbow. When he looked at her, she mouthed *I like her.*

He rolled his eyes, and dramatically for her benefit.

They hiked up the path to the wraparound porch of the cottage. It was quaint and rustic, bordered by mums overflowing from planters. From inside came the cheerful beats of Christmas songs.

Christmas songs?

Matilda led them through Eva's front door, and they entered what looked like a Christmas village.

From behind him, Millie gasped.

"I have never seen a more festive room," she said. "Outside FAO Schwarz, anyway."

"But isn't it supposed to be Thanksgiving?" Cruz asked.

Matilda laughed. "Listen, in this household, Christmas starts on September first. It's a Filipino thing."

"I can get with that," Millie said.

People were milling around though none paid them any mind. Some who recognized Matilda waved as she ushered Cruz and Millie deeper into the cottage.

The house itself was on the small side. To the left as they walked in was a large living room, which was now a winter wonderland, complete with a Christmas village on the windowsill. They followed a short hallway to the back room, which had an open-concept kitchen and a living room area where a television and a comfortable L-shaped leather couch stood.

What caught Cruz's attention was the gallery of pictures on one wall, with a family portrait right smack in the middle.

The image featured a family of four, with a younger Eva, a school-aged Gabby and a preteen, who had to be Frankie. And then him.

Louis.

Cruz had found out his name by doing a quick online search, starting with the B & B website.

Yes, he'd been curious, especially after she'd talked about being a soldier's wife at Jameson's. What was Eva's origin story? How had she gotten here? For a person to be as strong as she was, she had to have faced battles of her own.

With that quick search, Cruz discovered that Louis was killed on deployment.

Cruz peered closer. Louis had been handsome guy. With dark skin and dark hair, he was fit, with a chiseled jaw. His smile was confident; his pride evident in his posture, with his arm wrapped around Eva.

Eva had been a beautiful young woman. In this photo, her smile was sincere, expression open. It was an expression Cruz didn't see much of.

"That photo was taken about a year before Louis was killed," said a voice over his shoulder.

Cruz turned to Eva, who had a Christmas dish towel over her right shoulder. She was wearing an apron, and her hair was in a low bun. Wisps of baby hairs framed her face, and in this environment she was a different woman. Softer, at ease. Content.

"I'm sorry for your loss."

"I appreciate that. It was seventeen years ago. Some days it feels like yesterday, and others, like a lifetime."

"I know the sentiment. Every day brings something different," he said, as an olive branch.

"It's true." After a pause, she seemed to snap awake. "I'm sorry. I'm being such a rude hostess. Where's Millie?"

Cruz went with the change in subject. Distraction was an effective tactic of evasion. "Probably hiding among your Christmas decorations. With her no-bake dessert."

She threw her head back and laughed. "Of course she made a dessert even when I said it wasn't necessary. She's just as headstrong as her brother."

"Bite your tongue. She's way more stubborn than me. I'll have you know that she already ordered a new oven. It'll be at the house within a week."

Behind Eva, Cruz spotted Millie. Gabby was pouring her a drink, and they were with another younger woman with long wavy hair.

Eva followed his gaze. "That's my other daughter, Francesca. When you meet her, keep in mind that she's a lot more bark than bite." She cupped a hand around her mouth. "Frankie, sweetheart."

Frankie sidled up next to her mother and though she had suspicion in her eyes, she bore a polite smile.

"Frankie, this is Cruz."

Frankie's hand was warm when Cruz shook it, though there was no question that her firm handshake was on purpose.

"So you're the one who accused my mom of smoking, and then a couple of months later built her a fence."

In her grip, Cruz had no recourse but to tell the truth.

"That's me. The accusation was a mistake, and the fence was my apology. We're good now. Right?"

He looked at Eva to confirm that what he'd said was accurate.

Eva simply smiled, as if relishing this moment.

"That's good." Frankie dropped her hand. "We wouldn't want you to find out what happens when an Espiritu is angry with you."

He stilled for a moment, not knowing how to answer. He understood that she wasn't kidding. Not an iota.

Eva broke the silence with a laugh, and it allowed for him to exhale. "Okay, sweetheart, no need to scare him." She turned her daughter by the shoulders. "Though I do think that Liam's getting into something."

He followed their gazes to a school-aged boy who was cradling an armful of acorns. He was standing next to another guy.

Without a farewell Frankie took off, leaving him alone once more with Eva.

"I appreciate you saving me from the hot seat," he said.

She shrugged. "Eh, don't thank me yet. She's sure to corner you later on. But that's her Liam, my only grandchild. Next to him is Jared. My...son. C'mon. Let's put a plate in your hand. You can't come over without at least eating two helpings."

"No arguments from me," he said, realizing then, that for the first time, he had no desire to do so.

Though what struck him most was the sudden turn in her tone, and her crestfallen expression.

Rolling Stone,

It's Thanksgiving week and I made it out for a small hike. The weather's really started to turn, and I'm truly feeling festive.

I'm here mulling over your last note. As usual you asked a lot of good questions. To be honest, I'm not sure how to answer them.

I don't know that if we did see one another, if I would be as open. Maybe it's the act of me handwriting something that unlocks how I feel. Or maybe because this feels more like a confessional, where I don't have to literally face your judgment.

Not that I don't think you're a real person, because I do. But the anonymity helps, doesn't it?

I think what that says about me is that I'm not willing to let anyone see me like this: a little broken. That I'm not as strong as what everyone makes me out to be. And I have to be the strong one around here.

So I don't judge that you walked back wanting to meet in person. I don't think I would be ready for it. I don't think I would want to, either. I wouldn't want to lose this friendship.

Though, while I did my shopping this week, I looked for you in the people I passed by. I wondered what you were doing.

This Thanksgiving, I'm thankful for you.

Blue Moon

Chapter Nine

Though Christmas was undoubtedly Eva's most favorite holiday, Thanksgiving came in at a close second. There was something simply pure about getting together with her family and friends and being able to cook for them. It was the holiday when she could take out all of her recipes and simply let go, without worrying about gifts and the financial pressures of Christmas.

When she and Louis had gotten married all those years ago, she had envisioned a house full of kids and dogs and cats and plants. A home in which during the holidays, generations would fill it, from grandparents to grandkids, neighbors and acquaintances. Most of all, she had envisioned sitting across from Louis at the table with a child on his lap, and him slipping her his trademark grin, an expression that exuded gratitude and love.

But life never really did work out the way it was supposed to, even if at the outset, Eva had gotten exactly what she had wanted.

As a young couple, though they'd become nomadic with the army, she had opened her doors to other families. She had kept up the habit even after Louis's death, and over the years, instead of generations of family at the table, it was a houseful of peers seeking connection and found family. And now, while it wasn't Louis sitting in front of her, it was Frankie, with Liam hanging on her shoulder. It was Jared—however uncomfortable she might still be about him—her newfound son of sorts, and Matilda, who loved Eva as she loved her own mother. And of course, her youngest, Gabby.

Even Cruz and Millie were here, new acquaintances who seemed to fit in with the rest of her family. Cruz hadn't yet taken a breather from the sausage and apple stuffing, with dessert still to come. Millie, seated next to Gabby, was flushed with red wine and sugar.

All of her recipes had turned out.

Eva should be ecstatic.

Eva should be happy.

She had everything she needed, and most of what she wanted. Yet, a veil of grief remained.

Another glass of wine was passed into her hand by Matilda, poured from the bottle of a 1989 Cabernet Sauvignon from Kincaid Winery. Eva had purchased the bottle a decade ago, and this morning as she prepared Thanksgiving, she'd decided was time to pop it open. One of Rolling Stone's notes had come to mind, about leaving the world a better place, about legacy, and sharing this special wine had seemed like the best way to add to the holiday cheer.

"So there I was, looking for the perfect tree," Gabby was saying. She was full of mirth tonight, with her eyes glassy with drink.

It was a gentle pull back to reality, and Eva exhaled the last bits of her sad thoughts.

"Don't you already have two trees?" Frankie said as she stood from her chair and helped herself to another piece of apple pie. "Your cottage is, like, nine hundred square feet."

"So it's not just you who does this?" Cruz gestured to the two trees that were in Eva's great room alone. He wiped his mouth with a napkin, though he was laughing behind it.

He was sure to give her a hard time about this later on.

"What? It's cozy!" Eva said, biting the inside of her cheek, fully emerging into the moment. It was the way he was looking at her, like she was the only one in the room. She wanted to be present for him, and for the rest of the family.

"Ha!" Matilda added. "If you think Eva loves Christmas, Gabby is obsessed."

Laughter filtered along the dining room table.

"Anyway," Gabby said. "So I was there at Cloud Orchard to look for a tree for my front porch, because why not? And guess who was skulking around." She didn't wait for an answer. "Nathan."

"Um, that's his family's orchard though?" Frankie said. She was now tidying the buffet table before the next round— she couldn't sit still.

"You didn't let me finish. He was with a woman."

But by how silent the people were at the table, others knew about this other woman.

Gabby had picked up on it too. "Out with it if you know."

"It's someone he met at grad school," Jared said. From behind, Liam tapped him on the shoulder, and handed him an orange.

Liam hated peeling oranges, though it was his favorite fruit, never mind that it wasn't in season.

"I caught up with him at the farmer's market. He was there selling ferns and wreaths for the orchard, and she was there too." Jared peered at her. "Why are you so interested?"

The table leaned in to hear what Gabby had to say, no doubt wondering if she was finally going to admit that she had it bad for Nathan.

Except for Eva, who couldn't help but look at Jared.

At how he teased Gabby and was peeling an orange for his nephew. Eva suspected that later on tonight, he was going to jump right in to do the dishes without being asked, and put away all the leftovers in her mix and match plastic containers. Then, he was going to return home with Matilda.

In the last six months he had shown himself to be part of this family, but Eva had yet to reconcile this fact. A week ago, she thought she had made strides.

Now, sitting here, she realized her visions for the future hadn't included a surprise child.

Jared was her husband's legacy.

If someone left you something less than ideal, it's not on you to fix it.

More of Rolling Stone's advice.

But he was wrong. It *was* on her to fix it. Jared was here, in the flesh, working with her. He would soon live on the same property. There would be no getting away.

Eva's chest filled with heaviness. She stood. "I'm gonna make some coffee."

"We need more coffee beans, though," Frankie said.

"No problem. I'll grab them in the pantry downstairs."

It was just as well, because she needed a few moments of space. She stepped down the creaky stairs and then into the unfinished basement, to the corner where she stored dried goods, bottles of wine, and her much loved coffee beans that were sent to her by her family in the Philippines.

She touched the small bags that were stacked on the shelves and picked one. Then, she cradled it against her chest, and finally took a shuddering breath.

Was she ever going to get over Louis's betrayal? It wasn't for the lack of trying. Dealing with Jared felt like having to untangle Christmas lights that had no start or end.

She needed air, so she headed to the basement door, and it opened to the backyard and the path that would lead Spirit Trail. Above her was her balcony. All around came the laughter of the party, a happy background against the darkening sky. And when she stepped out, her motion sensor light turned on.

Staring out at the trees, past the picket fence Cruz had built, she imagined herself writing in the trail notebook.

Had Rolling Stone written her back?

Would the party notice if she took a quick hike? A notebook venting session would do her some good.

"Eva?" A voice knocked her out of her thoughts.

Jared.

She plastered on a smile and turned. "Hey. Did you need something?"

He smiled. "We drained the last of the wine too. I came down to grab another bottle."

"Help yourself."

"Okay." He started to turn, and paused.

Keep going, she thought. *Please, not now.*

He took one step, and in that short second Eva released a breath.

But he turned to her and took two steps. "Look, Eva. I'm picking up a strange vibe between us. I don't know if it's just in my head." He hesitated. "Did I do something wrong?"

"What do you mean?" Eva's voice felt strangled in her throat.

Eva had heard all the rumors that had circulated about her. She was serious and no-nonsense. That she was a professional, but never gave away her emotions. She heard that she was called ice queen, which was hilarious. One would only need peek into her home on a day like today to find out that it was way off base.

She never minded any of those rumors. People had a way of putting others in boxes. In her opinion, it was better than everyone seeing her exactly the way she was.

Somebody who couldn't get her shit together.

As a single mom, everyone was just waiting for you to break. When she used to run around town with her two little girls, and because she always looked younger than her years, Eva knew people had judged her. They pitied her too.

Over time she'd preferred to be known as somebody who had thicker skin, rather than somebody who was sensitive.

"I feel like you're avoiding me," Jared said.

"I'm not avoiding you." Eva's gaze trailed from his face down to his shoes.

"So, the times when I try to chat with you, when you step away from me or try to find reasons to walk away. How we text to communicate, rather than have real conversations? Are they made up?" He shrugged with one shoulder, and Eva spotted a glimpse of what Jared must have been like when he had been a child. A little vulnerable, a lot mischievous, and kind and honest.

And if it had been any other person, if it had not been Louis's child, she would have scooped him into a hug, and to reassure him that of course she wasn't ignoring him.

She steeled her voice. "I don't know what to tell you."

"Okay." Resignation flashed across his features. "Then whatever this is, whatever's wrong between us… I want to fix it. I want to make it better. I…love it here, Eva. This has become my home, and I love being part of your family."

Eva was bowled over by an emotion she couldn't discern, except that it was overwhelming. It filled her up in the chest and belly, in the throat.

"I am…glad you're here too. I'm sorry if I seem…to back away sometimes. It's just been…difficult. But please know that it isn't you, and I promise I'm not trying to take it out on you."

"I don't understand. You all came to get me in Louisville. You asked me to come back here. I wouldn't have come unless I knew it was okay."

"It *was* okay." Her voice rose, higher than she had intended.

His eyes widened. "So it's not okay now?"

"I didn't say that. I'm trying…to work this out for myself.

Can you give me a little time? It's not you, Jared. I promise."
Though her voice cracked, betraying her.

His expression was clearly disbelieving. But, he said, "That's
fair. It's been a change for me too." After a few beats of silence,
he said, "I'd better bring up a bottle of wine before they start
a riot. I'll see you up there?"

"Yeah."

Thank goodness, Jared walked back into the basement. As
soon as she could no longer see him, tears filled her eyes and
spilled over on her cheeks.

Oh God, she was a horrible mother.

She pressed her hands to her cheeks and wiped away the
tears. Somehow, she would need to head upstairs and rejoin
the holiday gathering.

But her feet remained frozen in place, unable to bring herself to face her family.

Her son.

Cruz spied his watch, noting that over fifteen minutes had
passed and Eva had not returned to the party. Jared had left and
returned with a bottle of wine, but with a somber expression.

It was a hikers survivability tool, to be able to keep track
of who came and left, and of noticing the small details. Of
taking stock of the vibe of one's environment, and listening
to one's instinct.

Ignoring one's intuition could mean someone injuring themselves, or getting lost entirely.

Not that Eva would've gotten lost in her own home. But she
didn't seem the type to stay away from her guests.

All around him, people were in the throes of celebration.
His sister was three sheets to the wind. Eva's daughters were
cackling and bantering, and Eva's grandson was playing video
games on the living room television. Wine was flowing. And

no one seemed to be the wiser that their matriarch wasn't in the same room.

Scratch that, except for Jared.

Jared was at the sink. He was putting dishes away, clearly unplugged.

He reached across to the bottle of Moscato, knowing that it was already empty, and shook it. He tipped the bottle into his glass, and only a drop was produced.

Someone said, "Uh-oh, looks like we ran out of this one too."

"Where can I get more?" Cruz asked.

"I can grab it," Gabby said, and set her napkin back on the table.

"No, no worries." Cruz stood. "Where is it downstairs?"

"You can't miss it." Gabby laughed. "My mother's got a whole system down there. Speaking of which, where is she?"

From the sink, Jared said, "Still downstairs."

Frankie's eyebrows rose, and she exchanged a look with Gabby.

Yep, Cruz's instincts were pinging.

"I'll hurry her up," Cruz said. "Besides, I want to see this system you're talking about." He padded backward, then headed down the stairs as everyone around the table continued their conversation. As he entered the dark basement, the temperature dropped. He found the pantry shelves, but no Eva, then spotted a light coming through a separate hallway to the left.

At the end of the hallway was an open door—Eva stood on the other side of the threshold under a spotlight. Her profile was in view and her hands were pressed against her face.

She was crying.

This should have been his cue to get the hell out of there. Cruz might have been raised by a nurturing woman and loved on by a caring sister, and he had no qualms hearing about and listening to emotions.

But he didn't have the ability to express them. His real thoughts, his real emotions were kept behind a locked gate. Sometimes he could see what was on the other side of it. Sometimes he could even touch it—he could write about it to Blue Moon. But let it go freely and in real life?

He wasn't so sure.

Still, he couldn't fathom walking away from Eva.

She was all sorts of strong and complicated and capable. And he suspected that she didn't cry often.

Strong people needed to be checked up on, too.

He moved toward the basement exit and hovered at the threshold.

He knocked against the doorframe. "Eva?"

"I'm fine. I'll be up soon." She turned away, voice croaking.

"It's obvious you're not fine." Damned the threshold and space. Yes, he was a person who kept his emotions at bay, but not when a person obviously needed comfort.

He tentatively approached her, then reached out and patted her on the shoulders. "It's okay." Then, he opened his arms, in an attempt to offer her solace in the only way he could think of.

This was an extension of him, of a friendship, maybe, but he also wanted her to make the decision.

To his surprise, she stepped in to his embrace. Welcoming it.

Perhaps he had been caught up in the moment, which was always a dangerous thing, but in holding her, he was comforted too. For what? For everything, for his own vulnerabilities. For his own fears that he can't run away from.

"I'm so sorry," she said, sniffing. Stepping back a half step, she wiped her tears away. Almost haphazardly.

As if embarrassed.

And he didn't want her to feel that. So he took his own thumb and wiped off her cheeks and said, "Don't be."

She gazed up in wonder. "It's Thanksgiving and you're a guest. This is supposed to be a happy time."

"Eh, a little drama never hurt anyone."

She half laughed, and leaned her forehead on his chest. As though she was drawing much-needed strength from him. Something about the moment sent a bolt of heat through his body, but he tried to ignore the sensation. "I don't let anyone see me like this."

"See you like what, as a human being? But, if you wish, I promise I won't tell anyone that Eva Espiritu has feelings."

She looked up at him, vulnerability in her eyes. Her arms were resting on his hips, like she was clinging to him. God help him, he wanted to be the person she needed. She felt right in his arms.

"Feelings suck," she said.

"I agree. But I'm here to listen, if you want to talk."

Could she feel how his heart had begun to beat like a drum? Their lips were so close, though he was already a goner, so lost in the way she was looking at him. He wanted to comfort her, to show her that in some ways, he knew exactly how she felt, of sometimes feeling alone even in a room full of people.

He cupped her cheek, and she lifted her chin higher so their lips touched. Though soft and chaste, it sparked an ember inside of him. His internal temperature rose, along with his need to know more about Eva. To be with Eva.

Then, Eva's lips parted, the invitation punctuated by her grip on the front of his shirt.

Cruz was more than willing to accept. He sighed against her mouth, relishing in the way their tongues danced. In the way her body felt, flushed against his. Along with the sounds of the forest, of the rustling of leaves, and the crickets, and the sound of her breathing.

And though it was cold enough to wear a coat, he was hot, and ready, and wanted more.

But the kiss started ended abruptly.

Eva had stepped back; her hand covered her mouth. "Oh my gosh."

Cruz was breathless, and as he inhaled, reality set in. "Oh, wow. That was—" *Fantastic. Amazing.*

"That...shouldn't have happened."

"You didn't want to kiss me?"

"I... I did...want to."

He inwardly sighed in relief.

"But... I don't..." She looked flustered. Unsure of herself for the first time since he'd met her. "I don't know why that happened." She cleared her throat, straightened her shirt. "What are you doing out here anyway?"

"I noticed that you were gone a while, and Jared looked upset." He raised a hand to redirect the conversation. "What did you mean you don't know why that happened?"

She frowned. "Did he say something?"

"Who?"

"Jared."

"No. Though, you kind of just told me that something's going on."

Her upper lip quirked and she took a breath. "You're observant."

"No, just paying attention." Now that they were a foot apart, he stuffed his hands in his pockets. Apparently, they were going to pretend the kiss never happened. He wasn't going to push, though, knowing the discomfort of having to express something one wasn't ready to reveal. "Do you want to talk about what was bothering you earlier?"

"It's nothing. I was just in my feelings."

"So this wasn't *about* Jared."

"No."

Cruz didn't believe her. She had zero conviction in her answer. And while he wished that she hadn't shut down just now, he felt compelled to share a little about himself.

His thoughts meandered back to New Year's Day, the ground white and pristine from newly fallen snow. He had been warm despite it, in waffle knit leggings and a long shirt. The house smelled of bacon. It was his absolute favorite. "My mom, she hardly cooked, and when she did, it was a big deal. And one New Year's Day she made a big ole spread. But, business didn't stop on federal holidays. The winter holidays meant it was the busy season. I knew that even as a young child.

"When Millie and I came downstairs, my stomach was grumbling. But my dad was dressed in a proper suit, all ready to go to work. He'd forgotten about spending New Year's Day with us."

"Oh no."

"Yep. My mother was so upset. *I* was upset too." He half laughed. "Not sure where that story came from, but I guess what I'm saying about all this is that I always expect for there to be a little bit of drama during the holidays, even if it's not a dragged-out fight. This is probably why holiday gatherings are bittersweet for me."

Her face softened, and she grabbed the two sides of her cardigan and wrapped it around tightly. He wished he could have done it for her and hold her again. "It's just complicated, you know?"

"Life is complicated. People are complicated. Work is complicated. There's a reason why I'm on these damn trails, Eva."

It was her turn to throw her head back and laugh, and the sound made his heart swell. She looked to Spirit Trail behind her, and her expression changed. "One day I'll get back out there for a long trip. I've only done day hikes since starting this business. Maybe that's what I need to clear my head, to get away."

"The open space makes everything less complicated, that's for sure. It's when I'm only worried about my next stop or my next meal or where I'm going to pitch my tent. Everything else goes by the wayside."

She nodded, though worried her lip. The act took Cruz's attention and his gaze, and heat shot down to his core.

Then, she said, "But then, doesn't it all just become an escape? I understand the freedom to be able to step away to think. But it doesn't really solve things, does it?"

He breathed out a laugh. This woman was something else. It was as if she cut off her memory to ten minutes ago, when their lips were locked. "Here I am trying to make you feel better and instead of thanks, you're calling me out."

"I'm not calling you out. I'm trying to work this out, for me." Her chest lifted as she inhaled. "When Louis was alive, he and I would take off. We'd get in our truck and drive for hours. We'd find a place to hike and camp out and stay away from the rest of the world. But I can't do that now, can I? Somehow I'm going to have to deal with this."

"*This?* So something *is* happening between you and Jared."

"Maybe? No? Yes? But I can't tell you about it. I…wouldn't want you to have the wrong impression of me."

"What impression do you think I have of you?"

"Well, you probably think I'm hard to deal with."

He tilted his head, debating the best way to answer that.

She laughed. "See!"

"I mean, I am not at all disagreeing." He was trying to remain serious, but couldn't help finding her endearing. Of how she could be so intense one moment and then light as a feather. "But I doubt that my impression of you would change that much no matter what you said. We're allowed to be multifaceted, Eva. I think it's part of being human, and especially as we get older. I mean, think about the experiences we've had."

"Right, but what's supposed to come with midlife is more wisdom."

"I don't know. I feel just as clueless today as I did even two decades ago. And especially right at this moment."

She was kicking a rock on the ground with the toe of her shoe. Cruz could sense her opening back up; he could feel it in the space between them.

It's because you like her. His conscience chimed in.

Of course he liked her. He wouldn't have come to Thanksgiving, wouldn't have built that fence had he not. But he couldn't be with her, and it wasn't just because of his own inadequacies.

She, too, had limitations. That she clearly put on herself.

On her heart.

And those limitations could very well hurt them both. Badly.

It was obvious right at this very moment.

"I should head upstairs." Her words caused him to exhale, but he nodded. "Thank you for…checking up on me." She pointed toward the door. "Is there anything else you needed from the cellar? I think Jared brought up a bottle of red."

"Yep, he did." He cleared his voice to move the moment along, understanding that what he truly wanted was more than what Eva could give at the moment. "We just need another bottle of something stronger."

Blue Moon,

I'm thankful for you, too, and do you know why? It's because you are so absolutely straightforward.

My Thanksgiving was...interesting. I ate my weight in stuffing, I was surrounded by funny and nice people, but there was also some sadness and confusion.

So I hiked a lot, too, to clear some of my thoughts.

The trail is where I feel most comfortable. But this isn't real life, is it? Real life is dealing with humans, which I'm not great at.

It also means dealing with stuff, like home repairs, and people divorcing, meeting new people.

I don't think I ever told you but the night I stumbled onto your notebook over a year ago, I was having a pretty rough time. It was a rainy night, and the truth was, I went on a hike knowing that it was going to storm.

I'd wanted to wash away the guilt I was feeling, because I'd just walked away from my responsibilities. To my family, and maybe myself, too.

I was soaked to the bone and was lying on the floor of the shelter resigning myself to the idea that I was selfish. Then, I spotted the metal box.

The entire discovery was a distraction for me: the box, the plastic bag, the notebook and the pencil. Then, I haphazardly flipped to the back page and found you.

Where is this going?

Had I not tried to escape my thoughts with a long hike in the rain, I wouldn't have found your notebook. And I wouldn't have gotten to know you, someone who I don't have to puzzle out.

See? This is what happens when I "people". And maybe it's

a good thing you don't know me in person? When I'm writing in this notebook, I have perspective. Better than seeing my grumpy self at Jameson's.

I hope your holiday was better.
Rolling Stone

Chapter Ten

Eva intended to improve her holiday weekend with retail therapy, shopping at her favorite local stores for Small Business Saturday. Looking at her watch, she had an hour to find out what deals her fellow small business owners were peddling, buy whatever made her feel good and head back to the B & B.

Though what she'd needed at that moment was to find parking nearby, all the while having Darcy, one of her oldest friends, in her ear.

"I miss your big dinners, Eva," Darcy said.

"Had I known you were going to be on your own, I would have insisted that you fly in. You know you're always welcome, right?"

"Right, and same to you. I just didn't feel like it this year. Sometimes having to put a pretty face on is tough."

She and Darcy had met in 2010, a few years after Louis died, through the Gold Star Wives of America. It was an organization that advocated for spouses and children of service members who were lost in war, so that they were provided their due benefits and not lost in the shuffle of red tape, especially in their grief. For Eva, it served as a network to tie her back to the community she had loved even if she no longer lived in proximity to a military post.

Eva hadn't realized how much she'd needed a friend who

knew exactly what she had gone through until she connected with Darcy.

Darcy's husband, Mark, had been killed in Afghanistan. She'd since remarried and had a child, but as with Eva and everyone she knew who'd been widowed, grief came in cycles.

"I completely understand. But I'm here whether or not you're fit for company."

"You're the sweetest, Eva."

"Well, you've taken care of me so many times...oooh, there's a space right there." Eva whipped into the roundabout on Main Street and screeched into a space that, thank goodness, was large enough for the truck. "Sorry, everyone seems to be downtown today."

Darcy laughed. "Did you get it?"

"I did. You're my good luck charm." She pressed on the emergency brake and unbuckled her seat belt, though she did not say her farewells. Darcy had been more somber than usual today, and she wanted to make her smile. "Guess what?"

"What?"

"There's...someone in my life. Sort of."

"Shut the front door!"

Eva scrambled to lower the volume. "Jeez."

"I want the short of it. Who, when, what have you done together."

Eva's cheeks warmed. "You're going to be disappointed at how mild this news is going to be."

"It's not mild if you're mentioning it. Is it serious?"

"We've only kissed."

"And?"

Eva shut her eyes, and the memory of his arms around her body rushed forth. "It was a good kiss."

A pause. "You *like* him."

"I think I actually might. And there's something about him.

Something deep. We didn't get along at first, but now…it's so hard to explain."

"Try. It's me, Eva."

She breathed out a laugh. Darcy reminded Eva so much of Rolling Stone—they were friends that knew the most intimate parts of her that she couldn't just show anyone. Kayla and Joy, and even her girls, were perfect people as they were. They had Eva's trust, but there were parts of her heart that only a few had access to. Rolling Stone had been able to tap into so many of her fears. And Darcy understood the nuance of a military spouse loss, of trying to move on after it. She never had to give Darcy any disclaimers, or had to explain the context of a spouse dying in a foreign land.

Darcy just got it.

"He challenges me, Darcy. But he knows exactly when it's time bring in humor, or to make me laugh. And he's strong… he built me a fence and he is…hot."

"He built you a fence!"

"It's a small fence."

"Still. Better than flowers."

"No doubt." She thought of the honeysuckle she'd mowed down months ago. The honeysuckle, which she'd planted years ago, had represented she and Louis. But after finding out about Jared, she'd done a number to the bushes, nearly destroying the plants.

"But," Eva continued, "he's emotionally constipated."

"Oh dear. Like someone I know." Her voice turned wry.

"I know. That was the difference between me and Louis. I could be a little withdrawn because Louis was expressive enough for the both of us."

Except about the fact that he slept with another woman.

She pushed the intrusive thoughts away. "And I don't know if I want anything from him at all. We're both so independent, both living our lives already. I don't know how he feels about me either. I wish he was more forthright too."

At times she imagined meeting someone who was the mash-up of Cruz and Rolling Stone. She smiled to herself. Finding a person like that would be virtually impossible. Though, Rolling Stone's mention of Jameson's had been curious. How often did he grocery shop? Did he start his shopping from the dairy side of the market, or from the produce side?

She shook her head. Thinking about who Rolling Stone was, was futile. He could be anyone.

Eva glanced to her left in time to catch Cruz walking out of Dr. Gerbera's counseling office, as if conjured. Startled, she watched as he slapped a beanie on his head and darted across the street to Winnebego's Plants.

"I bet by getting to know him, you might figure out that you share other similarities besides being so closed."

"Maybe," she said, belatedly, her mind on Cruz.

Had he been at Dr. Gerbera's office for himself? Judgment was far from her mind; she was pleasantly surprised. It had been a while since she'd gone to therapy herself, and seeing him there gave her another perspective to the kind of person he was. That he believed in caring for one's mental health.

"All right, my friend, it's time for me to go. The fam just walked in through the door," Darcy said.

"Call me later?"

"Of course. And you call me when you finally get in this man's pants."

"Darcy!"

"What? I'm just saying. Love you."

"Love you." Eva hung up, and sat in the silence of her truck. One of her destinations was Winnebago. Was it a good idea to "accidentally" run into Cruz? Their conversation at Thanksgiving was stilted and awkward, not helped by her inability to say exactly what was on her mind.

And with Rolling Stone's last note with his own mess of a holiday, she wondered: Was she someone that he would have considered frustrating, too? Did she frustrate other people in her life?

She didn't want to be that person people ran away from or complained about, and especially not by the people she cared about.

Okay, she was going to do it. She was going to say hi.

One, two...

Eva climbed out of the truck and straightened out her clothes, then darted across the road. As she entered Winnebego's, she braced herself for Cruz and for the serotonin that coursed through her whenever she entered this shop.

Because...plants.

Inside was a cozy jungle of green. Winnebego's focused on indoor plants, and the shop extended farther to the rear. Though she was distracted by the newest succulents that came in, she made her way to the back, toward the greenhouse.

Cruz was easy to spot. He was leaning toward a potted spider plant and touched its leaf. He then picked it up, only to set it down. He seemed hesitant, almost afraid.

Her heart softened at the sight of it.

"Mom?"

Eva spun at the M word. It didn't matter if she was at the grocery store, at the beach, or at a restaurant, her reaction was automatic. "Yes?"

It was indeed Frankie. In each hand was a potted philodendron. "Playing hooky, eh?"

She hoped that Frankie hadn't seen Cruz. "I can't resist Small Business Saturday."

"Same." She nodded over to the left, where a man weaved through the crowd. He had dark brown skin, was of Asian descent—he might've even been Filipino—and handsome. And Frankie's age. "Mom, meet Julian."

"Hello." Eva stood straight. Frankie, hanging out with a man?

"Hi, auntie," he said with a grin.

Yep, he was, indeed, Filipino.

"Julian kindly stepped up as the vice president of the PTO and he's also the dad to one of Liam's friends. Just so happened to have run into one another. Here's your philodendron, Julian." She handed him the pot. "It's a present for his wife."

"Thanks," Julian replied. To Eva, he said, "My wife's a certified 'plant mom' and thank goodness Frankie was around to help me out. Well, time for me to pay. Have to head out. Eleanor has swimming. Talk soon." He raised his potted plant.

"Nice to meet you, Julian." Eva watched him get swallowed up by the browsing plant shoppers.

"I saw that look, Mom."

"What look?"

"That you hoped he was single."

"Was I that transparent?"

"*So* transparent." She rolled her eyes. "Please don't worry about my love life. I am fine. Things are good and I'm not in any rush to turn my life inside out for a man. I did that already, remember?"

Eva nodded. Frankie's relationship with her ex-husband was fraught with complication. But Eva wanted love for Frankie; she wanted to see her daughter doted upon, to be cared for.

But she kept her thoughts to herself. Frankie was a grown woman, and Eva was the last to give her advice on matters of the heart.

Frankie sighed. "I'd better go. Lots of work ahead today. By the way, we need to discuss Snowball Royalty."

Every Christmas, the town voted on upcoming Snowball Royalty. It was announced during the tree lighting ceremony.

"We should vote for Gabby," Frankie continued.

"But Gabby isn't dating anyone. Or is she?" She attempted

to keep herself calm, so Frankie would continue to dish the gossip.

"She's *not*, but you know how she's enamored with these things. And she deserves it, with all the work she's done for the B & B. She plans everyone's big day, but she never really gets hers, you know?"

"Aw, that's sweet." Eva's heart squeezed. Her daughters were typical in that they fought over the smallest things. Their conversations could turn on a dime, and no one was safe from their banter. But then there were moments such as these that made Eva feel as if she'd done something right.

"Mom." Frankie's face switched to mischief. "Don't look now, but Cruz is here."

"Oh?" Eva infused faux-surprise into her tone.

"Oooh, he's headed our way. Now, smile okay?" Frankie's own grin spanned from ear to ear. In a sudden movement, she turned Eva by the shoulders.

Just in time for Cruz to walk up.

"Ladies." His serious expression was incongruent with the fact that he was carrying four potted plants in his arms.

"Hi, Cruz. Well, I've got to go. See you later." Frankie scurried away, leaving the two of them in an awkward silence.

Eva knew that it was awkward because of her, because despite what she'd told Darcy earlier, Eva might actually beat out Cruz in the emotionally constipated department.

"So." She dug in for the words as a child would carve a pumpkin. "Nice picks."

He returned a curious expression.

"The plants. You picked out some nice healthy ones."

"You know plants?" The relief was palpable in the slump of his shoulders. "I have no idea what I'm doing."

"Oh, well…" She pointed to each plant. "That's a spider plant, a pothos, money plant and Chinese evergreen. They're all easy to take care of. Are you decorating?"

"Me? No. This is a new…project for me."

"Ah. Good choices then for a first-timer." Eva shifted her weight from one foot to the other, unable to cover up their last conversation with small talk. It had everything to do with the flutters in her tummy. "Hey, I know you're probably busy, but I was wondering if we could talk, about Thanksgiving."

His expression seemed to cloud slightly. "Sure. There's really no need, though."

"I know, but I want to. Um…how about tonight? Or whatever night works for you…"

She held her breath, feeling like a rookie.

"Tonight's good. Where should I meet you?"

"How about La Calle? Tacos, at seven?"

"I can do that."

"Great." She couldn't read the expression on his face. Was he upset? Angry? Though, her own cheeks were warm from relief. "I'll see you tonight then." She made to turn.

"Wait. Eva?"

She halted, though her heart rate spiked. "Yep?"

"If you have a couple of minutes, I would love some help with these." He gestured to the plants. "Do I need anything else? I really don't want them to die."

"O…okay." She released a breath, relieved that perhaps his expression had been all about the plants rather than her. "You stay right here, and I'll be back with a cart."

Eva might not be great at expressing all of her emotions, but she was adept at being a mother. To people and to plants.

When Cruz walked back into his house to see Millie vacuuming, three hours after his appointment with Dr. Gerbera, he barely recognized it.

For a beat he forgot about his eventful afternoon.

"Hello?" he called out, setting down the plants on the foyer, while his eyes roamed what had been a sparse living room.

Millie turned off the vacuum, smiling as if she hadn't just turned his house upside down. "Welcome home, honey."

"What in the world is all of this?" Cruz liked wood and metal and hard surfaces. He preferred cool tones and understated furnishings. What he was seeing now were flowers and soft pillows, a fluffy couch and a brand-new rug.

"I decorated." As if that wasn't a strange thing to do. "And, you read my mind. Plant babies." Milly skipped to where he was standing and picked up the spider plant, inspecting it and placing it on his coffee table. "Ah, she's going to thrive in here."

Millie was trying to distract him, but he wasn't going to fall for it. "Not sure if you've forgotten, but this isn't your house."

"I know." She returned a satisfied smile, the kind that said that he couldn't do anything about it. "You've lived here a year, and it still looked like a college dorm. You're a grown man. You should have real furniture."

"I had real furniture. And by the way, where is it?"

"Oh I had it relocated. Paid a couple of college kids to move that uncomfortable loveseat to the office, and the side table up to the loft."

He shook his head. The audacity, and also, the resourcefulness. Like, how did she arrange all of these things while working remotely? He couldn't even be angry. Knowing Millie's penchant for multitasking, he'd expected something this drastic in her arrival. And, perhaps a few hours ago he would have insisted that she return everything right that second, but now...

"So the appointment went well?" Millie said, falling into the couch as if it was a chaise longue. "Seeing that you're walking in here somewhat in a good mood, bearing living things."

He nodded, plopping down into an armchair. Also new. "Thank you for the suggestion. It might work out."

She leaned in. "Can you say that again? Did you admit that I was right?"

"Yeah, okay, you were."

It had been years since Cruz had gone to therapy, and he only had a handful of sessions under his belt. But what Millie had said in the car on Thanksgiving Day, and then what Eva had hinted at—that he'd wanted to escape—became a nagging earworm overnight.

He was lucky. Dr Gerbera had a cancellation this morning, so he jumped into the hotseat. "My next appointment is in a week and a half." He gestured to the foyer with his head. "Until then, the plants are my assignment."

Her eyebrows rose. "Really?"

"Something about me taking the time to ground myself without having to head onto the trail. And that by taking care of something else, it might get me out of my head. As if having a business allows for me to stay in my head all day."

"That's an interesting approach. But, I can see what she's saying by it."

He shrugged. "I just hope I don't kill them. What would that say about me?"

She laughed. "I'm glad you went. What happened during Thanksgiving anyway?"

"Nothing specific," he lied, crossing the room, still shaking his head because on his kitchen bar island was a decorative bowl with fruit in it.

The truth was that seeing Eva in pain had been a trigger. He'd felt helpless, which had been reminiscent of his lack of control when he was sick. It also had been the sting of Eva's rejection after they kissed.

"I'm sorry I didn't notice that you were upset," Millie said.

While opening the fridge, he smiled at her. "It was Thanksgiving. And I could have told you, too. I'm fine though, okay?"

He sounded so self-aware, but even today, in seeing Eva, he hadn't known how to react.

"Eva asked me out. Tonight," he said.

Millie sat up. "What? I can't believe you didn't lead with that. When?"

"At the plant store. She helped me pick stuff out for the plants. I've got a trunk full of soil and rocks and bigger pots and I don't know what else."

Millie's laugh resounded through the room.

"You think it's funny? I have three different kinds of soil, and gardening gloves and something to rest my knees on. For four house plants."

She snorted. "Well, now I'm really glad I decorated. This place has to look better when Eva comes over."

"No one is inviting Eva over to this house. We're meeting at La Calle." That would be open season in the Forrester clan. There was a reason why he never brought anybody home. Especially not in the last five years, when everybody—specifically his mother and sister—had increased the pressure in finding his person, as she put it. In starting a family, even.

"Then I'll I invite her over."

"Decorating my house doesn't equate to inviting whomever you want."

"You know that's not how this family works, right? What's yours is mine and what's mine is yours? Except your mattress in the guest room. That can remain yours. I'm seriously thinking of ordering a new one so my back doesn't ache so much when I wake up."

Cruz had reached into the refrigerator for a sparkling water, only to retrieve Millie's vice: canned ice coffee. Looking in, he noted that there were more than a dozen cans on the shelf.

Millie only drank a can a day.

He trudged and sat on his leather armchair. The pillows had taken most of the real estate, and he tossed them to the ground.

"Cruz! I fluffed them to perfection."

He grabbed one of the pillows and lobbed it, and it landed on her face.

"Hey! What are we, ten?"

"We need to talk about what's going on here. Call me enlightened since this is my first therapy session in four years but… You insist on coming to visit, you mention a retreat at the B & B. You decorate my entire house to look like yours, and you're saying things like what's mine is yours and what's yours is mine. It's like you're moving in or something." He laughed, though it died in his throat when he realized what he'd said. "Wait. Are you really moving in? Is this about our conversation before Thanksgiving dinner?"

"Dammit. I was hoping that we were going to sweep that under the rug." Her hands landed on her lap, and she laced them.

"Millie?"

She shot up and began to pace the living room.

Now Cruz knew that something was terribly wrong.

"I'm here because I miss you. Mom misses you. And I'm here to see if there's room for us to live here."

"Live here as in live in my house?" He had visions of his mother sweeping into the living room, her Louis Vuitton luggage filling the front hallway. That, and her incessant little yapper of a dog.

"No, what I mean is living here in Peak. You've been gone for the last three years, Cruz, and we are the only ones left in our family. Unless you can find a way to spend more time with us, then Mom is hell-bent coming to live here. My kids are close to graduation. Mom's duties have dwindled with Forrester, and she refuses to wait any longer for you to come back home."

"I don't think any of this is necessary. There are planes. I can visit."

She slapped her hands against her thighs. "Cruz. The only time you go to Colorado is for your appointments, and that just won't do. Not for Mom and especially not for me. Life is too short," she said.

"I know that."

Though Millie didn't say the word *cancer*, Cruz heard it underneath these conversations with his sister. He hated that word with a passion. He despised it in every cell of his body.

He hated it most of all because he'd caused Millie and his mother worry and hurt and pain because of it.

"Then you should know how important it is that we try to spend time together," she said.

He shook his head, disbelieving and also in disagreement. "I need my space."

"You are running away."

Eva's words came to mind, and he winced. Was there something wrong with space? Wasn't it his God-given right to seek his space?

Certainly, finding it on a trail—which was a healthy way of finding his peace—was better than other coping measures. "You make it sound as if I've been living aimlessly. I learned a lot about myself hiking, so much that I've opened two trail shops since the beginning of all of this. I also physically labored to maintain at least a half a dozen trails. This is where I've dedicated my life, to trying to put something good out into the world."

"And yet, how about the people who love you?"

"We're not going to talk about this."

"You can't *not* speak about it." She shoved her hands in her pockets. "I didn't want to bring this up, but me and Mom coming to live here also has everything to do with bringing Forrester to *you*. Our father left this business to you and me. Since you left, I've been on my own. True, we have the board. But it's the family decisions that push Forrester along.

Mom, thank goodness, has been a good sounding board, but ideally, I should have been making those decisions with you. All these years, we have been in a kind of limbo, and guessing, in a way, that I'm making decisions that you agree with."

And there it was. The whack of the gauntlet. The reason why he had avoided spending too long of a time with Millie. Only she could hold his feet to the fire.

He dipped his chin to his chest, understanding that he couldn't refuse to respond. This was Millie putting the ball back in his court.

"And what if I don't want to be a part of Forrester?"

A beat of silence passed. "It would suck, but we'd need to make some business decisions to restructure your position in the company. But it wouldn't change that Mom and I would want to live here, near you."

Restructure was the nice way of saying "cut out" and the thought of it brought a newfound slice of pain. Sure he'd left to pursue his own path, but inside, he'd still been a part of this generations-long establishment.

Where would that leave him, if he was cut out? Would he still be a Forrester? And wouldn't that make him a coward?

All of those thoughts, though, remained stuck in his chest. Instead, he said, "So I'm stuck with you no matter what?"

She half-laughed. "Yeah, you are."

He cleared his throat. "What would that look like if Forrester came here?"

"We build an office here—there's enough land to do so. You'd travel a bit, but this would be our home base. It'll take time, so we may rent out an office space until then. This is your decision, though."

He nodded.

Millie sat on the coffee table and faced him, a slight grin on her face. "But whether or not you're in or out with Forrester doesn't mean we won't try to keep getting close to you. Mom already has a Realtor on speed dial."

All of this was causing Cruz whiplash.

She reached out and squeezed his knee, grounding him. "We are all in this world together, Cruz. Get to know your niece and nephew. Talk to Mom. Deal with Forrester."

She leaned in and gave him a hug. It was strong hug, a mother's hug. "I know I haven't been around for you lately."

"I'm not mad." Millie straightened. "I just want your attention sometimes." A smirk appeared on her lips.

The tension in the room fell away. What was left was his sister's underlying mischievousness. "So much that you're actually thinking of buying a new mattress," he said.

"Actually, to be honest…" She gritted her teeth.

"You bought it, didn't you?"

"I did. It has all the bells and whistles. I can even control it with an app." She shrugged with a satisfied look on her face. "Are you mad?"

"About the mattress?"

"About everything I brought up."

The answer came quickly. "Not about you and Mom hanging out here at Peak. Though I'll have to get used to it. About Forrester, though? Not sure what to think."

She stood and offered him a hand. "While you think, we might as well empty that car of yours. Don't you have a date in a couple of hours?"

He groaned and got to his feet. "It's not really a date."

"Whatever, dude." She snorted, leading the way to his Outback. Her jaw dropped at the gardening gear that filled it. "Holy moly."

"Like I said I couldn't say no."

Her expression turned mischievous. "It's better. It's more like you wanted to say yes."

Rolling Stone,

Whew. That sounded like a doozy of a Thanksgiving, and I'm sorry it didn't go so well. Mine was...okay, too. As I write this though, it feels like a million years ago.

Or maybe, I'm already trying to move on from it.

I hike to get away, too. But unlike you, I don't go very far. Reality and my responsibilities always pull me back, and there's no choice but for me to check in. Connection is important to me, as much as solitude.

It was really why I started this notebook in the first place. With that first note, I guess I was just looking for someone to connect with, even if it was with myself. I didn't think someone would write me back. And continue to write me back, especially these days.

I think my problem is connecting, honestly. I can't just be, and say what I mean, and show people everything.

I want to try though. No matter what, I need something to change. The betrayal I talked about a couple of months ago? My feelings for it are the same. There's no peace in sight.

At the risk of digging into more personal information, but is home base nearby? You mentioned Jameson's so casually. I admit, that while we agreed not to meet, I'm curious as to who you are.

But we know what curiosity did to the cat, don't we.

Safe hiking,
Blue Moon

Chapter Eleven

"What are you doing?" Eva said to her reflection in the hallway mirror.

She had gone all out. Fixed her hair. Put on makeup—not much, just a bit of mascara and gloss, but certainly a little more than she wore in the day-to-day. In less than a half hour, she was seeing Cruz. To do what? She wasn't sure. Except that she wanted to see where that kiss would lead, if anywhere.

It was a kiss that made her lightheaded. It was a kiss that made her knees buckle.

But how did one do this—talk about their kiss, and on that end, dating, moving forward, share oneself—as a widow? Looking at herself now, at her fifty-year-old face, at the experience in the lines that graced the sides of her mouth and eyes, it was all so different.

Yes, she'd kissed other men since Louis died. She'd made love too. But her expectations in this season of her life might be too high for anyone to meet. It took more to impress her, or more specifically, it took authenticity instead of things. She looked for realness.

A knock on her front door dragged Eva out of her thoughts. Exhaling, she opened it, to Matilda.

"Hey." Surprised, Eva looked at her watch. It was well past Matilda's usual shift. "Everything okay?"

"Yes, um…but it looks like you're headed out. We can speak another time."

"We can walk and talk. Hold on a second." She grabbed her purse, coat and keys from the kitchen and stepped out, locking the front door.

The weather was a crisp forty degrees. The night was clear the moon was high and bright. A perfect late fall night.

"How was today?" Eva got into step with Matilda as they walked down the path. Beyond, the lights of the B & B and her daughters' cottages illuminated the otherwise dark property.

"It was good. Guests were happy. We received another glowing review online."

"Wonderful." Matilda was truly a blessing, to Eva and to the B & B. She kept everyone and everything straight with her organization and focus. Though sometimes blunt, Matilda wanted to please people.

"I'm here to talk more about something personal rather than work, actually."

"All right." Eva inhaled slowly, though kept her expression still. There was only one topic of conversation in Matilda's life that was both business and personal...

"It's about me and Jared. We'd like to get married here. If that's okay."

Eva halted; they were at the edge of the B & B patio. Thankfully, they were also in a dark spot, in which Matilda could not see Eva's expression.

Because she was stunned.

"Married, here?" Eva's voice strangled in her throat.

"I talked to Gabby this morning, and there are a couple of dates available in the spring."

"Wow." Eva's brain had frozen.

"And of course we'd pay for it. But we thought, where else would we want to be married, but where we met? I mean, we met at Mountain Rush, but we fell in love here. It's perfect, too, because by then we would have moved into his cottage, so everything will be happening in our backyard."

Eva opened her mouth, but nothing came out, stuck on the fact that yes, they had met at the B & B when Jared had not disclosed his true identity to the Espiritus. Matilda had kept his secret, until a picture on social media had outed their relationship.

"Eva?"

Then, she felt the cool touch of fingers against her forearm. She startled.

"I'm sorry. I'm shocked...and honored." Eva rallied. Their engagement *had* been a happy moment, and so was Jared's acceptance of the job as full-time chef at the B & B. He wasn't hugely well-known, but his regional brand had brought in some additional guests eager for a "foodie vacation."

It would make it easy for their families and friends to attend, since the wedding would be right here, in town.

And, not only was Jared her son despite all of her inner turmoil, Matilda was important to Eva, and loved by the whole family.

It *was* an honor. Jared and Matilda's love for one another had been a joy to witness.

"Of course. Of course you should marry here." She leaned in and scooped Matilda into a hug. A tight one, to communicate how much she cared about her.

Because, at the end of the day, she loved Matilda. And she loved Jared. As she'd promised to Jared on Thanksgiving, it wasn't about him. It was about Louis, and her getting over what Louis did.

"Thank you," Matilda said, stepping back. "Oh my gosh that was nerve-racking."

"What do you mean?"

"It's this whole situation. You're my boss, but also my future mother-in-law, but most of all, like a big sister to me. I wasn't sure how to ask. You and your family matter to me so much, in all ways, and not just because you're Jared's family. You mentored me in the hardest transition time of my life."

"You matter to us too, Matilda."

"I know, it's just…with what happened in the spring, with my involvement. I know you said that things are fine and I believe it, but I find myself double-checking that you and I are okay."

Eva was mollified by Matilda's words. At how honest and evocative they were.

Why couldn't she be the same way?

"You and I are absolutely okay," she said, reaching for the nearest thought despite the heaviness she still felt.

"Okay. I'll give Gabby a call. I hope that you have a good night. Are you headed out to see Cruz?"

"How did you know about that?"

"Millie, his sister, said so. She called earlier to speak to Frankie about a professional retreat for Forrester employees. It could be great for us—I think they would take over the entire B & B! Anyway, make sure to get the fish tacos. They're the best." Matilda smiled. "And you look really nice, Eva."

"Thank you." How the conversation continued to ping-pong rendered her unsteady. "I'd better head out."

But as she watched Matilda enter the back door of the B & B, Eva hesitated making her way to her car. Suddenly a dinner at a lively restaurant among acquaintances who surely were going to be watching her and Cruz sounded taxing.

She took out her phone; a text had buzzed in and she hadn't noticed. Cruz. Running late. Hiking group delayed.

A hike. That sounded good right about now. A hike and a cigarette, though she could only have one of those things.

Though a night hike was an immediate no. The night she'd met Cruz had been a safe lesson that it could have ended differently. With the increase in hiker traffic on Spirit Trail, she was sure to run into a stranger.

Her fingers flew on her phone screen. It's fine. And actually, I need to cancel.

Everything ok?

Eva eyed the text and contemplated if and how to explain her situation. At how she needed to find a way to process these feelings for Louis. She no longer wanted these negative emotions so she wouldn't push people away.

As she'd written Rolling Stone earlier, her problem was connection. She continued to allow the past to disrupt it.

Eva then knew what she truly wanted to do tonight. She only had one real safe space these days. It had only been a couple of days since she'd written her last note. The chances that Rolling Stone had written back was unlikely, but even sitting in that trail shelter, surrounded by the sounds of the forest, sounded perfect.

Eva: Not really. Not sure I'm fit for company.

Welcome to my one-person club.

I'm sorry. I'll make it up to you another time?

Eva had started to walk back to her cottage, when another text from Cruz flew in.

Want to make it a two-person club? I know a couple of trails.

Eva climbed up her stairs. It was like he'd read her mind. Night hike?

Why not? It's gorgeous out there. I've got all the right gear.

When else could she hike with the safety of an expert? And someone who she had, in a roundabout way, learned to appreciate and trust.

I'll be ready in 10.

Meet you on your front porch in three.

You're that close to my house?

She started stripping out of her clothes, starting with her shoes at the front door. From her dresser she grabbed a T-shirt and a long-sleeve shirt, her hiking pants and socks, tugging them on swiftly. Her phone beeped.

Chip took the hiking group the rest of the way back to Peak. I'm coming to you now.

An unexpected need bloomed in her core. Yes, she was reading too much into the text, but the way he'd quickly changed plans at the last minute, and the tone of that last sentence…

Like nothing was going to stand in his way to see her.

She pressed her hand against her belly to steady herself, understanding now that what she was feeling, and what she'd felt earlier, was giddiness.

She shook her head to clear it. There was no time to mull over it now. From her hallway closet she dragged out her day hiking gear: a small pack with an attached whistle and a water bladder, which she filled, and her walking stick that could double as protective equipment for the random, assertive critter.

Then, from her pantry she grabbed a couple of high-protein granola bars and nuts. And an apple for good measure.

Finally, her portable phone charger.

Yes, she overpacked even on hikes.

Her phone pinged.

I'm outside.

The message rocketed her heart into space, though some-how she kept it together in time to throw her hair up in a po-nytail and snatch her windbreaker from the coat closet. Then, breathless, she opened the door to a man who looked as beau-tiful as he was rugged.

"Ready?" he asked without preamble.

Was she ready?

She had a feeling that with Cruz, once she got on that trail with him, it would be an adventure. Whether or not she knew what she was doing.

"Yes."

"Still doing good? Tired?" Cruz looked to his left, at the outline of Eva walking next to him. They'd been hiking for two hours on one of the trails that looped out and back. They would soon come upon the junction behind the B & B, where they could choose a longer trail to maneuver, Spirit Trail, or cut through the B & B to her cottage.

The sky was a navy blue, illuminated by the moon and stars. Beyond her outline were the Blue Ridge Mountains, and there was a definite chill was in the air—a sign that it would likely snow soon.

But he couldn't quite focus on the beauty of all of these things, because Eva had hardly spoken throughout the hike, engaging in small talk but not much beyond that. She had seemed in good spirits in her cottage—he'd just finished up writing a letter back to Blue Moon when he'd texted her—and when she'd opened the door with a smile, he'd thought that this hike would be full of banter. At the very least, he'd thought that she would vent, from her mention of not being fit for company.

But perhaps she was more like him than he'd thought when it came to hikes; perhaps she was processing something.

So he hadn't pushed it. He had enough on his plate with what Millie had thrown upon him earlier today. Having to guess another person's intentions was a bridge too far, especially when she'd been clear that she was having a bad night.

But he'd wanted to know how far they were going, seeing that he would like to have a good night's sleep. "Or," he continued, "should I map out a trail to West Virginia?"

"No. Not tired," she muttered.

Okay then. No jokes tonight. He strode out and kept in time with her footsteps. The round spotlights of their headlamps bopped on the horizon. Eva clearly felt comfortable on the trail, and it was one more thing that drew him to her. Every time they saw one another other, she seemed to unfurl a petal at a time. What other talents and gifts did this woman have, and what other secrets did she carry?

"About Thanksgiving." Eva's voice cut through silence, causing Cruz to whip his head toward her. "I don't think I said so, but thank you. For being there."

"You're welcome." Satisfaction mixed with relief coursed through him.

"And thank you for not pushing too hard about what I couldn't share."

"Yeah. Of course. I get it. It's not any of my business."

"Well, the thing is—I did want to tell you. But I haven't even told the person themselves how I feel, and it doesn't sit right to talk about it to others. The last thing I want is to create a rift, you know? Working and living with family can be tricky."

He smiled to himself. "If there's anyone who knows about the family business situation, it's me."

"Huh. What's your role in Forrester these days? I assumed that since you're out here that you've stepped away."

"Not quite." Now, with the business back on his mind, a trace of anxiety whirled in his belly. "My father left Forrester to me and Millie, but I'm in this in between space."

"So...technically you are *the* Forrester."

"A co-Forrester, I guess."

"Wow."

He waited for more. "What do you mean by 'wow.'"

"That's a huge deal. Money. Power. And yet...that's not quite you."

Hearing Eva speak in the dark was like a confessional. It unlocked some of the thoughts he couldn't access earlier, with his sister. "That's exactly how I feel. It feels incongruent, and yet, who in their right mind would walk away from that? I could do a lot with that money. Not only for me, but for others."

"What's holding you back from staying with Forrester?"

"Me."

"I mean, obviously." The humor in her voice caused Cruz to exhale. "But what *in* you is holding you back."

"This." He raised his hand to the space in front of them. "And everything that comes with this." In the pause, he thought on it some more. "Freedom, the air, the sky. To explore, I guess."

"But you have a responsibility, right? To your family. To work. And to whatever your dad left? Where does that come into play? There's a great deal of privilege to be able to just go."

The questions were direct and fair. It mimicked Blue Moon, and it allowed for him to say more. "I hear you. I know I'm able to take off and create the life I want because of Forrester. But shouldn't everyone seek what they think is good for them?"

"Good is a relative term. Because what's good for you sometimes ends up bad for others."

He frowned at the edge in her tone. Definitely *not* like Blue Moon. Now he really knew that this wasn't about him. He gently tugged her back by the elbow—she'd been speed walking. "I know you're not judging me on what's going on in my family, right?"

She halted, shoulders drooping. When she turned to him, the glare of her headlamp caused him to squint. She laughed, reaching up to turn off her lamp. "Sorry."

He did the same to his, blinking for his eyes to adjust. "It's fine."

"No, it's not fine. Because I'm sorry for what I said. I'm not judging you. This is why I'm not fit for company tonight. I'm dealing with my own stuff, and it comes out and you're the lucky guy who happens to be around." She heaved a breath. "The mention of you leaving the family, of seeing other experiences does something to me."

"This has something to do with Thanksgiving too."

"Yes. With Thanksgiving, with months before then. And why I'm walking around with you in the middle of the night. Though, you must be kind of tired of me, sulking."

He frowned; the comment was strange. "Why do you say that?"

"Just that, I don't know how to do this, you know? Like just come out and tell you how I feel."

"You've told me how you felt all along, from day one."

She dipped her head. "I mean, it's easy for me to stand my ground. It's easy for me to love on my family. The rest takes me some time."

He stepped in closer, now wishing that he could see her face in full, though hesitating for a beat. "May I?"

"Yes." Her answer was a breath, tugging him closer.

Though they weren't touching, he could feel the heat of her skin.

"You just told me a lot about you in the last few minutes," he said.

"Yeah?"

"Yes. That *you* find family important. That *you're* loyal and reliable. And that you're someone people rely on. Though I already knew that from the way people talk about you."

"I never meant you weren't loyal."

"I know that too." He grinned. "What I'm trying to say is that if you know someone well enough, or get them, the understanding is there. And right now, I understand that we both have things that we need to work out. That you and I both needed this hike tonight."

"More than a big Mexican dinner."

"And miss out on the granola bar I chowed down an hour ago? No regrets."

"You know what I regret? That I cried. Into your chest."

A smile threatened to burst out of him, in a teenage boy kind of way, but he tried to keep himself somewhat cool. The way the conversation had meandered had him wrapped around Eva's pinkie. She had layers of complexity. "My chest didn't mind it."

"It wasn't a bad chest."

"And the kiss?" The words broke out of him before he could stop them.

Silence descended between them, and he wondered if that question was too forward.

He'd heard once that when a person aged into their fifties that they no longer cared what everyone else said. And while some of that was true—these days he'd wanted to achieve his own goals versus others'—he'd become more empathetic.

Which was also the reason why hiking was the most perfect activity: he only needed to mind himself.

In a softer voice, almost shyly, she said, "I liked the kiss."

Part of him wanted to whoop and yell. Her answer felt like a reward for all the good things he'd done in the world.

But would there be a second?

Testing, he reached out for her hand. For as much as he wanted her at this moment, he didn't want to move too fast. He understood that in addition to her treasured privacy, Eva valued her personal space too.

The touch of her skin was like the crackle of electricity. Their fingers interlocked, and engaged in a gentle play.

With his other hand he cupped the back of her neck, his thumb resting on her pulse point. To his pleasure, her heart beat a strong, steady pace.

Heat flared inside him. "If you want, I think we can make that happen again. As early as now."

She inched closer to him so there was only a breath between them. He watched her eyes shut in anticipation. It was a small gesture from her end, but the satisfaction, knowing that she trusted him, that she wanted this, ignited his insides.

Leaning down and keeping his eyes on her parted lips, he thought about the first time he'd met this woman face-to-face at Cross Trails. At how these same lips put him in his place.

He was going to make this kiss miles better than their first.

The touch of his lips against hers was like the sunrise against a mountain range. While the first kiss they'd had was tentative and sweet, this one was more intense, hungrier, clamoring with the promise of more.

Against his lips she said, "I want to go back to my place. Right now."

He laughed though didn't dare disengage. "I'll follow you anywhere, Eva Espiritu. Just lead the way."

Blue Moon,

What would you do if I said: curious cat be damned? I'll soon have to leave town once more, to see my doctor for a follow-up, and I'm tempted for us to keep in touch. Could we text?

Is that too much? Sharing our cell numbers is a step toward revealing who we are. Is that something we want? Can we be friends in real life, too?

Speaking of growing relationships...this might be strange to bring up now, but I am seeing someone, or hoping to. She's beautiful, special, so many things. As I'm writing this, I realize that I don't know if you have a partner. I suppose it never did matter, because it feels like this friendship is so distinctly ours. When I'm in this trail shelter, writing to you, everything kind of fades away. But in the talk of meeting, or even considering it—I have never mentioned your existence to anyone. Should I? Have you mentioned me?

On the subject of peace. Damn. Is there such a thing? I have been searching for it for years now, and even in the last few weeks, it has fully eluded me.

No, that's not the complete truth. Because when I'm with this person, I get a taste of it.

Rolling Stone

Chapter Twelve

Eva's adrenaline was on overdrive as she pulled Cruz by the hand up the path to the B & B. Her vision swam with excitement.

All they'd shared so far was a kiss, but her imagination, her senses, her hormones were doing all sorts of wild things in her body. And her only focus was locking this man in her bedroom.

It had been how he'd listened. How he'd validated the importance of her emotions.

It had been how he seemed to accept all parts of her, even when her emotions were a mess.

Yes, these where the gestures she'd needed to ramp her up. Not even Cruz's attractiveness, which was next level, could compare to the way he listened. It was his care for her, his concern for her, and his ability to liquify her insides with one singular kiss.

She wanted him now.

But as they crossed the patio, a spotlight turned on, halting them in their place.

"Dammit. Let's cut across," she hissed, gripping his hand. Since the B & B started holding public events and because of the increase in hiker traffic, they'd installed state-of-the-art security lights and cameras all over the property.

"Where?" he whispered back.

She squinted against her diminished sense of direction.

"Hello?" It was Frankie.

Eva let go of Cruz's hand. Looking back, he had a grin plastered on his face.

Oh no.

"Mom?" said another voice. Gabby.

"Sorry. Ignore us." It was Jared, this time. He grunted, saying, "Let go of the freaking door, Frankie. Gabby, quit it..." And after what sounded like a squabble came the slam of a door.

Then, silence.

A rumble of laughter came from Cruz. "What the heck was that?"

"My children." At the words, at calling Jared her child, too, brought only a smidge of mixed emotions, but humor remained. She breathed a sigh of relief and chuckled.

He slipped his hand into hers. "Should I go?"

She turned to look at him. One more turn-on? That he didn't flinch at the Espiritu chaos. "Hell no."

They held hands as they walked up to her cottage, and while the tension between them had been turned down from boiling to a simmer, Eva could feel her heart threatening to burst from her chest. His grip was firm. He wasn't going anywhere, at least tonight.

"Kind of reminds me of how Millie and I were as kids. Double trouble."

"Yeah, those three are peas in a pod." She thought of her girls pre-Jared and post-Jared, at how he was that missing puzzle piece between them. He was the connector between the two, easing the communication flow. "Jared evens them out. He's a good buffer for the girls. I don't hear them fight nearly as much as they used to before he arrived."

"Arrived? Where was he?"

She slowed. "You don't know?"

"Know what?"

"Wow, that's a shock. I would think you'd have heard the story around town." They were three-quarters of the way up the path, and her heart sank a little. By the time they got up to the cottage, this man was going to spin right around and leave.

"Want to tell me?"

She steeled herself. "Jared is my late husband's—*Louis's* son with another woman. We only met him when he came to Peak in the spring and took a job as our temporary B & B chef. Matilda found out the truth first, but Jared asked her to keep his identity a secret until he was ready to tell me…us, the truth. They fell in love in the process. Then, one day, I found out. It was…a tumultuous time for all of us, but we got through it. In fact Matilda and Jared are getting married in the spring, right here."

Eva didn't disclose her feelings for Jared, keeping her tone light. But as she stepped up the porch stairs, unlocked the door and stepped inside, she noted that Cruz was no longer behind her.

He remained on the other side of the threshold.

She exhaled, unsurpised. He was a man who'd admitted he liked freedom. Why would he want to get tied up with a woman who had so much drama?

"So, Thanksgiving had something to do with Louis *and* Jared?" he asked now, expression serious.

She nodded, eyes darting to the ground. Still, she didn't want to say it aloud. Jared had to be the first to hear it.

And yet, with the admission came a smidge of relief.

"Can I come in, still?"

The question startled her, though hope flared from within. "You still want to?"

"Do you still want me to?" Then, seeing her confusion, he said, "Eva, I didn't want to assume, especially after that conversation. I want this to be your choice."

Relief and joy burst in her chest. This man. He continued to surprise her. From his stubbornness, to his attitude, and to the ways he was also compassionate.

Now, she wanted to know more about what's under all those clothes. She wanted to show him how she appreciated that he cared enough to listen.

She stepped forward and pulled him in, then shut the door in earnest.

"Here's what I choose," she said, leading him to her bedroom. She turned on a lamp on her oak dresser, and gestured to her queen-sized sleigh bed, dressed with a simple white down comforter. "I choose you, in my bed." Saying it drew heat to her own core. With every step into her cozy room, a room that was normally only inhabited by her alone, her body temperature ratcheted up by a degree. She was burning up, dropping her backpack, toeing off her shoes, shrugging off her windbreaker. Cruz did the same, pulling his shirt off, snatching his webbed belt from its loops, the sound melting all of her inhibitions. Then, he uncuffed his watch and gently set it on her bedside table.

Looking at him now, she wished to be touched that way. She wished to be doted upon, gently handled, cherished. The idea that he was capable of both—of being able to endure the outdoors, and then to appreciate something he clearly found important—encouraged her to lower the last of her outer clothing, leaving her underwear.

With Cruz's gaze trained on her body, Eva paused.

She was proud of her body. She'd birthed two children, survived tragedy. She'd built this business with her mind and internal muscle. She was a strong person.

But it had been over a year since she'd taken off her clothing for a man. And the light was on, with all of her imperfections on display, imperfections that she'd accepted of herself. Imperfections that she'd dared casual partners in the past to dismiss, because she didn't care about them the way she cared for the man in front of her.

Somehow, this was different. For the first time in a long time, she was nervous.

"Come over here." Cruz's voice echoed through the room, and it took hold of Eva's spiraling thoughts.

She did as he asked, reaching out to take his hand. Closer, bodies touching, he planted a gentle kiss behind her ear, his breath against her neck eliciting desire that caused for her to shut her eyes.

"You're beautiful, Eva." He trailed his lips across her cheeks to the tip of her nose. "Every part of you."

She reveled in his encouragement, in the fact that he knew her thoughts. He could read her so well, as if their friendship, and whatever this was had spanned longer than the two months it had.

"Will you let me?" His fingers lingered across the waistband of her underwear, waiting for her permission. Delicious shivers ran up her spine, melting off all of her doubts.

"Yes."

He pressed his lips against hers. As he kissed her, he slowly inched her into frenzy, and his hands and fingers worked their magic all over her body as he led her to bed.

"Cruz," a voice said in the distance.

He was floating, face up, taking in the sun's rays. Buoyed and relaxed, he watched the clouds pass overhead.

"Cruz," the voice said again.

He didn't want to move; it was perfect exactly where he was.

Peace. This was the feeling he'd been searching for and what he'd tried to describe to Blue Moon. But he couldn't convey it in words. When he was with Eva, though, it was as tangible as the ground he hiked on.

Blue Moon.

Eva.

One a friend, of sorts. The other, now a lover. Their figures materialized above him. Of Eva as she was on the trail last night, and of Blue Moon, though hers was a shadow. Then the two grew closer, their outlines converging.

"Cruz."

The water around him rustled; he was being shoved from the side. Water splattered into his nose and mouth.

"Cruz."

His eyes flew open; Eva was above him. She had a tank on, and her hair was down. She smelled like toothpaste, and her smile grounded him to the moment.

He'd been dreaming.

The breath left his lungs. Blue Moon and Eva in the same dream—that was…strange.

In the next second the memory of he and Eva's night flooded his senses, ushering him into the full reality of the morning, dashing the last of the dream. He wrapped his arms around her and kissed her. "Hi."

She bit her bottom lip. "So, don't be alarmed."

His eyes darted around, noting the sun was streaming through the sheer white curtains on her windows and French doors. Their clothes were in little piles around the room, like lilypads.

It was only then he noticed how light and cheerful Eva's bedroom was, without a stitch of clutter. That, on top of her dresser was a vase full of wildflowers.

But nothing seemed amiss. "Now that's a way to start a sentence."

A sheepish smile appeared on her lips. "Remember when we got caught on the B & B patio?"

"Yeah?" His mind, though, was wandering. Because he'd just noticed that Eva was wearing a tank and underwear and nothing else. That she looked ethereal and innocent when she had been anything but last night. He shoved the covers aside and hooked an arm around her waist, tucking her back into him.

She yelped, followed by a giggle. "I'm trying to explain."

"I like it better when we're touching. Then you can explain." Her body was warm against his, a key to his lock.

"Who knew you were so cuddly." Though her tone was humorous, she wrapped her arms around his waist and squeezed. "Not that I'm complaining. I could stay here all day."

"Why don't we?"

"That's what I'm trying to say. My girls? They're here."

He stilled. "Here, as in…"

"They're in the kitchen, making breakfast as we speak."

It was only then that he noticed the scent of bacon in the air. "Are we in trouble?"

"Maybe?"

He loosened his hold on Eva. He'd found last night's spotlight situation hilarious, but he noted the tension in her body. "Should we go out there?"

"No! Absolutely not. I'm their mom. They can't see me like this."

"Like what?"

She whispered, "Naked."

He barked out a laugh. This woman was going to be the death of him, at how she continued to show different sides to herself. "Don't look at me like that—I don't know what to do either. This is your family." Her face skewed into mortification, and Cruz reveled in the idea of teasing her. He kept his smile in check and said, "Unless it's because you're ashamed of me? Of this? Because maybe you're slumming it, too."

"What? No. Of course not." She sat up. "Is that what you think? I said that months ago, and it was during our trail maintenance phase, and I was annoyed that you came up to the festival through the back way. I know I can get ahead of myself when I'm frustrated. I don't think you're slumming it, and—"

"Eva, I'm just kidding."

"Are you sure? I don't want you to think I'm judging you—"

He pulled her down to kiss her deeply, to squelch her panic, but it was also for himself. Because his chest had expanded in a way he hadn't felt before. It was almost too much to feel it.

Their kiss eased. Eyes locked, he said, "I'm sure. Though I didn't realize there were phases."

She nestled into the crook of his arm, and she rested her hand on his chest, trailing her fingers across his abdomen. "I just made that up. We could probably break it down even more: the mistaken for smoking phase, the…"

But the rest of her words faded away as she unknowingly came upon one of his scars from his surgery. He had three quarter-inch long scars on his body—the colectomy was done laparoscopically—but it was somewhat concealed in the dark hair on his lower abdomen.

With the women he'd slept with since his surgery, he'd never felt the need to tell them anything—they were flings. But this, with Eva, was decidedly not one.

From somewhere, a phone buzzed, and Eva gasped. Eyes locked, she said, "I bet that's them."

He swallowed his thoughts, grateful for the distraction. "What do we do?"

For a beat she just looked at him. The situation seemed to play out in her eyes. He felt himself grinning at her seriousness, and potentially what she was planning. "What's going on in that head of yours?" he asked.

"I refuse to go out there."

"There's really no choice." Would it be awkward? Yes, it could be. But he and Eva's relationship, or whatever this was, had been an unconventional path thus far. Everything was on the table.

"There's always a choice." Her eyes wandered to the French doors that led to her balcony.

"Hold on a second. Are you really proposing we escape?"

"It's easy." Totally focused, and utterly irresistible, she used her hands to emphasize her points. "That balcony wraps all the way around, to the front porch. It does, however, pass the living room and kitchen windows. We'll need stealth—"

He stifled a laugh. "Stealth?"

"Absolutely."

"Eva, we're grown adults. As you said, you're their mother. And we're, like, super-adults. Adults max. If they're willing to see us the day after, then bring it."

Her expression clouded. "You don't understand. This isn't just about seeing their mother come out of a bedroom with a man. It's them putting expectation on this." She gestured between them. "How else can I explain it…do you know any divorced couples?"

"Yes."

"Okay, so, I have divorced friends with children, and they are so careful at bringing another person home to meet their kids. The kids could get attached in ways that might not yet be appropriate. What if the couple breaks up? Then the kids suffer, too."

He nodded. "I see what you're trying to say, and I'm not dismissing you, I promise. But your children are in their twenties."

"Kids are kids are kids no matter what ages they are, Cruz. When they walk through that door, I'm their momma. So any man coming out of my bedroom has to be, well—" she winced "—a for-real relationship."

He clutched his chest in jest, though he felt the implication deep inside him. "Youch, what a way to find out that I was just a booty call."

"Cruz." She shoved him playfully. "You're not—"

"I mean, you didn't even give me a second chance. I thought I did a pretty good job for our first time." Though he grinned, he was filled with unease. He sat up in bed, and rested his back on the headboard, to right his brain so he could sort out how he felt.

He hadn't thought of *her* as a one-night stand in the slightest.

She climbed into his lap, and tilted her chin up at him, pulling him from his thoughts. "It wasn't just good. It was… amazing and wonderful, and hot." She pressed a kiss onto his lips, parting it gently with her tongue. Cruz responded with a growl as the rest of his body came to attention.

Literally.

But he couldn't let his thoughts go.

In truth, knowing that she was a widow, he wouldn't have fallen into bed with her had he wanted it to be a fling. Especially after what she'd revealed about Jared.

While Cruz was a rolling stone, he was still careful where he trod. He understood loss in its full circle, of both losing someone and being the one who caused grief.

"So, you're okay with this, Eva?" He spoke in between kisses.

"Of course I'm okay with it." She moaned into his mouth.

"I mean, this arrangement?"

She lifted her lips from his, and ran her fingers through her hair. "This feels like a serious conversation now."

"It's just us talking." He inspected her face and noted no fear or doubt. Her confidence was admirable; she seemed to be unshakeable. "I don't want a misunderstanding."

"If we're honest, there won't be one."

"I'm not sure that's true." He smiled. "I've worked with a lot of people, and transparency can still lead to misunderstanding."

"Well—" she readjusted herself on his lap "—I know I like

this, and you. But I'm not looking for anything serious. I've... got my whole life where it should be."

He nodded. "Same. I've got my business. Travel, too. I'll be gone most of the winter. But—" he squeezed her thighs gently, hoping he could channel his feelings for her "—I like you, too."

"There's no one else?"

"No one." Though, Blue Moon's signature flashed in his head. That, he shoved away.

"And we'll tell one another if there is someone else, or when things no longer feel right?"

"Cross my heart."

A smile that reached her eyes grew on her face. "Well then, it sounds like we're on the same page."

"So I get another night?"

"Maybe," she said mischievously.

"Dammit, Eva." He heaved a sigh, vision swimming with ways he could take her. Then he glanced toward the kitchen. "What do I need to do to get rid of them?"

She frowned. "I don't think that we can. But we can go with my first idea." She raised her gaze to the French doors once more.

"So, what's your plan?"

"We sneak out to your place."

He shook his head, excitement waning. "No can do, my sister's working from home. She's got a whole video chat set up where it has to be silent. Which I know you're not capable of."

Her face twisted into disappointment. "I feel like a high schooler with no place to go to make out."

"We can go to Tin Cup Café and take food to go. I know a spot for a picnic. But are you sure? How about work?"

She took a beat to decide; Cruz assumed she would say no. All signs had pointed to the fact that Eva lived and breathed the B & B.

Then she said, "The B & B can survive for a couple of hours."

"All right then, let's go."

They both dressed in record time. They exited through the French doors and skirted the wraparound porch, ducking under windows so as not to be seen. With the back door, the final obstacle, up ahead, Eva counted to three, and they both sped past, laughing as they belatedly heard Frankie and Gabby calling them to breakfast.

Rolling Stone,

It's still December as I write this, and I hope that these few days have been all right. Can you let me know before you head out to your doctors appointments? Maybe I can send a prayer or good vibes and thoughts—something that might reach you somehow. Do you believe in that?

I'm not sure what I believe in. I was raised to have faith with a capital F. I did everything I was supposed to do, and things still happened. I supposed that's when the capital F was downgraded to a lowercase f. And I struggled with it for a long time.

These days, though, that f is getting bigger, growing a millimeter or so. To answer your last question, I do have a partner, though it's recent. It's so fun. I laugh a lot. I do other things besides mull over the betrayal, that yes, continues to plague me. Though at least now, I have this person to turn to.

But no, I haven't mentioned you. We're not in a place in which I need to. Though, if the days continue to pass with this feeling of being light on my toes, then that might be a possibility, only because he would need to know all of me.

Might this person be the closure I need? Is that healthy? Then again, I've been looking for ease, and I've found it.

Safe hiking, Rolling Stone.
Blue Moon

Chapter Thirteen

Eva stretched out like a cat under her sheets, the fabric against her skin delicious and luxurious. But the best thing was the man lying naked next to her.

Cruz's profile was beautiful. The curve of his nose, the lips that had roamed over her body, his strong arms that wrapped her into himself, made even more sexy by the sunlight coming through her cottage's bedroom window.

Then, it hit her again—she was in a bona fide sexual relationship. One that had no guilt attached to it, at that.

She bit her bottom lip to keep herself from giggling. No, this whole arrangement hadn't gotten old yet. It had been only a couple of weeks, but it had been like a honeymoon of sorts. She couldn't get enough of him.

"Are you looking at me right now?" His lips spread into a Cheshire grin. Then, his right eye popped open.

"What are you going do about it if I am?" She rolled on top of him and rested her cheek against his chest. His skin was warm, the thumping of his heart as comforting as her comfiest blanket.

"I can think of a few things." His hands trailed down her vertebrae, eliciting a gasp, then down to cup her bottom. He squeezed gently.

She lifted her face to his and kissed him on the chin, trailing her tongue underneath and down to his Adam's apple. "I wish that it was the weekend."

He groaned. "Killjoy."

"The girls have been complaining that I haven't been around. So today's the day I go in." Now with work fully in her conscience, she rolled off him, though turned so she faced him. Cruz's short hair stuck up, and a shadow of facial hair speckled his chin and upper lip. He blinked ever so slowly that she could imagine how he looked as a child. At the moment, he exuded both maturity and youth. A little bit of wisdom and innocence.

She didn't want to leave this bed.

"What did you tell them?" he asked.

"I gave them a lot of reassurance that they could run the place. And it's not like I'm out of reach. I do have a phone."

In truth, Joy and Kayla's cruise proposition for Frankie's birthday had been on Eva's mind. Her friends were right, she'd rarely taken off since opening the B & B a decade ago. Work was a priority. The survivability of her business took all of her attention.

She'd also had no one to frolic with. That was, no one like the man next to her, who continued to bring her out of her shell.

But she didn't want her children angry.

"Do you think they're still sore from when we snuck out?"

Eva thought back to that day and laughed. She and Cruz had cracked up all the way to her car and gone speeding into town for that promised picnic. Her girls had given it to her that night; Frankie and Gabby nagged at her as if the tables were turned and she'd been the child.

She shrugged. "They really overstepped."

"They might think I'm corrupting you."

"I like being corrupted by you."

He tugged her closer by the waist and kissed her on the fore-head. "Have I told you how pretty you are in the morning?"

She laughed, though she could feel herself flush from the toes on up. "God, you're so sappy."

In the last two weeks, Eva had also discovered another side of Cruz. The hard outer shell he toted around was simply a facade. Inside, he was soft and sweet and thoughtful. It was remarkable how he could be both, iron rod straight to every-one else and a marshmallow to Eva.

She didn't quite know what to do with it. It rendered her unsteady.

Louis was the same way.

She dashed the thought away. She wouldn't think of Louis.

He tilted her chin up to face him. "I'm serious."

"You're not half bad yourself," she said, her face still burn-ing from the compliment.

Cruz's phone buzzed its alarm, intruding on the moment, and they both groaned.

Checking her phone at her bedside table, Eva noted that there were no major emergencies overnight. She headed into the kitchen to make them both some coffee.

"Can I grab some paper and a pen? Just got a long voice-mail about our December hikes and I want to jot some notes," Cruz called from the bedroom.

She fiddled with the filter. "I have some in the cabinet next to my office desk, though don't judge me. It's a mess in there. You're still hiking?" Eva thought of Rolling Stone. It had been several days since she'd visited the trail shelter. She should check in.

It dawned on her—the hiker circles in town were tight. Had Rolling Stone met Cruz already? Did he go to Cross Trails for equipment?

"Oh yeah, winter hiking is pretty awesome. It's a great

skill-building season. But I'll be out of town most of the winter. I have to visit family and the new trail shop in Georgia."

She smiled to tamp down the disappointment that rose within her. She selfishly wanted to spend as much time as possible with him this winter. And with Rolling Stone gone, too...

She was mid-scoop of the coffee grounds, and she stilled.

Were the two gone at the same time?

Was there a connection?

Looking over her shoulder, she spied her lover's back. He was digging through the cabinet.

"Nah," she said aloud. Cruz couldn't be Rolling Stone. They were...different. The cadence in how they communicated... while Rolling Stone was so expressive in his words, Cruz was sarcastic and a jokester when not grumpy.

Except for mornings when he was sappy of course.

Her insides went mush.

"Whoa..." His exclamation was followed by thumps.

Eva abandoned making the coffee, convinced that there was no connection, and padded to the other room, only to find a half-naked Cruz in front of her office cabinet, scooping up fallen pieces of books and papers.

He looked up. "No worries. I've got this."

From afar, though, Eva could see Louis's yellow hardback recipe journal. It was in Cruz's hand.

Eva was swept with a myriad of emotions that rendered her slightly unsteady. She approached him with a hand out. "Can I have that, please."

"Sure." He stood, placing the journal in her palm.

She pressed it against her chest. "I'm so sorry. This was Louis's."

"You don't have to apologize."

Except, somehow, she felt she needed to explain. "It's a journal of his recipes. I found it recently and thought..." She hadn't really known what to think or what to do with the book.

She'd shuffled it around from her office, to the kitchen and back. Once she'd been tempted to throw it in the trash.

"Does it bother you?" she said now, opting to pivot her thoughts. "That you're involved with somebody who has all this baggage? Because I have my moments. Not so much the last couple of weeks…"

"Because I'm amazing and wonderful and hot." He grinned, repeating what she'd said the day after they'd made love the first time.

A marshmallow, he was.

"Exactly," she answered back, and meaning it.

Cruz perched on her desk, and he pulled her to him. "We had lives before meeting each other, Eva. If one gets to this age without some kind of baggage, I would be more suspicious, wouldn't you say? So the answer is no. It doesn't bother me a bit."

Relief rushed through her. "What kind of baggage do *you* have?"

To her surprise, he stiffened. For that brief moment, Eva regretted asking. She looked up at him and said, "Not that you have to say anything to me."

For as much as they had spent a good deal of time together the last couple of weeks, they hadn't really talked about serious matters. It was still early days. Sure, they'd discussed work and their plans for the day. He knew about Jared but hadn't asked further. And he not once had mentioned visiting Dr. Gerbera.

Besides Millie, his family history and childhood were unknown to her, too. Then again, there wasn't the pressure or the rush to examine each other's résumé. Eva had been satisfied by the little said of him online.

Cruz didn't pry about her life, and she found relief in that, too. She enjoyed him as he was, she appreciated the compliments, the comfort he gave her. He validated her feelings without centering himself.

Though now, she was curious.

"My baggage is being part of the Forrester clan," Cruz said. "Which brings about a whole host of pressures."

"I have to admit that I did a little stalking." Her face warmed at the thought of the time she had spent looking him up. "Only to find that there really wasn't much about you."

"My mother was really good at keeping our private lives to ourselves. Or at least, she hired a bunch of PR folks to make sure we didn't reveal too much online."

"So you *do* have secrets?" she teased, though curiosity ran through her.

"No comment." He planted a brief kiss on her forehead and slipped away from her. "Speaking of work, I'd better get back to this voicemail. Chip's going to be handling the shop while I'm gone for the winter, and he's eager for plans."

"Chip? How does the guy even have time?" Eva asked, though tried not to take his avoidance personally.

She, after all, hadn't told him about Rolling Stone. He didn't know that her closest friend might be a person she had never met or even seen online.

Besides, she had a full day at the B & B to manage, a family to take care of and had herself to improve before she could demand anything from anyone.

"He's got a lot of irons in the fire, but you can't tamp down his enthusiasm." He half laughed. "I don't have any doubt he'll do a good job."

She finished up making the coffee. "When are you leaving?" She'd known about his winter plans, but when he'd told her, it had felt too far away. But here they were, over December's threshold.

"Christmastime."

She nodded, tamping down the dread. Her most favorite time of the year, and she wouldn't be celebrating with him.

A lover does not make a relationship.

"I'm going to jump in the shower," she announced, to wash her thoughts away.

When she got out, a little more clearheaded and awake, Cruz already had his clothes on, his backpack zipped up and was ready to go.

She tried not to take that personally either. "Heading out already?"

"They need me at the shop. What are your plans for to-night?"

"We have Liam's holiday show at elementary school."

"A holiday show?"

"Yeah. It's *A Christmas Carol*, and Liam's the Ghost of Christmas Past. Frankie's been stressed. I think more than she was for grad school." Eva laughed. "I remember being that way with the kids. I wanted to make things perfect for them."

"Yeah, well, I never had kids, so I don't have experience with that."

The downturn in his voice was unexpected, and Eva wasn't sure how to take it. She didn't judge him for not being a fa-ther. At the same time, she didn't want to downplay her own life and her experiences. "Do you want to come?"

"Seriously?"

"Yeah. It should be a good production. With a lot of laugh out loud moments for sure. And we can head to the tree-light-ing ceremony at the town square right after. Or you can skip the program and just meet us at the tree lighting?"

Was she sounding desperate? She let out a laugh. "Sorry. I guess you can tell that I wouldn't mind seeing you tonight." She mindlessly pulled at the sheets of her bed to straighten them, and hurried into the kitchen area to fix her coffee to go.

Looking at the clock she gasped. "Ack, I'm late. I'd better go. I have a meeting with the girls and Jared. We're planning Valentine's Day weekend."

Cruz joined her at the counter as she filled up two to-go

cups. She dropped a couple of sugar cubes into his, and one into hers. "Valentine's Day already? It's not even Christmas."

"It's never too early to plan Valentine's Day." She grinned at him. "I know, I know people complain that it's a retail holiday, but we are a retail establishment in a way, and February is a big month for us."

"Damn Februarys."

She snickered. "Typical. Louis didn't like Valentine's Day either."

Eva brought her cup to her lips. Was it kosher to compare her late husband to a person that she was sleeping with? She hissed at how hot the coffee was.

"Mine doesn't have to do with Valentine's Day per se." He had made it to the foyer and slipped on his boots. She waited for him to continue, standing by as she held his coffee cup, but he didn't. Instead, after his shoes were tied, he took the cup and hooked her gently around the neck, hugging her. "I can't make it to Liam's play tonight because of a staff meeting. But I'd love to meet all of you at the tree lighting. It's going to be right outside my door." He pressed the kiss on her forehead— a surprise—and said, "Got to go."

Eva exhaled at the strange tone in his voice, watching him as he hiked down the path.

What just happened?

Behind her, her cell began to ring. Her daughters, she was sure of it.

Eva's ruminations would have to wait.

But now she couldn't help but wonder what happened in February. And why the timeline sounded all too familiar.

The problem with reminders was that they were in fact a call back to reality. Eva's question that morning regarding Valentine's Day, and now, a calendar notification that prompted him to buy his tickets back to Colorado, to see his oncologist for his six-month follow-up, were a clapback to all of the fun he was having.

He had, admittedly, forgotten. With his nights spent with Eva came a denial that the days were clicking by, and that February was a mere two months away.

February meant grappling with the idea that life could flip on itself. February meant facing his mortality. Yes, he was in remission, but the consequences of the disease would last his lifetime. It included the mental health implications, hence his follow-up therapy appointment earlier today—which didn't feel quite as productive as their first meeting—the plants and the constant anxiety of his cancer returning.

He clicked his phone off and stuffed it back in his pocket, refocusing on the staff meeting wrapping up around him. Dean was back in town to help train the guides for proper winter hiking.

Dean was talking about increasing safety measures during the cold hiking months, and their current plan to shut down hikes between late January and March, where snow was at its abundance in the Shenandoah Valley.

"It will also give Cruz and I time to make final plans for the spring opening for Cross Trails Club number 3 in Dawsonville," he said.

The rest of the staff gasped in surprise.

Cruz remained seated, his mind circling back to the task at hand. "Since the pandemic, the market for hikers and gear and tours have grown. The quarantine and shift to working from home amped up the interest in outdoor activities. When I opened the first Cross Trails in Boiling Springs, I quickly realized the great impact we made to the hiking community. We got to educate novice hikers, and help maintain the very thing that brings us joy. And well, as you can tell with how quickly this Cross Trails has grown, we are truly fulfilling our mission. But I feel that Cross Trails could do more. Hence, Dawsonville, which reminds me so much of Peak."

"The plan is to launch by spring of next year. The building has been constructed, but we're setting up shop in January," Dean added.

"Cruz, does that mean you're moving? Just like you moved down here from Boiling Springs?" Paul, a man in his midsixties, and a four-time Appalachian Trail thru-hiker, asked. He was the most experienced hiker in their crew, and a volunteer guide.

"I'm not sure yet," Cruz said.

"It's because of Eva, isn't it?" Sydney said, then slapped her hand over her mouth. "I'm sorry. I didn't mean that. It's none of my business, although the whole town is talking about it."

Leave it to Sydney to continue to be the eyes and ears of Peak gossip.

He barked out a laugh. It wasn't as if he and Eva had been keeping their relationship a secret. While they weren't big on PDA, they caught lunch and shopped together. Still, he had to draw boundaries at work. "You're right, it's definitely not any of your businesses. But if it's going to be placed on the record, I think Peak is a beautiful town, filled with wonderful people. I've really liked it here."

Sydney nodded, triumphant. "I knew it."

"All right." Dean cleared his throat. "That's the end of our meeting. If there are any questions, of course we're both available to answer them. But enjoy the tree lighting tonight. And stay warm."

Chairs squeaked and jackets rustled as folks zipped into their coats, and one by one staff members bid their goodbyes, leaving Cruz to lock up. Dean gathered up the trash to deposit in the outside garbage can; Cruz cut the lights. And as they both walked out the door, they were met with the loud siren of the fire truck coming through town with Santa driving.

In the hour and a half of the staff meeting, downtown had turned into a winter wonderland. A dusting of snow covered the surfaces of the town square. And now that the sun had set, the Christmas lights set the holiday stage. Couples and families milled around, and a few vendors sold snacks under white tents. It could be a scene out of a Christmas movie.

Cruz hadn't lied—he found Peak special, and Eva surely contributed to it. But this morning had been…a lot.

"Perfect timing." Dean snapped him out of his thoughts. He tossed the garbage into the outdoor receptacle and said, "Want to join me? I'm meeting up with a couple of thru-hikers."

Normally he would say yes. He loved the spontaneity of meeting strangers who were coming off the trail. Hearing their adventures, newest tips and what their stories were gave him perspective to be largely thankful about his life.

And he needed it right about then.

"I'm meeting up with Espíritus for this. They're somewhere around here. I didn't realize that there was all this hoopla."

Dean laughed. "It's not hoopla. It's Christmas. Did I partner up with a Scrooge?"

"I'm not a Scrooge. I just don't celebrate at all that heavily. My family's pretty low-key about it all actually. We have dinner and get together with friends but nothing like this. New Year's Eve is more our speed."

It had always been that way though. His family had big Christmas celebrations until their father passed away. After that, quiet Christmases had been what was preferred, though it had become a tad livelier when Millie's kids were much younger.

"Give me a buzz if you need to get out of here. We'll probably hit one of the bars later on tonight."

Cruz bid him goodbye with a handshake and a shoulder bump. "Will do."

A beautiful woman came through the crowd, heading their

way. Her hair was up in a ponytail, her ears and head wrapped in a furry headband. Her lips were painted a cherry red, and her eyes were lit up with the joy of the season.

Eva.

His body reliably melted like snow on a warm day; he surrendered to it, mind wandering back to the highlight reel of their lovemaking the last two weeks. Yes, his mind worked that quickly.

"Maybe we *won't* look for you." Dean waved in her direction and nudged Cruz forward. "For the record, Sydney was a hundred percent right. I'll catch you later."

Cruz's heart was in his throat as he met Eva halfway. She threw her arms around him, and he bent down to kiss her cool lips. He was warmed instantly. Gone was the period of awkwardness this morning upon finding the journal, or the discussion of him leaving. And gone was the whole town—at this moment, it was them alone.

Let them talk, was what she'd said once.

It had taken him by surprise. He oftentimes lived in the privacy of his thoughts. And though two weeks had gone by, he hadn't had the bravado to tell her the real reason why he despised February. Nor had he mentioned Blue Moon.

He forced himself into the moment. "How was Liam's play?"

"It was amazing, of course. He was the best actor out of all of them, even the older kids."

"Spoken like a grandmother."

"It's the best, being a lola. That's grandmother in Tagalog. It is one hundred percent a reward for all of the hard labor raising the girls. All the heartache they cost me, and now I just get to spoil Liam to my heart's content." She pulled Cruz by the hand. "Come on, the family's set up on the other side of the street."

Cruz was thankful for the distraction as they traversed the

square, his hand in hers. Eva spoke with such joy about being a grandmother and a mother that he never quite knew how to respond. His thoughts about his niece and nephew seemed a little thin compared to the experience she had, raising kids and now helping with a grandson. But it wasn't as if he had avoided becoming someone's husband. It was just that the window closed when the wind had become too strong.

Cheers and welcomes came from Eva's family as they crossed the street. They'd set up seats in a circle, and a cooler sat in the middle of the group. Someone had mugs of hot cocoa; one was placed in his hand. And all around them were the sights and smells of the holiday season.

He felt cocooned in cheer whenever he was around the Espiritus and all of their chatter. Admittedly, his small house had felt cavernous since Millie had returned back to her family. He had no one to talk to but his plants, who continued to survive.

Off to the right, Liam was attempting to form a snowball, though there wasn't quite enough powder on the ground. It reminded Cruz of him and Millie, praying for enough snow for a snowman. He strode over to Liam. "Hey, little man, I heard you were pretty awesome tonight."

Liam stood and arranged his knit cap, his smile wide and gleeful. "I kicked butt."

"Yeah." He offered his fist, and Liam bumped it. "I'm sorry I couldn't make it. I had work."

"That's okay. I think I'm gonna try and get a part in the spring play. It's supposed to be *The Wizard of Oz*. I think I would make a good Lion. Will you come to that one?"

"Oh yeah, sure." Cruz's heart dipped the small fib. He didn't know where he would be in the spring, though he charged through the thought by bending down, and saying, "I don't think you're gonna get much snow from the sidewalk."

"But I want to make a snowball so bad."

Not wanting to disappoint him, Cruz scanned the area for

untouched snow, finding a bird water fountain that might have at least a handful. He pointed to it. "Why don't we go that way."

"Okay. I'll go tell my mom first." He jogged off to Frankie, who gave Cruz a thankful smile. She had definitely begun to warm up the last couple of weeks. She no longer leveled him with an icy stare, though her questions were direct and challenging.

She was definitely her mother's daughter.

His heart swelled at the thought of Eva raising her daughters on her own. It must have been difficult. He would have helped her had he been around.

Where had that come from? He shook his head, feeling discombobulated. It had to have been the snow, or maybe this morning's conversation with Eva.

This was simply a consequence of him settling in. Of getting to know her beyond the basic facts of her life.

A frisson of discomfort ran through him, though it came from left field. But he shoved it away as Liam rushed back at him, grabbing the sleeve of his jacket. "Take me to the snow!"

"This way." He led him to the fountain and to his relief, there was enough snow for a proper snowball.

He scraped the sides of the bowl and packed the snow into Liam's hand. It was the size of a baseball, and the sight of it brought both of them to laughter. Cruz felt himself glow from the inside out.

"So you have one chance here, buddy. One throw. Who will the unlucky person be?" They both scanned the crowd.

Eva was standing next to Jared and Matilda, and the couple had an arm around each other. Jared threw his head back in a laugh.

Was Eva over the discomfort of Jared's presence? Cruz hadn't asked, not wanting to place pressure on their relationship. Talking about these deeper things felt out of reach still, because it would lead to more topics he wasn't quite ready to talk about.

"Tito Jared." He passed the snowball from one hand to the other.

"Think you can make it from here?"

"Yep. At school, I got my principal in the dunking booth."

"All right. But if you hit him, I'm going to claim innocence. I can't be attached to this crime."

"I won't throw you under the bus." His gaze narrowed at his target.

My God, he was like Eva too.

Liam took a pitcher's stance, wound up, stepped forward and threw the snowball. The smack on Jared's right shoulder could be heard across the street. Spectators gasped and laughed.

Cruz didn't have the heart to run away. He was overcome with awe. The kid really did have an arm! "That was pretty amazing."

They bumped fists once more. "You're the best, Cruz."

Cruz could only smile. Because he wasn't sure if he really was.

Blue Moon,

I'm still here. Obviously. Ha.

I keep changing the date of my departure.

Like you, I've found a bit of a groove. Maybe it's the holiday cheer, or the snow on the ground, but it almost feels like I'm getting ready to hibernate, and yes, with that person I'm seeing.

Can I be honest though? Everything feels too comfortable. It feels too...still. This isn't how I've managed my life the last few years. I created it so I could continue to move, to grow, to not be entrenched.

You're probably thinking that I'm a commitment-phobe. But I don't know if it's commitment that I'm worried about. Or if it's because I haven't felt this way before.

Nonetheless, here's my take. I wouldn't lean on another person for your closure. The closure should be from within oneself, don't you think? What happens when that person is no longer is around?

Sorry to be such a bummer. You deserve cheer, Blue Moon, not my morose thoughts.

Rolling Stone

Chapter Fourteen

As was tradition, after Santa passed through town in the fire truck, the festivities at the town square before the tree lighting ceremony geared up. The band began to play, and the square filled so every free space was taken up by a camp chair.

Throughout it all, Eva could not keep her eyes off Cruz, especially as he interacted with Liam. They were so good together, and Liam appeared comfortable, that she couldn't help but envision Cruz as a bonus grandfather.

Was it possible to be so attached to a person only after a few weeks? Especially someone who at the beginning she couldn't stand, much less admire?

"Mom." Frankie sidled up next to her, lacing an arm through hers. "Want to get in line for a churro?"

"Sure." They snaked through the crowd, heading toward where the food trucks were lined up.

"You're deep in thought," Frankie said. "Are you okay?"

"Yes, sweetheart. Of course I'm okay." She did a double take. "Why?"

"Just saying. I'm thirty. You can tell me anything."

"I know you're grown." Eva took her daughter in, at the new wrinkles that had appeared at the corners of her eyes. At the few strands of silver hair.

Eva's sister Carolyn had dealt with premature gray hair. The difference was, while Carolyn dyed her hair to this very day even at the age of sixty, Frankie was intent on embracing her natural hair color.

"Then will you tell me what's going on with you and Cruz? I can tell the two of you like each other so much."

"Of course I like him. I wouldn't have brought him around to my family if I didn't."

They found the churros truck, named Chugga Chugga Churros, and got in line.

"But this is different," Frankie whispered. "Do you think that maybe…"

Her words trailed, though Eva picked up on her sentiment. It was the word that she had not uttered to anyone else besides her children and her grandchild. The word that she kept so close to her heart.

Love.

"Oh… I don't know if that's it." She looked down at her feet. "It's a little too early for that."

Yet, as the words left her mouth, she found that it wasn't a hundred percent true.

When she and Cruz were together, she felt whole. Rolling Stone might have warned that relying on a person for closure was unwise, but Eva couldn't deny that Cruz seemed to heal that part of her.

Was that love?

And was she capable of it? Though she didn't want to admit it, these last few months had challenged her love for her late husband.

As usual Frankie was undeterred. "It's just as well. Cruz deserves to hear it first anyway."

"How would you feel about that?" Now that Frankie had brought it up, she was curious. "If I was in love, I mean."

Part of the reason why Eva had been so careful with the girls wasn't because the guys she'd dated were awful.

Eva had been well aware that they were being compared to

Louis. Louis, who had died on deployment. Louis, who had been a doting father, who cooked meals when he was home. Who mowed the lawn and took the girls fishing. Aside from their break, she and Louis had a perfect marriage.

Or so you thought. The words came unbidden, and Eva inwardly winced.

"Gabby and I have already talked about it. Jared too."

"You talked about this with Jared?"

"Yeah. Because he loves you too. And he's our brother. In fact, he had the best thing to say."

"Oh?"

They'd arrived at front of the line. Frankie ordered five churros sprinkled with extra cinnamon and sugar. Directed to the other window for pick up, they meandered and stood off to the side for their number to be called.

Frankie shoved her hands in her coat. "He said that if anybody deserves to fall in love again, it should be you."

"And you agreed with it?"

"Heck yeah, Mom. To see you with somebody you really like is pretty cool. Cruz has changed you a little."

"I don't think I've changed, have I?" Worry spiked her.

After all, she had made it to fifty on her own. She liked herself the way she was.

"Maybe changed is the wrong word." She paused for a moment. "I guess, to say it more bluntly, you seem to feel *more* when you're around him. Your smiles are bigger. When he speaks, your eyes light up. When he's around, it feels like you're standing a little bit taller, which is an improvement with how short you are."

They both laughed; the humor allowed Eva to think. Had she appeared less than herself? "I'm not sure how to take that."

"Mom, you've been a little sad since you found out about Dad."

Her breath hitched. "You noticed?"

Frankie nodded. "Me and Gabby chalked it up to meno-pause." A quirk lifted her lips.

"You are too much." Eva couldn't get over this daughter of hers.

"You're saying that it's not menopause then?"

"No doubt those changes are going on and it's contributing to what I'm feeling. But it's more than that. Though, I want to keep it to myself right now."

She hesitated on what else to say. She didn't want to tar-nish her daughters' relationship with her brother. Together, the three of them had made a team. "But I promise it's noth-ing bad. It's just stuff that I have to go through."

"Order number sixty-two!" one of the churros cooks called.

Frankie grabbed the snack and they made their way back to the town square. The cinnamon and sugar wafted in the air; Eva's taste buds clamored for a bite. But her belly had started to turn.

It didn't stop Frankie, though. With a mouthful, she said, "Then I'm really glad you and Cruz are hanging out. If you're in your feelings, Mom, you should talk to someone about it."

Eva couldn't help but feel touched at Frankie's awareness of the emotional storm brewing inside of her. Considering her daughter's words, she thought of Cruz leaving Dr. Gerbera's office, then shoved that notion aside. She had her friends. She had Rolling Stone. And yes, she had Cruz too, if she chose to reveal more.

Mayor Sylvia Cortez ascended the stage. She tapped the microphone, the feedback capturing everyone's attention. Her earrings blinked green and red, and her Santa hat stood tall on her head. "Hello, Peak! Are you ready for our tree lighting?"

The crowd clapped; Eva and Frankie got back to the group.

"Let's call up Santa!"

Santa stepped down from the truck, waving, his beard halfway off his face. He joined Mayor Cortez; he was handed a clicker. "All right. Let's count backward from ten. Ten…"

Eva made her way next to Cruz, who called out the numbers along with everyone else. He slung an arm around her shoulders and looked at her for a beat. He was enthralled, like a kid in a candy store.

"Three…two…one…"

The town square tree lit up, bright with multicolored bulbs. Cheers and clapping followed.

"Isn't she gorgeous?" Mayor Cortez said. "But that's not all, folks. It is our most favorite time of the year. It's time to announce our Snowball Royalty."

"Oh yay!" Frankie said, unironically.

Eva stifled her own excitement. When the ballot entries were announced online, she and Cruz had voted for Gabby, as Frankie had suggested weeks ago. At the moment, her unassuming daughter was helping the tree lighting behind the scenes.

As the mayor explained the Snowball Royalty tradition, which included having an appearance at the Love Day Festival in February, Cruz leaned in and whispered into her ear, "Do you think that Gabby will win?"

"I hope so. I think she's going to get a kick out of it." Their faces were close, and she was tempted to get on her tiptoes and kiss him. "Thank you for coming."

"It's been fun."

"It's been fun *all* this time," she said, with Frankie's observations running a loop in her head.

These weeks with Cruz *had* been a dream. Why couldn't they take the next step?

His eyes twinkled. "Are you thinking naughty thoughts?"

She laughed. "Far from it. I'm actually thinking serious thoughts."

His expression changed. "Serious, huh?"

"Drumroll please!" the mayor said as she tore open an oversize envelope.

At that moment, Gabby arrived with Chip. They were splitting a soft pretzel and wore open-mouth smiles.

Which was interesting. What happened to Nathan?

"Eva Espiritu and Cruz Forrester!"

Clapping exploded around them, and Eva froze.

"Us?" Cruz coughed.

In front of her, Frankie and Gabby high-fived, proud of themselves.

"Get onstage, you two," Mayor Cortez said into the microphone.

"Lola and Cruz won! I knew they would win." Liam cheered. He grabbed both their hands and pulled them onto the stage.

There was no choice but for Eva to smile. Looking back at Cruz, he had a deer in the headlights look, though he followed her up to the stage.

"I swear I had no idea." She stood next to Cruz though he didn't hold her hand. "This is fine, right?"

He mumbled something unintelligible.

Last year's snowball couple approached them. Marlene and Patricia Cowell were the powerhouse beekeepers behind the Queen of Bees, where they manufactured wellness items made with honey. They were a stunning couple.

She tipped her head forward, as did Cruz. The sashes were placed over their shoulders and the two women curtsied.

"Should we do that too?" Cruz whispered.

"I… I don't know." So, Eva attempted a half bow, half courtesy.

Then, the microphone was shoved into her hand. A glance up at Cruz—he rigidly shook his head. Eva cleared her throat. "We want to thank you for this great honor and hope that we can be as amazing as these two women have been."

The crowd clapped. Looking out into the crowd, Eva spotted her daughters' joyful expressions.

But when she turned to Cruz, he avoided meeting her gaze.

"You're avoiding the question," Millie said. She was on video chat, though he could feel judgement through the computer screen.

"I don't know what you want me to say." Starving, he was rummaging through his pantry. He had lost his appetite after the Snowball Royalty hoopla, and now that he was in his own sanctuary, he needed calories.

Though, nothing looked good.

"You can start by telling me why you're being so cagey. What happened tonight? Is everything okay with you and Eva? Though—" she waved the air in front of her, as if to disregard her comment "—you two seem so perfect."

"No one is perfect."

She rolled her eyes. "Obviously, Cruz. What's up? I know you didn't video chat me just to give me your flight information. You could have texted that."

He took a breath to help regulate his insides. After the tree lighting, he found all sorts of reasons to head back to his house despite his and Eva's initial plans of spending the night. "We were picked for this Snowball Royalty thing."

"As in, like, homecoming court?"

"Yep."

Millie's expression softened. "Aw. That's so cute."

"Not cute."

"Okay?" She frowned. "Help me out here, Cruz."

"But it wasn't just that."

"That's not very specific."

"Her grandson liked me and invited me to his play. In the spring. Eva said she was having serious thoughts about us."

But it wasn't what she said more than the way she'd said it.

Millie's eyes widened. "She wants a commitment. I mean…
what's there to think about? You're already there."

"Are we?"

"Are you not?"

Cruz found a snack bag of Cheetos in the back of his pantry and he all but dumped the entire contents into his mouth.
He chewed against the dry puffs until they became powder,
threatening to choke him. He grabbed a glass and filled it up
with water—glancing at one of the plants near his sink and
watering it first—then chugged half a glass and all the tension that had surfaced in the last twenty-four hours. "Also. I
found her husband's recipe book."

"Oh." A beat passed, then two. "How did that make you
feel?"

"That this is all too much. This relationship was supposed
to be fun. I care about her, Millie, but I don't know if I can
do serious."

"You're assuming a lot right now without having a good
long conversation with her. You're talking yourself into having cold feet."

"It's not cold feet." This wasn't an engagement or marriage;
this was a relationship that had just gotten started. "I don't
know if I can do this much longer."

"Don't say that." Millie stood and went to the bar behind
her. She grabbed a glass and poured herself wine, then came
back to the screen. "Don't say that unless you mean it, and I
really don't think you do. You haven't said one negative thing
about Eva, and you were just spooked today."

He shook his head. "So much talk about the future. We
spend all our time with her family. Her daughters. The expectations…and I got to thinking."

"You got to thinking she shouldn't share or talk about the
important things in her life? You knew she was a grandmother

and a mother and a widow. She's allowed to celebrate and mourn these things. I mean, what do you talk about?"

"I don't know. I talk about hiking. My business. Sometimes about Forrester."

"She knows that you're building another trail shop in Georgia, right?"

"Yes."

"She knows about Dad leaving you and me the business?"

"Yes."

"Have you told her that you're not going to be there in February because of your oncology follow-up?"

He shut his trap.

Across from him, his sister's chest rose and fell with her deep breath. She sipped her wine. "I see."

"I shouldn't have to tell anybody about what happened to me."

"No, you don't. But when you get romantically involved with somebody, it might be the kind of thing you should bring up."

"I'm not ready to tell her."

"Then don't. But you might have to ask yourself why you're not ready to tell Eva." Milly swirled the wine in the glass. "Only you can determine if somebody is trustworthy enough, kind enough, important enough to share that part of your life with. But here's my question: if you don't feel in your bones that Eva is trustworthy, or kind or important enough, why the hell are you with her?"

He couldn't talk about this. He and Eva had been sleeping together for two weeks. How did it get here? "Look, no need to be my therapist. I already have one, thank you."

Millie chugged the rest of her wine and winced. "You can't keep running, Cruz. One day, you'll stop, and you'll notice that you've dusted people who love you. Including Eva."

"First of all—love? It's too early for that. And second of all, you're talking as if Eva and I are done and over."

"You're halfway out the door—I can feel it."

"You know, that's actually a good idea. The trail and the woods don't talk back, or assume, or judge." Blue Moon wouldn't either.

"Sure, Cruz. I don't expect any less."

For seconds they looked at one another. His fingers itched to click on the red button to hang up. But long ago they'd promised to one another not to hang up angry, and he wouldn't be the one to break it.

"Love you," she said, breaking the stalemate.

"Love you, too," Cruz answered back.

Once the screen turned black, he shut his laptop harder than usual.

What the hell was that? He'd called Millie for support, and instead, he got a lecture. Worse, it had been a preemptive lecture over something that hadn't happened.

You'll notice that you've dusted people who love you. Including Eva.

He snorted. Love? That was impossible. What they had was a purely physical relationship backed by friendship. That, he could confidently say. They also had connection and spark. All that didn't equate to love.

Cruz took the stairs by two to the loft, into his bedroom, to his pile of gear. A quick look outside and he confirmed that the snow had indeed stopped. Still, he packed extra layers. He only planned to be out a couple of hours, but preparation was key.

As he pulled on a long-sleeve shirt, his phone chimed with a text. Eva. Hey, just thinking about you. Sure you can't come over?

He deliberated his next words, fingers poised on the touch-screen keyboard. *OMW* was instinctually his first answer, but he couldn't, not until he could source out this negative energy running through his veins.

In her arms and in her bed, he wouldn't be able to think, either.

Headed on a hike tonight. I'll be back late. See you tomorrow?

Text bubbles appeared, then disappeared, then appeared again. All the while, Cruz continued to get ready, then got into his car. It was a dark night, with only a sliver of the moon helping to illuminate the road. Finally, he parked at the trailhead, where he was the only car in the lot.

His text remained unanswered.

For a beat, he considered going back home. Hiking alone, at night, in the cold was ill-advised—he'd told other hikers that same thing time and again.

But the itch to get on the path was strong.

He switched on his headlamp, donned his gear and allowed the woods to swallow him whole. Hooking his hands under the straps of his backpack, he stepped out, one foot in front of the other, until he fell into a groove in his stride and in his breathing. Occasionally, he was greeted by the hoot of an owl. Otherwise, he reveled in the aloneness.

Soon, the energy that had been teeming off of him had settled into a low simmer. Then came the zone that he loved the most, when all thought left him, including the worry that plagued his brain, and the choices he would apparently need to make: the family—and the business—and Eva.

Finally, he came upon Spirit Trail, and turned into it, his steps confident in this familiar route. At the thought of the trail shelter and the notebook, he picked up his steps.

But when he stepped into the path that led to the trail shelter, the bulb of his headlamp flickered, then turned off.

"Dammit," he whispered. He blinked to adjust his eyes to

the moonlight. Thank goodness he'd packed an extra flashlight.

He was digging in his backpack when the sound of voices brought his gaze up.

He stood corrected; there was only one person. A woman. It sounded like she was talking on the phone. The beam of her flashlight bobbed; she was heading away from him. Still, he heard the words *Liam. Frankie. Christmas. Cruz.*

Cruz.

The hiker was Eva. He could only assume she was coming from the trail shelter.

He opened his mouth but nothing came out; instead, his brain spun with questions as to why she was out hiking by herself.

Safe hiking, Cruz.

Words that Eva had said to him at one time or another in conversations came to him suddenly, like shards of ice on the wind.

Betrayal

Woman

Gen X

"No way," he said, his voice nearly silent in the chill night air. Once he found his flashlight, he booked it to the trail shelter. The box was where it should be. So was the notebook. When he opened the notebook to the last page, there was a freshly written note.

Staring into the night, the realization hit him like a wrecking ball.

Eva was Blue Moon.

Rolling Stone,

Someone's definitely in a morose mood, and it's not me. :)
    I do appreciate your advice, though. Maybe you were right to tell me that I shouldn't lean on a person for closure, because things have felt different between this person and me.
    There's change in the air.
    It's not so much what he has done or said but what I feel.
    The sad thing about this is that I thought that this was going somewhere. I thought he and I were in a place that I could reveal more, that I could allow myself to open up. That maybe I could even tell him about you.
    See, I never thought I'd feel the same way again, for anyone.
    Here's the thing, though. I don't want to let this opportunity, him, slip through my fingers. I don't want to write about this next year, feeling regret that I didn't put myself out there.
    I'm going to throw caution to the wind. I'm going to tell him how I feel.

Safe hiking, Rolling Stone.
Blue Moon

Chapter Fifteen

While Cruz tinkered with the wind chimes at Chime O' Clock, a gift shop downtown that specialized in chimes and clocks, Eva stared at his profile. She inspected it for anything out of place. A bruise, a scratch, a new wrinkle.

Because something was different.

She rewound her memory of the last twenty-four hours. They'd spent last night together at her cottage. This morning they'd had breakfast together. They talked about their morning before they went off to work. Now, they were doing last-minute gift shopping with only a week left before Christmas.

But they'd settled into an every other night sleepover situation, though he'd attributed it to being busy at work. He was taking off in a few days to head to Colorado to visit his family, and he seemed distracted.

While his explanations made perfect sense, she felt unmoored.

Was she being paranoid?

She was new at this kind of dating, where even after sex there was no real title for them. Previous relationships after Louis hadn't been emotional, nor had they lasted this long. With Louis—it was a whirlwind. They'd fast-forwarded to love in no time flat, and they'd attached labels to themselves immediately.

She needed a status.

"I think I'll take this one," Cruz said, snapping her out of her thoughts. He tapped the chime once more. "What do you think? For Millie?"

She smiled. "She's going to love it. And the best thing about this place is that they'll wrap it up for you. Madison can turn any old ribbon into a beautiful bow. I know Millie's going to appreciate it."

"Thanks for coming with me. It's hard to figure out what to get for someone who already has everything." He bent down and kissed her on the forehead, then searched the shelves for the box for the correct chime.

See? she told her conscience. *That was the sweetest, sincerest kiss. You're overreacting.*

She exhaled her worry away as they made their way to the cashier's counter. The store, which had been overstuffed with product, had barely any room to walk with so many patrons for the holiday rush.

At the counter, she and Cruz stood only inches apart. She was warm under her coat. "Did you figure out what to get your mom?"

He shook his head. "I saved her for last. She's the hardest to find a gift for."

"Well, what does she like?"

"She is a definite matriarch. A hard-ass. Also sensitive. Very much like you, I guess, except that she's in her eighties. Which makes her a little bit ornerier and a lot more stubborn."

"I'd love to meet her." She envisioned a woman with white hair, but with a fiery personality. A woman with fair features, and like Milly and Cruz, with a strong personality but soft insides.

He hummed noncommittally, which shoved Eva from her meandering thoughts.

She'd said what she said as a general statement, something

she could have said to any one of her friends. Meeting a part of one's family felt like it was the next step in any friendship.

At the moment, it felt like a rejection.

Stop it. She was thinking too much. She'd met Millie after all. Though Millie was back in Colorado, she'd been commenting on the B & B's social media posts, and sharing them, too. All good signs, right?

It made it more imperative that Eva speak to him about where she stood in his life. This limbo put her on edge, and she was overthinking.

Cruz paid for the wind chime, requested for it to be wrapped and made arrangements to pick up the package in an hour. The perfect amount of time to grab something to eat, and maybe to discuss the thoughts that had overtaken her since the night of tree lighting.

"So what do you feel like having for dinner?" she said as they inched their way to the front door.

"Anywhere you want."

"I'll go where you want," she said.

"It doesn't matter to me."

They'd made it to the wet sidewalk—it had been flurrying the last couple of hours, and though nothing was sticking, the air was chilly. Weather reports called for a white Christmas, and Eva had been looking forward to it. The last couple of Christmases had brought forty-degree days.

Though it wasn't the weather that caused her to tighten her arms around her chest. It was his tone.

"How about Korean barbecue?" she asked.

"Sure." Then, as if completely preoccupied, he stepped out toward the restaurant, making it half the block before noticing that she'd stayed back.

Cruz, who naturally tracked everything, had forgotten to look back to see where she was.

It was wrong. It was all wrong.

A memory rushed back at her, of her and Louis, days after she had expressed that she'd missed her family in Oregon. It had been their first duty station as newlyweds, and she'd cried almost every day, having moved to a military town where she felt alone and overwhelmed. They had been in this strange state of quiet. Where the conversations weren't occurring on the same plane. When everything he said made her hackles rise, and whatever she did would elicit an annoyance or a negative reaction.

The disconnect had been so drastic that they hadn't known where each other was in their tiny apartment.

It was soon after that they'd called for their break, the six months during which she'd moved back to her parents' place. And when Louis met Sharla.

Then Jared.

Repercussions and consequences ran deep.

Now, Eva and Cruz looked at each other from half a block away for a beat, and she caught up to him.

"What happened back there?" He half laughed though his expression was tight.

"You forgot me."

"What? Never." He wrapped an arm around her, but she didn't feel the usual comfort.

"It's our Snowball Royalty!" Mr. Jeung greeted them when they entered the restaurant.

"Oh, there's no need," Cruz started, but it was too late—the patrons in the packed dining room began to clap.

"Thank you," Eva said, not quite sure how to respond.

They were led to an intimate booth to the rear of the restaurant, lit from above by a cone lamp. In front of them was a gas burner and grill. Soon, after they sat, banchan was served, the colorful bowls of side dishes cheerful despite the mood between them.

They ordered, and once they were finally left alone, Eva

opened her mouth to confront this strangeness head-on. But a text from Jared buzzed in.

Eva, can I have an appt with you pls.

What is this about?

Admittedly, since after Thanksgiving, she and Jared hadn't had another one on one, their interactions limited to B & B planning sessions with others.

I have an idea for our Christmas guests. How do you feel about offering a Noche Buena meal?

Filipinos celebrated Noche Buena, or "the good night" on Christmas Eve. Traditional celebration foods were served on that night, and the suggestion conjured a memory of Eva eating comfort foods like arroz caldo, or chicken and rice porridge, and lechon baka, or roasted pork, after Christmas Eve mass.

That sounds wonderful. Go ahead and write up the menu, and send it to me. If it's well received we can do media noche. We are full for New Years Eve too.

It'll be faster to talk through versus writing it up. FYI I did run it through Matilda, and she is for it.

Eva shook out her shoulders. Her schedule was packed. This wasn't a hard request.

A few notes will suffice and if I have questions I'll get back to you.

She clicked her phone off. By then the meat had been brought by the server and Cruz had begun to grill. His expression continued to be serious, though he engaged in small talk. Small talk that Eva couldn't follow, with the noise in her head.

"What's your favorite dipping sauce?" he asked.

Belatedly, she answered, "What?"

"Dipping sauce."

"Oh, sesame oil with sea salt."

He kept on, talking about soy sauce with vinegar, with some kind of Worcestershire sauce concoction. Yet, all she heard were words without substance.

He was stalling.

To a point that Eva finally could not keep her emotions in place.

"Is there something up?" she asked.

His expression was nonplussed, and that alone spoke volumes. After a beat, he said, "Actually, I do have something to tell you."

The bulgogi was cooked through, and he placed some on her plate. "It's about my trip to Georgia."

"Yes?" She ate, though she was far from hungry. The food, which would have normally given her joy, felt pasty and dry in her mouth.

"We've got a lot to do to prep for the club's opening. Besides the retail front, we have to plan the trips. It looks like there are a couple of trails that will require some maintenance, so that needs to be organized, though it's nothing as demanding as Spirit Trail."

His voice had such an ease to it. It was like he'd practiced it.

"That makes sense." Eva drank her water, taking in an ice cube and crunching it to release some of the tension in her body.

"But I'm a little concerned it all won't get done as fast as I want it to if I'm not in town."

"I thought that you planned to hire a manager for that?"

"I still do. But it's important that this club launches well.

There's another shop in the same vicinity, and I want to get ahead on marketing and all that. You know how business goes."

"Huh. So, you're saying…"

"I'm saying that I might be moving to Georgia."

Her body had frozen in place. She could feel how she was clenching everything.

This wasn't happening, was it?

What the hell happened?

"What?" She swallowed against the shock that had lodged itself in her esophagus.

"Looking back, the main reason why Cross Trails launched so well is because I moved to Peak. It only makes sense that I should move to Dawsonville."

"So when you leave for Christmas…"

He isn't returning.

"But what about your plants?" she asked. "Who will take care of them until you decide what to do?" It was a reach, a foolish question, out of all she could have asked, but it was the first thing that came out of Eva's mouth.

He shrugged. "I'll probably leave them at Cross Trails."

"And not with me?" She was mincing words, she knew, but all the details were critical. She was trying to find a connection back, or a reassurance that she'd been thought of when he'd made these plans.

"I guess, I didn't think to ask. And Cross Trails does need a little greenery in it."

"But you'll come back often, right?"

"I'll try to visit when I can."

Try.

It was coward's word.

Dumbfounded, all she could say was, "Okay."

"I'm sorry for springing this on you now. It was a change in plans. And it doesn't mean I won't keep in touch. Because

I will." As if infused with newfound appetite, he shoveled the food into his mouth, leaving Eva to process what he'd just told her, but also to pretend that she was good with it.

After all, she hadn't required anything from him. They had gone into this relationship without discussing boundaries, and now wasn't it a little too late?

So she ate quietly, and allowed the numbness to set in. She went along with the rest of the small talk, unable to get above the confusion that had set in.

What the hell just happened?

At the end of the evening Cruz dropped her off at her cottage instead of spending the night, because of work, or so he said.

But as she got ready for bed, climbing into what had become her side, and noticing that Cruz's was empty, she remembered that unlike those years ago with Louis, she was a different woman. Today, she was a woman who knew how to speak up, and who never walked away without the answer she needed.

While lying in bed that night, Cruz pressed the pillow onto his face and growled into it, thinking of the words he'd said to Eva at dinner.

I'll try to visit when I can.

He was such a jerk. Eva would have been a fool not to pick up his insincerity.

He'd read Eva's thoughts, though. She'd known he was lying and he was running away. When she didn't fight back or ask more questions, he'd understood that he'd insulted her by not telling the truth.

But Cruz couldn't promise what he knew he couldn't give her. In the last few days, as he fully comprehended that Blue Moon was Eva, that their lives had been intertwined from the very start, he couldn't bear to disappoint her. Eva was a woman who deserved the whole package, a man who was going to give her the world. A man who would be around until the very end.

She couldn't know that he was Rolling Stone. What if February brought bad news? What about the following August?

He couldn't be one more person in her life that she should be responsible for. Or someone that would leave her.

Especially not that.

It was better just to go, to leave, to move on. To remember their relationship as it was: full of passion and banter, despite it being fleeting.

But now, for all the food that he had placed in his mouth, he felt sick. Sick of the things he didn't say, sick of his own bullshit.

Sick that he was walking away from the woman who, it turned out, was everything he'd ever wanted in a woman.

Thumps from his front door dragged him from his thoughts. He removed the pillow from his face and stilled his breathing. The lights were out.

Thump!

The sound was coming from downstairs. He clicked on the security cam app on his phone; the black-and-white image reflected back Eva.

He pulled the covers off of his body and hopped off his bed, padding down the stairs. No good news arrived at two in the morning. For Eva to come to his door meant that it had to have been an emergency.

Eva's back was to him when the door opened and she spun around. She wore pajamas under her long trench coat. On her feet were socks and Birkenstocks. Her face was screwed into a frown. "Hi."

"Come on in, you must be freezing. Is everything okay?" He moved aside, and she stepped over the threshold.

"I'm sorry to bother you this late."

"No, it's okay. Can I get you anything?" He closed the door

behind her, belatedly shivering, and combed his hair back with his fingers. He shuffled toward the kitchen. Though when he turned around, Eva was still at the threshold. "Why don't you come all the way in?"

She shook her head. "I just need to know. Are you breaking up with me?"

"What?"

"I couldn't sleep. After our conversation at the restaurant… I don't know what that was about. When you say *I'm going to try*, it tells me that more than likely, you won't be visiting. And I need to know, is that just another way of you breaking up with me?"

"Eva, I—" he started, then understood innately that this conversation was happening right then. That she wouldn't let him get away without hashing it out. "I'm still figuring this out. Work…"

"You're talking to someone who has lived and breathed work, Cruz, and work is an excuse. We're not kids. There's no room for mind games between us."

And yet, we have the notebook, he wanted to say. Because that was the only place where they had been the most honest. Unbeknownst to her, she knew everything about his life.

"I'm not sure what you want from me. We talked about this our first night together. We decided that this wouldn't get serious."

She sniffed. "A person can change their mind. Did we not become a thing? Was our relationship really that casual for you?"

The question stung him. "We *are* a thing, Eva. And I care about you."

"Then what is this?" She raised both arms, beckoning him. "What's happening here?"

He returned where she stood, but he wasn't sure what to

say. The pain in her expression hurt him from the inside out, especially knowing that he was the cause of it.

He drew her to him by the waist, resting his forehead on hers. The air between them crackled, as it always did whenever they were in proximity to one another. It was all consuming, how she made him feel. "Eva…"

Eyes shutting, she went on her tiptoes and captured his lips. Their tongues tangled in earnest; she gripped his shirt so there wasn't a second of breath to take. He became lost in it, in the knowledge that what happened hereafter would be his choice. That if he walked away from this, he was risking losing someone special.

The pain of her pulling away woke him from his thoughts. Stepping back, Eva's expression was serious and sad. "I no longer want to live my life in regret, which means I can't not tell you this before you leave. I love you, Cruz."

The words swept over Cruz like a gust of wind and he was a feather. All he could do was look at Eva slack-jawed.

He couldn't remember romantic love. He'd had it once, when he was younger, and so long ago. Before five years ago. Not since he got sick.

How could he love, when the future wasn't promised?

"Eva, I… Love is such a strong word."

"That's it?" Her eyebrows furrowed, and she stepped back.

"And…" He tried again, because he was doing this wrong. He was supposed to say that he loved her back. But there was too much in his head to sort through. All he could say was, "Thank you."

She laughed, though her eyes glassed over with confusion. "Thank you?"

"Eva, I feel so much for you. So much, but I can't."

"Love just *is*, Cruz. Love just is."

"Eva, I can't," he said softly. It was more to himself than

to her. "You're a mother, a grandmother. You deserve a happy ending, and I can't give you that."

"What does that even mean, happy ending? What we have right now is good, isn't it?"

"Yes, but…" Frustration coursed through him. She had no idea that signing up for him was signing up for the unknown.

She shook her head as if in disagreement, though she didn't say a word. Which was a good thing, because Cruz wouldn't have been able to explain. No one knew what somebody's path was like. And certainly, Eva would never know what he had gone through to get to the space where he was now.

He couldn't let this go on; he couldn't give her false hope. "If you're asking me if I think we should break up, then yes, I do. Because what you're expecting from me is more than what I can give."

Her face changed. On the inside Cruz winced, but he stood firm and strong.

He didn't want to hurt her. But this was exactly why he couldn't be with her for the long term. He didn't want to be the cause of her pain. She'd had enough.

"I see." Her arms lagged by her sides though she raised her chin to him. "Goodbye."

Then, she walked out the door.

He didn't stop her.

Blue Moon,

This will be my last note for a while. It's that time. Time for me to head out to see my family, and then for my appointments.

I'm not sure when I'll be back to check in. It looks like there's another trail for me to explore, and I'm afraid it's a little farther away.

I'm going to miss you, though. I flipped through some of our notes, and we've talked about everything under the sun. I want you to know that I consider you a friend. That I hold you in high regard. And that I'm not sure if I'll ever meet a person like you again.

I've been thinking about your betrayal from earlier this year. I wish it didn't happen to you. No one, and especially you, should have had to endure that. Please remember that none of it is your fault, and there's no right way to grieve from that.

With that guy you're seeing, if he's a fool to walk away, it's his loss. It's about him, and what he's going through. I can guarantee with every cell of my being that he'll regret it, because he'll miss everything about you. You deserve your happy ending.

I'll think of you every day.

Safe hiking, Blue Moon.
Rolling Stone

Chapter Sixteen

Two days before Christmas, Eva sat in her cottage office, working on the accounting spreadsheets on her computer. Outside, snow fell in sheets. The weather reports were turning out to be correct—they would be having a white Christmas.

It should have been a magical season, but it was far from it. He left.

Cruz *and* Rolling Stone.

When she'd walked away from Cruz's home a few days ago, she'd thought that Cruz would reach out to her. She had confidence in what they had built.

Her hope for a text or phone call had held out until yesterday, when the sky had turned dark and a snowstorm was announced, and she'd read Rolling Stone's note.

Like she'd ushered in the gloom.

Would she miss Rolling Stone? Unequivocally. He was her friend, her confidant. But she'd known he was leaving. His trail name managed that expectation.

But Cruz...

She thought that he would stay despite the biggest red flag of all: he'd believed that being alone, that hiking, was a proper way to cope. While Eva thought herself independent and understood how to survive without a man by her side, she fell for this idea that he would change for her.

Now she realized that she'd been so desperate for him to

fix the hurt Louis had caused, that she'd allowed herself to fall headlong into a relationship that was doomed from the start.

Cruz was her rebound. And those never did last. Even if every part of her wished for the opposite.

Eva pressed her fingers against her tired eyes, heavy with work and lack of sleep.

Her phone buzzed, and she looked down at more than a dozen unanswered texts. They'd arrived nonstop since she wrote her simple message about Cruz's departure in both her family and friend group chats: *Cruz left for the holidays and for Dawsonville and we decided to not do long distance.* Everyone meant well, but she was tempted to power down her phone. Alas, work remained.

She also estimated that everyone in town would find out before Christmas, which would make her and Cruz the first Snowball Royalty to not make it to the Love Day Festival.

More salt to the wound.

A knock sounded on the front door, and Jared stepped in a few moments later. And for the first time since finding out that he was Louis's son, Eva was not filled with dread at his appearance. Her entire body was spent. She had no energy. "How can I help you?"

"I'm here to turn in the estimated accounting for the holiday dinners."

She beckoned him over, and he walked in, shrugging his coat off and hanging it on the coat rack. "I told you that you could email this to me."

He placed the papers in her hand; she set them in her inbox.

"I also wanted to see if you were all right."

"I'm fine. Thank you."

"And…" He gestured to one of the side chairs, requesting to sit.

She shook her head. Today was not the day. "Jared."

"Please. This will take just a few minutes of your time."

She nodded.

Jared sat at the very edge of the cushion, hands resting on his knees. His looked down at his feet before meeting her gaze.

His usual jovial nature was missing. "If you look at the papers I handed you, you'll see that one is my resignation."

It took a beat for what he'd said to settle in, not until she fished the letter from her inbox and began to read. The first line: "This is my notice of resignation."

Eva sat up, vision clearing. A heavy weight settled in her chest. "What's this about?"

"Eva, I get it, okay? You've been kind enough to allow me to work here, but I understand that it's not for you. That *I* am not for you."

"You're quitting?"

"Isn't that what you want?" His face switched to indignation. "You've systematically ignored me the last six months. I've not been alone with you more than a handful of times. So, while I've taken part in all the family things, it's clear that only my sisters accept me."

"I accept you. And on Thanksgiving I asked for patience."

He raised a hand. "Things haven't changed since Thanksgiving, though I wished every day that we could get back to the way we were in the beginning, when you welcomed me back to the B & B. But there's this barrier, and this vibe...I haven't been able to speak my mind with you around. You and I haven't even had ten minutes alone with one another before you walk away. I can't work in this environment."

"But where will you work?"

"Is that all you're concerned with? Where I'm going to work?" He raised his eyebrows and gave her a dubious expression.

"No, that's not what I meant..." Eva's words and thoughts and feelings were scrambled in her chest and her throat. "You're just catching me by surprise."

He half laughed, gaze darting to the ground. "That's sad too, that this caught you by surprise. Frankie, Gabby, and Matilda have noticed. And did you not think that at some point I would get tired of feeling this way? I mean, do you not care?"

"Of course I care."

"Okay." He smiled, though it didn't make it to his eyes. "I'm not worried about finding a place to work. I've taken lesser positions—I'm willing to do a different position alto-gether. But I would rather work a less than ideal position in a place where I'm wanted rather than work in my dream job with people who wished I wasn't around."

"It's not that you're not wanted, Jared. I want to be able to explain." And yet, she couldn't put words to the jumble in her head, and the sadness of this whole situation.

Because Eva had known she was pushing him away, and she didn't do enough to stop it.

It was one more failure.

He stood then and took a step back.

"Matilda knows about all this. And we've worked it out so I can transition the next chef before I exit. I have some chef leads for Matilda to follow up with. After last spring's suc-cess, it won't be hard to get someone in here.

"And for the record, I've worked really hard to come to a point where I too can work here, because it hasn't been easy for me either. I've had to grapple with the fact that I lost so much time with my sisters, and knowing you were hurt too. But I'm not doing this alone. I have Matilda, and I have a ther-apist. I have my family to speak to. I hope that you don't find offense in this, but perhaps you need to talk to somebody too."

Eva nodded, belatedly, dumbly. Like she was simply an observer.

"I'm leaving now."

It was the story of her life.

Louis left, once in their marriage, and then forever. Rolling Stone. Cruz.

She hated it.

For the first time in a few days, she was filled with conviction rather than hurt. Because she wouldn't stand for it, not anymore.

She stood. "No. Please. Don't go. Don't quit. I'm sorry, Jared."

Jared had already taken steps toward the door. He shook his head.

"I'll do whatever you want me to do. Just stay."

He opened the door so light spilled into her foyer. "Up to a week ago I would have thanked God for that. But I realize this is really not about me. This is about you and Louis. I'll see you at work, Eva."

Eva watched Jared walk out the door and down her porch.

At the crack of dawn Christmas Day, Cruz walked out to the living room of the Forrester family home, dressed in the requisite Christmas pajamas—this time candy canes printed on a red background—given to him by Millie, but without a lick of holiday spirit inside him. Situated on the outskirts of Denver, built into the mountain, the home was a sizable cabin, with windows that overlooked the Rockies. The start of morning light shone through to the open living room and onto the sparkling Christmas tree, gifts burgeoning beneath.

"Merry Christmas!" His mother, Samantha Forrester, entered the living room from the kitchen. She wore the same candy cane pajamas and a matching robe, and held two cups of coffee; she handed him one. It was her favorite Christmas blend from the local roasters down the hill. He sniffed to fill the void in his chest.

Though it didn't work. And neither did a hike yesterday, and the day before that.

"Did you sleep well?"

"Yes, thank you." He kissed his mother's cheek. She smelled like lavender and vanilla and baking bread. Very much not like her weekday boardroom persona, with her prim suits and Chanel N°5. Though she was a figurehead these days, she still looked the part.

At the moment, she was just Mom, and Nana.

As if conjured, his teenage niece and nephew took the stairs down two at a time, also in candy cane pajamas. Their faces were lit bright in anticipation of opening their gifts, reminding Cruz of him and Millie diving headlong under the tree to tear open boxes.

Millie and Max stepped down afterward. Both had sullen expressions despite their own candy cane pajamas as they got to the first floor.

It was Christmas after all. Everyone had to be on their best behavior. They had to summon cheer, even for the moment.

Samantha ushered everyone to the kitchen first, where breakfast was set up: sausage casserole and cinnamon rolls, bacon and eggs, coffee and hot chocolate, all handmade by her. Once everyone plated their first round; they headed to the living room so the kids could open their presents.

Chaos ensued with chatter and cheering, at the consumption of coffee, the tearing of paper and the opening of boxes. As the excitement died down, and the kids and Max settled in for a post-breakfast nap in the living room, Cruz followed Millie to the kitchen to clean up from the morning. She leaned over and asked, "Have you heard from her?"

He shook his head. "I sent her a text this morning, to wish her a Merry Christmas."

"With that text, did you admit that you made a mistake?"

He shook his head. "I didn't make a mistake. I'm not right for her."

"Two things. One—it bothers me that you think of yourself like that, and I hope that you wake up from this thought process soon. Two—you'd be hard-pressed to find a woman who loves you just the way you are. Oh, and three—if she was one of my friends, I would have told her to block your number. I can't believe you had nothing to say to her after she told you she loved you."

"My God if you like her so much why don't *you* marry her. Oh wait, because you're still unhappily married," he said through gritted teeth.

"I'm gonna let that pass. Just because it's Christmas, and I don't want to make a big scene and because I know you're projecting."

"Now what's going on in here?" his mother asked, walking into the kitchen.

"Cruz is having woman problems."

"Millie." He rolled his eyes. This was starting to become very reminiscent of their younger years.

"Really?" His mother raised her eyebrows, clearly awaiting an explanation.

"Yes, Mother. And his fear of commitment has brought him all the way home for Christmas instead of spending time with her."

"I've always known of his fear of commitment, but I just thought that it was with me or with Forrester."

"Nope, and that poor unsuspecting woman—who's so great by the way—fell for him. She's in Peak."

"Peak! So this is why he was there for so long."

Cruz raised a hand. "Hello? Am I not in the room?"

Millie bit into another piece of bacon. "We only speak the truth."

With the two most important women around him, women who he couldn't hide from or lie to, the resistance to face what he'd done fell away. He forced the words out of him, though resisted telling them about his and Blue Moon's—or Eva's—letters. "I just…don't know what to do about all of it."

"About what, sweetheart?" His mother approached him. She got to about a foot away and placed a hand on the countertop.

He shut his eyes and spit out the first thing he could extract. "I don't know if I can do it, if I can tell her everything. Eva needs someone who's whole, who will be there for her. Time is already against us, but to add…" He trailed off, though saw understanding in the expression on his mother's face. February loomed in his mind, knowing too, that beyond February, there were all the years ahead, if he was lucky to have them. "She was already widowed once."

"Honey…"

"No one is guaranteed tomorrow, Mom. Dad was the epitome of health. He had nothing wrong with him, and he was there one second and gone the next. And I mean, I'm not even you. You must've felt horrible."

"It was horrible. And I miss him. We all miss him. But I also see him in you and with Millie. He's in all of you so he's still here."

He shook his head. These were encouraging words, true, but they were words that fell flat.

Seconds passed when his mother didn't say anything. Then, she said, "Everyone—quick change." She walked into the living room. "Everyone in the car in thirty minutes."

The kids looked up from their devices, Max rose from the couch.

"Where are we going?" Cruz watched as his mother ascended the staircase.

"Time to go to work, son."

Chapter Seventeen

"**P**our it all the way to the top." Eva nodded at Joy as she tipped the champagne into the glass of orange juice.

Kayla raised an eyebrow. "It's nine in the morning. Are we sure this is a good idea?"

"Are you kidding? In an hour we're going to be bombarded. Yes, this is a good idea," Eva said. Under her breath, she added, "I need this mimosa. It's been a difficult week."

Understanding rippled through her friends' expressions. "How are you, for real?"

Eva scanned the room, at how picture perfect it was. Garlands trimmed doorways and windows. Ribbons and poinsettias everywhere one turned. Christmas music piping through the speakers, and the hint of pine smell just behind the savory and sweet of her planned Christmas breakfast. "You're seeing all the efforts right here." She jutted her chin toward the living room at large.

"You *are* pretty good at channeling energy," Joy said.

"It's either that, or cry." Which she also had done a good deal of, and which, surprisingly had alleviated some of the anger inside of her.

"He'll come back. Surely," Kayla said. "Or I read him all wrong. The both of you were so cute. We thought for sure…" She glanced at Joy. "That he was the one."

"He sure looked like he loved you," Joy agreed.

Eva had gone over everything in her head a million times, and where she could have done better, not only with Cruz, but with Jared. What could she have done more to prevent them from leaving?

"Did you make that telehealth appointment?" Kayla asked.

She nodded. After Jared's resignation the other day, Eva had been left bereft. She'd called Kayla and asked if she could sift through her health care contacts and suggest a therapist. "I have one the day after New Year's."

Joy gripped her forearm. "I'm glad. And until then and after then, we're here when you need us."

But she wasn't sure if they would feel the same way after she told them the rest of the story. "You guys are so good to me. Here you are, missing some of your Christmas with your families to make me feel better, but you might think differently after I tell you more."

"I don't think you could do anything that would make me not like you. Annoyed maybe, but not dislike." Joy winked.

"This isn't about Cruz. It's about Jared."

Her two friends listened with serious expressions as she explained the trouble she'd felt connecting with Jared and that it had culminated in his resignation. "I don't know how to explain it. I was sincerely happy about Jared being here. I wanted him here, with the girls, with me. He reminds me so much of Louis, and it was like having another piece of him. But that slowly changed. I was left with a lot of questions. And I took it out on Jared. He said something the other day: that he knows it's not him, that it has everything to do between me and Louis. And dammit, I can't argue with Louis, can I?" She pressed a hand to her chest. "I can't believe that I'm losing Jared too. Despite it all, he's my family. My son. On top of Cruz…how can I be happy and smiley for my Liam? He deserves a good Christmas."

Joy sniffed—she was crying.

LOVE LETTERS FROM THE TRAIL

"I'm sorry." Joy wiped her cheeks. "I don't have any right to cry. But it's just that I empathize. I know you don't want to feel this way."

"I don't."

"What are you going to do? With Jared?"

"I don't want him to leave the B & B. But I don't know how to fix it."

They came around the kitchen island. Joy put an arm around Eva, while Kayla reached across to take her hand. "You can tell him exactly what you told us. You can tell him that you love him."

"I've already told him that." Though, in hindsight, had she? Had she told him how important he was to her? Had she used the word *love*?

"I wish you could have told us sooner," Joy said. "You've been carrying this for too long."

"I didn't want to admit it."

"Do you regret telling Cruz that you love him? Even if he did leave?"

The question elicited a double take from Eva. "No. I don't." It was the one thing she had peace with.

"Then, you know what to do from here on out."

"I won't hold back." Eva pressed her hand against her cheeks, which was wet with tears.

She didn't know why she felt she needed to carry it all, but she didn't want to anymore. It was too heavy. "I love you both."

"We love you too," Kayla said.

"I do...have something else to tell you."

Kayla shook her head vehemently. "Not until I have my own drink. This has been a lot and not what I expected on Christmas Day."

It was Eva's turn to make her friends' mimosas. They toasted and drank, and she pressed her lips against the tartness of the orange juice.

"I've had a pen pal."

As she expected, her friends returned a confused expression. Joy swallowed her drink. "Should we sit for this?"

She nodded. "And maybe open another bottle of wine. We might be tipsy by the time everyone comes over, but for this next part we're gonna need it."

Cruz watched the horizon go past, of mountains and blue sky, of ranches banking each side of the road, the commute so familiar that it made his insides turn.

This drive had been his life. Riding shotgun while his father drove, then doing it on his own, with his sister in the passenger seat.

It was a short ten minutes from the front door of their home, but Cruz absorbed the trip as if the drive was going half-speed.

Then, the sign for Forrester came into view.

Why they were headed in made no sense, but when Samantha Forrester had her mind set on something, everyone jumped on board.

Forrester headquarters and its manufacturing plant were located in a building that spanned ten square blocks. His great-grandfather had been intent on manufacturing and shipping all their watches from their Colorado location, and he made it happen through sheer grit and competitive salaries to convince people to move to the Rockies. The building itself was nondescript, however a gate enclosed the entire piece of land.

The gate slid open as the car rolled up. In the parking lot were a handful of cars.

"Can we try on some watches, Nana?" Jamie, Cruz's niece, asked.

"Sure, honey. You can hang out in the showroom."

"Now will you tell me what we're doing here?" Cruz asked from the passenger seat.

"You'll see," Samantha said.

Cruz knew better than to argue. His mother was the queen of lessons and always punctuated one with a show-and-tell. It wasn't good enough for her to make a point but to ensure that the other person had no doubt that she was right.

But this must've had everything to do with what Millie had discussed with him during Thanksgiving. Time for him to decide if he wanted to exit Forrester.

They entered through a side door, where security guards met them and ushered them into the inner hallways of the building. It was silent, except for their footsteps.

They followed Samantha through a series of lefts and rights, a route that Cruz had memorized from the myriad of times he had traversed these halls. He had grown up here. As a toddler, he ran through the hallway. As a teen, he'd casually learned the ins and outs of watchmaking. In college, he interned with sales, then marketing. He'd been groomed to ascend the ranks with Millie, and then take the company to the next level.

They entered an elevator. Samantha punched a code in to a keypad for the top-most floor, to the executive offices. After several moments the elevator door slid open silently and they headed down another hallway. His niece and nephew, as well as Millie and Max, entered the showroom, but Samantha continued on.

Cruz and his mother were headed to the boardroom, *the* room where all the magic happened, and where all the money was made.

Another keyboard punch, and the lights turned on, illuminating the windowless room, the whiteboards full of handwritten ideas.

He sucked in a breath, impressed at the enormity of it all. These were ideas, secret ideas, innovative ideas. Within these walls was the next big design, the next bestseller, the next source of fashion inspiration.

He'd written on these boards long ago.

"It's amazing what we've been able to get done the last quarter," his mother said. "Millie has great marketing ideas that I think could elevate us in the European market."

"That's amazing." He meant it, though inside his unease lingered. He should've been helping her. Then again, he didn't want to be here. This dichotomy took up so much of him, because he was proud of the Forrester brand. He felt no shame in his family's success. But it didn't fulfill him.

"Millie has such a gift. It blossomed after you left." She faced him. "She was always a little bit in your shadow. And with you away, she grew into the role."

"I'm super happy and proud of her."

"Me too. I'm assuming she told you about the decision you must make in your role in Forrester."

"Yes."

"And that I'm thinking of buying a home in Peak to be closer to you. Although it sounds like that's something I should put on hold until further notice."

"No comment."

"It's a shame. I have a Realtor all ready to go." She heaved a breath. "When it comes to Forrester, though, it's about contracts, Cruz. Having true boundaries will allow for you and your sister to grow."

"I understand. I know I've been…"

"Avoiding it?" She smiled. "It's all related, you know—how you feel about work, about your family, and I bet with this woman you fell in love with."

"I'm not in—"

She put up a hand to halt his objection and gestured for him to sit on one of the leather chairs. "When you said you wanted to take extended time off after your surgery, I admit I was worried. It was as if you wanted to erase those months of your diagnosis and treatment. But I continued to hold out hope that you would come home.

"And then you didn't, because you found purpose out there. It took a while, but my opinions of your new life changed. The joy was evident in your face, and all I wanted was for you to be happy, son. I'm proud of you, of what you've accomplished. I admire that you found something that aligns with your beliefs and you're willing to grow it. And I had hoped that by telling you this over and over it would change the way you feel about coming home. But you continued to avoid us. And it hurt."

"I know it did." The honesty in her words were cuts against his skin. "I'm sorry."

"I thought it was because of the memories you held of this place. But then you said something in the kitchen today that threw me, son. You questioned how you can be there for some-one if tomorrow isn't promised. I realized—you were stay-ing away from us, from work—you're staying away from this woman not because you don't care, or don't love us enough. It's because you do.

"Cruz, just as you've learned to live your chosen life by doing exactly what you want—" she leveled him with a stare "—when people connect with you along the way, you need to trust that they're capable of deciding their own path. It's our decision to love you and miss you. We're willing to put our-selves out there for you, to ask you back home, because we want to. Making this decision for us, assuming that you know what we need, and thereby staying away, not only hurts, but is pretty insulting. You don't have the right or the power to keep us from loving you."

"I'm so sorry, Mom."

Cruz started to shake. The tears that he had kept inside threatened to burst through. He shut his eyes, he willed his tears away. Because what he'd done to his family, he had done to Eva too. To Blue Moon.

Only then did he understand what he'd done. While he

had only lost one person—Eva—Eva lost two, him and Rolling Stone.

"*I'm* sorry. I should have figured things out sooner. I want to be there for you, and I mean it." Samantha sat on the chair in front of him and placed a hand on his knee to steady it. Once he calmed, she sat back. "The good thing about all this, is that taking that first step of making things better is as easy as spending time during Christmas and by talking things through. Though one is much easier to accomplish than the other."

The memories of Eva flipped through his mind. The comfort he felt; how fun being with her had been. The banter, the squabbles. The letters they'd written to one another. Their last conversation in which he could have told her who he was. He croaked out his next words. "Mom...."

His heart. It hurt.

"What's the matter?"

He told his mother about Rolling Stone, Blue Moon, and their letters. Eyes wide, she listened to their story.

"I walked away from her, Mom. She told me she loved me, and I still walked away. How do I make that better?"

A smile appeared on his mother's lips. "Well, sweetheart, the Christmas season isn't over yet."

Chapter Eighteen

After breakfast, everyone migrated toward the large tree in the great room of Eva's cottage. Looking out from the kitchen as she cleaned up, Eva took in the bodies that now filled her home. Her girls, Liam, Joy and Kayla, Jared and Matilda. And though they were all wearing silly, ugly Christmas sweaters—as coordinated by Gabby—the mood was far from rambunctious. There was a delicate vibe over the room, like they'd been wearing lace, in fear of tearing it with a sudden raucous laughter or joke.

"This is all my fault," she said, as Matilda came up to refill her drink.

Matilda hadn't mentioned anything about Jared's resignation; she was so professional, though Eva knew that her fiancé leaving the B & B had to have hurt her. Still, Matilda said, "Don't say that. It's not anyone's fault."

Eva shook her head, though she lowered her voice to a whisper. "There's no need to sugar coat things. Matilda, I'm worried that this—" she gestured between them "—our relationship won't be the same. You've been like a sister to me. Despite it all, and maybe because of it all."

Her face softened, and she reached out and held Eva's hand. "I feel the same way. You mean so much to me. But I admit, this has been difficult."

Eva looked toward the living room, to Jared sitting in between his sisters. The inseparable three. She couldn't imagine them apart from one another. If Jared left, their holidays might never be the same. "I'm going to make this better. I will."

After her mimosa morning with Kayla and Joy, she'd resolved to continue what she'd begun before Cruz left, and that was to put herself out there. To lay it on the line.

Matilda's lips turned up into a smile. "Just so you know, Jared cares about you. And I think, with Cruz leaving, he's more worried about you than he is about him leaving. You, the person, matter more than anything to him. But that's just Jared. He doesn't want others around him to be bothered, to hurt. Then again, you're the same way."

Eva inhaled a sharp breath against the tears that threatened to flow.

"Mom!" Gabby called from the couch, jostling the moment. "Mom!"

"My goodness, it's like I'm not literally right here," Eva whispered.

She and Matilda burst out laughing, then Matilda gestured that she was heading back to the couch.

"Mom!"

"Gabby, what is it?"

"Ate Frankie said you found her yearbooks. Can I have them? I want to show Kuya Jared her eyebrows in high school."

"Cruel. You're cruel," Frankie said.

"Yes, I'll grab them." It was a good enough time to excuse herself from the room. At her office, she opened the cabinet, and some of the contents spilled out, including Frankie's yearbooks and Louis's notebook.

She really needed to declutter that thing.

While picking up papers, the yearbooks and the journal, she was struck with a bittersweet déjà vu, of Cruz doing that very same thing.

In her hand now, the journal felt foreign. Maybe it was her

still grappling with not knowing everything about Louis, but it was clear that this journal was never hers.

Because it was a book of recipes. It belonged to a cook.

She fanned the pages one last time, coming upon a folded note tucked between pages. Her chest hammered as she pulled it out; it was a torn Steno page, almost sheer and yellowed, and written on with black pen.

Steno top-spiral notepads were Louis's favorite.

My dearest Eva,
I'm writing this the night before I leave for deployment.
You and the girls are sound asleep, but I can't relax.

I hate leaving you again. I hate leaving our girls. It's the worst part of my job, hands down. To be away from you all, it tears me up.

But knowing the girls are with you, I can breathe. You are the love of my life. You are the best mother to our girls. You are the thing that makes me whole.

I write this, even when I know our marriage isn't perfect. We have both made mistakes. I, for one, carry guilt even from when we split up long ago. We never talked about it, you said we were starting from scratch. But there was someone else, Eva. It was one night, a lapse in judgment, and I own my actions.

I'm sorry. I hope you can forgive me. I've written a version of this note before every deployment and thrown it away whenever I returned. Maybe I'll throw this away too. But I can't leave without saying that even through this guilt, through our hardships, our moves, there was never a question that you were always it for me.

You are it.
I love you,
Louis

Eva set the page down, her vision swimming.

It was what she'd wanted. An admission, in black-and-white, by Louis's own hand.

And yet…acknowledgment made it all even more real. Because yes, she realized now that she'd hoped that it was all a lie or a mistake.

Every new discovery unearthed another layer of grief. Each truth came with the requirement of acceptance.

But it was clear that Jared was one hundred percent right. This was all between Louis and her.

I own my actions.

And she would spend her life if she had to, to make up for it.

"Eva, where do you keep your balsamic—" Jared walked into the room. "Can I…are you okay?"

She looked down at herself; sure enough, she was sitting on her knees, with everything scattered around her. "I…" The yellow journal was in front of her, Louis's note to its left. She picked up the journal.

She then understood who this journal needed to go to. "I went down memory lane is all."

He approached her and offered his hand. But instead of taking it, she placed the book in his palm.

"What's this?" He crouched, so their eyes met.

"I found it, and it's clearly for you. It's like he knew."

"Knew what?"

She shook her head. This was hers to work out. "Just look. It was your father's."

He opened the book, then, as if captivated, lowered himself to the floor too as he turned the pages one at a time. He worried his lip; he ran fingers on the pages. He glanced up, eyes glassy, though he didn't shed a tear. "I can't take this."

"It's yours." She took one of his hands and once more threw caution to the wind. "This B & B too is yours…oh, Jared, I'm sorry. I'm sorry. I want you here. I can't imagine you not being here. This was never about me being angry with you—you were right. I knew in my head and in my heart that this was all about processing what Louis did, but I didn't know how to tell you. Instead I held back, when I should have continued to say I love you. You are a part of this family, a part of me. And I'm so very sorry for how I've acted, for how I took this out on you, Jared."

"I don't know what to say." His voice was gruff.

"I hate that I haven't asked how you felt with all these changes, too. I was in my head. I thought I was in it alone."

"But you're not."

"I know that now. And you aren't either."

He smiled wryly. "I'm surrounded by those three women over there. I don't think I could forget."

"Four." Eva squeezed his hand. "You've got four."

"Four." A beat of silence followed, where he looked down and away.

Eva bit against her cheek. "I'll accept whatever answer you give me, and you don't have to make the decision now, but whatever you choose, you will never stop being my family, Jared. I love you."

She leaned in and took him into a hug, belatedly realizing that the last time she hugged him was months ago.

She wouldn't let that happen again. Jared was her son, after all.

The front door blew open, startling Eva, and Chip walked into the office, along with the cool refreshing wind. "Sorry I'm late. I had to check into Cross Trails. I like being the manager but dang is it high maintenance."

Eva met Jared's eyes, and though no words passed between them, it was understood that their conversation would continue at another time. Jared got to his feet, assisted Eva up.

"No such thing as being late," Eva said to Chip as he shoulder-bumped Jared. "We still have a lot of food left over."

The vibe changed as Chip charged into the great room; the playlist switched up. Someone brought out board games. The only thing, or person, missing…

No, Eva wouldn't think of him.

"Hey, y'all. I need help with something." Chip plopped down on the couch, so there was no space between people. "It's time for me to pick a trail name."

"But doesn't a trail name get picked for you?" Jared asked.

"Yes, exactly. So name me, please. I'm the only one at Cross Trails without a trail name."

The conversation piqued Eva's interest, and she neared the group holding a plate with another helping of French toast. She realized that she didn't know Cruz's trail name. She'd avoided the conversation about trail names with him, intent on staying far away from topics that could lead to her letters with Rolling Stone.

"What do you want to be named after?" Frankie asked.

"What do you think I look like? It has to match to something in personality or the mannerisms."

"How about Squirrel," Liam suggested. "You know, like when a dog goes 'squirrel.'"

The entire room burst into laughter, though Eva stifled hers, watching Chip. She hoped he wouldn't be insulted.

"Hmm." He looked at Liam in what seemed like agreement. "I mean, that's not bad."

"What's everyone else's name?" Jared asked.

"Sydney's 'Jumping Jack' because she works out every morning even when she's camping. Dean is 'Chatterbox' because he doesn't shut up while hiking. And Cruz has a couple."

"You can have two?" Frankie asked.

"Yep, you can be renamed when you take on another trail. He's done the Appalachian Trail twice, and he stuck with his second name when he got to Peak, was Tickety Tock."

"Ah, because of the family business," Jared said.

"Yeah, and of course to no one's surprise, he's always on the go." At the words, Chip's face reddened. "Oh my God, I'm so sorry, Eva."

"No, no, it's fine," Eva said, exhaling, realizing she'd held her breath. "I'll just eat my weight in French toast."

"Honey, I'm gonna make you another drink." Kayla stood and headed to the table.

Laughter rippled among them, and Eva didn't want to squash that. It was Christmas! She gestured for Chip to go on.

"Okay." Chip cleared his throat.

"So I asked Dean, about Cruz's first name, since they've known each other years. And he said that his name was Rolling Stone."

Eva coughed and almost spit out her food. She looked over at Kayla and Joy, whose faces transformed into shock. After swallowing her food, she said, "I have to go."

"We're coming with you," Joy said.

"Where are we going?" Frankie asked.

She couldn't focus on the questions, nor could she provide any context, her body already in motion. Grabbing a waterproof jacket from the coat closet, slipping on waterproof boots. Donning a hat, and then jogging down to the basement and out the back door. Passing the fence Cruz built for her.

Cruz.

Rolling Stone.

Cancer.

February.

I hold you in high regard.

I'm your guy.

As she trudged through Spirit Trail, the vision of who Cruz was melded together with her letters to Rolling Stone. When she turned down the path to the trail shelter, her heart grew by tenfold.

It was hope.

Hope that their friendship would reign above what they couldn't piece together as lovers. That their story wasn't at its end.

Reaching the trail shelter, she bent down and fished for the box. She had read Rolling Stone's—Cruz's—last entry days ago, but hadn't responded.

She scanned for the line in the note that caught her attention for a millisecond, though was overtaken by the sadness of Rolling Stone's departure:

You deserve your happy ending.

The same words that Cruz had said the night they broke up. Words he couldn't explain, though now made perfect sense.

He had figured out that she was Blue Moon.

Like she had been, he hadn't wanted to be vulnerable. He hadn't wanted her to know that he was Rolling Stone.

Like her Louis, she started writing despite her fear. But unlike her late husband, she would write it to make sure it gets into Cruz's hands.

And this time, she sent it through the modern way—email.

Cruz,

This is Eva.

I know this is you, Rolling Stone. I don't know how I didn't figure it out before today, but now that I have, everything makes sense.

I understand why you pulled away, and why you left. I know why it's so hard for you to stay in one place.

And I'm furious with you. Steaming mad. That you knew I was Blue Moon but didn't tell me. That because of this, we lost out on being more to one another. And that you couldn't risk letting me in deeper into life.

But I can't make you do that, even though I tried in the end. You have to do that. You have to decide how and when to open up, and to whom. It's something I learned, too, from my friends, from my son Jared, and from my dear Rolling Stone.

Rolling Stone, who I care about. Who didn't shy away from me when I was sad, and confused. Who kept me company for months. Who was my friend. And I'm not letting him go without a fight.

So I'm not going away. I will be here, for when you're ready to be honest. For when you're ready to square off.

We didn't get off to a good start when we first met, but it never stopped us from trying again.

Blue Moon

Chapter Nineteen

Cruz couldn't drive fast enough. He read the last lines of Eva's email while keeping his gaze focused on the dimly lit gravel pathway of the Spirit of the Shenandoah B & B. After parking in the first available spot, he jumped out, leaving his carryon tote behind.

Dammit. He wished he had two flashlights on him. But as it was, he would need to take care with the snow on the ground, and the lack of moonlight up above. He turned on his phone flashlight and traversed the path toward the left side of the B & B, to the Espiritu cottages.

Finally, Eva's cottage came into view. Its windows glowed, inviting, and it was enough of an incentive to get him through to the finish line. It had been a long day, full of decisions and travel and all kinds of doubt. Up to when he went through TSA, he wondered if Eva would be able to hear him out. If there was room for forgiveness.

And then he got her email.

She knows.

Not only did she know that he was Rolling Stone, but that he knew that she was Blue Moon. His need to explain as well as the relief that she accepted him ratcheted his urgency to get to her door.

Because he made a mistake. And he hoped that it was truly not too late.

Cruz felt himself welling over with emotion as he circled around the house toward her front porch. His heart was beating in triple time, and he readied to pound against her door. Only to pause to heave deep breaths and run his fingers through his hair.

He checked his watch: 12:26 in the morning.

Maybe this was the wrong time to come. Perhaps he had been too hasty. She was surely asleep.

But he rang the doorbell anyway and attempted to settle his heart rate. He glanced at the security camera at the corner.

Would she open it?

I will be here, for when you're ready to be honest. For when you're ready to square off.

The click of the front door stirred him from his thoughts, and it opened an inch. An eye peeked through and a gasp followed before the door opened to its full width.

Eva was in an ugly Christmas sweater and leggings, mouth slightly ajar. "Am I dreaming? I drank a *lot* of mimosas."

She was...just everything. How had he walked away for the past several days? He leaned in and scooped her into his arms, and to his relief, she wrapped her arms around his neck.

"I'm really here. But I'm an idiot." After setting her down. "I don't even know where to start."

"We're going to start by closing the door." She shivered and shut the door behind him. Then, she said. "Then you're going to kiss me until I can't catch my breath."

"Yes, please," he managed to say as she pulled him down by the coat, their lips crashing in a desperate kiss. She tugged his coat off, and he toed off his shoes. He pulled off that dreadful sweater down to her warm skin, all in between frenzied kisses.

"I'm still so mad at you," she said, before she kissed him in the underside of his jaw.

"Please forgive me," he said, before unsnapping her bra.

They were naked by the time they made it to the bedroom,

and in the dim light the energy between them changed. In bed, the air between them became heady and serious; their foreplay slowed to a crawl. Their touches were deliberate, and he watched her with fascination. Because this was also Blue Moon. And she knew everything about him, absolutely everything.

She was still here despite it.

"Cruz." Eva was above him, and was breathless, though wore a concerned expression.

It was time to square off.

He rolled her to his side, and they faced one another. He took deep breaths to settle himself, and he waited until her eyes cleared, that they were both free from that rush of need.

He swallowed against his rising fear. "I was on my way here, when I got your email."

Her eyes widened. "You were?"

He nodded. "I knew it was a mistake for me to leave when I did it. But I couldn't wrap my mind around you knowing all of me. I didn't want to have you…" His voice trailed off, replaced by the pound of his heartbeat.

"Have me what?" she asked.

"Worry about me."

"Oh, Cruz."

His chest felt hot; his lips trembled. He could feel himself unravel. It was like cresting the top of hard-won mountain hike, where he knew he was seconds from falling over from exhaustion.

But then, she pressed her hand against his heart. It wasn't the first time she'd done it, but it settled his nerves. Enough for him to go on. "I didn't want to be your sadness," he said.

"But if I want that? When that means you could be my happiness too?"

"Could I be that? Now that you know that there's February, and six months after that. And then who knows?"

She looked away for a moment, then said, "You hiked the Appalachian Trail twice, right?"

He nodded, unsure where this was going.

"You hiked it knowing you might hurt yourself, that you might get trench foot, Lyme disease, or that you might not finish it at all. But why did you do it?"

"Because the AT's beautiful. And the journey's life changing."

"Because the journey is life changing," she whispered.

He shut his eyes, and felt her snuggle into him.

Eva changed his life.

"I love you, Eva."

"I love you too."

"I can't believe you didn't shut the door in my face."

"I meant what I wrote. Once I found out you were Rolling Stone, I understood why you left."

"But you said once that intentions didn't matter, that the execution mattered the most."

"I had people forgive me recently, Cruz. Kayla and Joy and Jared—they didn't turn me away after I made the same kind of mistake. They empathized with my situation, they sympathized, too. I want to be the same way. People are allowed to make mistakes. So are you." Then, after a pause she said, "But that's your one pass, buddy." Her lips lifted into a grin. "Because I'm ready to be someone's person. I want someone who'll stay, in here." She pressed his hand to her heart.

Cruz understood what she was asking. "You have it, Eva. You have me."

"You have me too, through it all," she said with firm resolve, with the same conviction on that first night that they met.

He kissed her then; his heart released all of its doubts. Between them came newfound energy as they worked back into foreplay. The heat rose in the room and so did the volume of their voices.

"I want you now, please," Eva pleaded, and the sound of her begging for him was almost enough to do Cruz in.

Almost. He retrieved a condom from the box he'd left her bedside table and sheathed himself. She straddled him, but before she made love to him said, "I love you."

He barely got to say it back.

After their lovemaking, as they looked at another, still on top of the sheets, a question struck Cruz. "How did you find out that I was Rolling Stone?"

She yawned, eyes shutting. "Oh, who else? Chip."

Epilogue

February

The blaring alarm shocked Eva awake, her eyes flying open. "Nooooo."

Every part of her body didn't want to get up. They'd returned from Colorado a couple of days ago, but she still suffered from jet lag. She'd barely traveled over the years, so entrenched in work, and she had underestimated what a two-hour time change did to a body.

She stared at the clock, though attempting not to move a muscle. It was eight in the morning.

And since today was the Love Day Festival, she and Cruz had to get to City Hall early to check in with the rest of the VIPs.

But she noticed that there were no noises coming from the great room. Cruz, she'd learned, was never quiet. Every step was a stomp, every whisper a declaration.

And his side of the bed was empty. Except for a note on his pillow.

Sitting up, she combed her hair back with her fingers. She'd slept like a rock, apparently.

She read the note:

My Blue Moon,
I'll see you at our trail shelter.
Rolling Stone

My Blue Moon. She loved when he called her that, which he had begun to during lovemaking. Was it possible to have something be romantic and erotic all at once? If so, then she could put that act firmly in that category and wanted more of it.

But what was this about? They hadn't written to each other on paper since their notes at Christmastime.

The exhaustion left her as she jumped out of bed and got into hiking clothes, layering extra clothing for warmth and grabbing her cold weather gloves. She sent the family group chat a text to remind them of the City Hall meeting, tied on her hiking boots and headed to the path.

The cold air woke her the rest of the way up. As promised, February was gloomy and frigid. They hadn't had snow for almost a week, though patches of ice showed on the path. It was virtually silent, with no birds to welcome hikers, and one could see deeper into the woods without leaves to block the view.

And yet, despite it, she could have skipped down the trail. It had been a good month, culminating in Cruz's clear colonoscopy and favorable lab results. She, Cruz and his family had breathed a collective sigh of relief. Though, as Eva faced her own fears while she witnessed his, not a doubt existed how much she loved him, or that whatever would come would not deter her from standing by his side.

Eva turned down the small path to the trail shelter, anticipating Cruz, but there was no one in there.

That was, nothing but the metal box, now sitting on top of the bench.

She pressed her hand against her chest; her heart was beating so fast that it seemed to leap out of it. This was…strange. Her hands shook as she popped the top open. Inside was a velvet box.

She gasped.

"Eva."

She looked up; Cruz stepped from behind one of the large oak trees, with a tentative expression.

"Hi." Her voice shook. "What's going on?"

He took long slow strides toward her; his cheeks were pink, though she could tell it was from nerves rather than the chill.

Stepping up to her, he kissed her gently on the lips, then reached for the velvet box in one hand, opening it to a cluster ring of three stones.

She inhaled, looking up at him.

"Three stones for three children," he said.

Her eyes watered; he knelt down on the icy ground, holding her hands.

"Eva, will you do me the honor of spending the rest of our lives together? I can't imagine not being a part of you and your family, or you being part of mine."

She blinked away the tears that clouded her vision. "Yes, to forever." The breath left her body. She was weightless. She was looking at this scene from above.

Eve knew she was lucky enough to have fallen in love and married once.

Nothing could have prepared her for this second chance, and she wouldn't waste it.

* * * * *

Don't miss Gabby's story,
the next installment in
USA TODAY bestselling author Tif Marcelo's
new miniseries Spirits of the Shenandoah.
Coming soon to Harlequin Special Edition,
wherever Harlequin books and ebooks are sold!

And catch up with Jared's story,
It Started with a Secret.
Available now!